"What can I say?" L'Hero laughed. "The people love me, 'evil demon' as I am. They know very well that I am a vampire."

"I protect them and care for them. They know that I have certain . . . limitations, such as moving freely by daylight, and they help us. In return, I treat them well. I give them bread, and a place to sleep. And if they truly merit the honor, I promise them eternal life . . . once we have overthrown the monarchy."

"Treason!" Edmund cried, as, without a moment's hesitation, Marie-Christine withdrew a stake and prepared for attack.

L'Hero guffawed. "Slayer, in your journeys through the fair city of Paris, have you not come to realize that the King and Queen are worse vampires than I? That they have sucked the lifeblood of their people, until they are driven mad with hunger and pestilence? The Queen herself has said, 'Let them eat cake.'

"I say, 'Let them drink blood.' "

Buffy the Vampire Slayer™

Buffy the Vampire Slayer
  (movie tie-in)
The Harvest
Halloween Rain
Coyote Moon
Night of the Living Rerun
Blooded
Visitors
Unnatural Selection
The Power of Persuasion
Deep Water
Here Be Monsters
Ghoul Trouble
Doomsday Deck

The Angel Chronicles, Vol. 1
The Angel Chronicles, Vol. 2
The Angel Chronicles, Vol. 3
The Xander Years, Vol. 1
The Xander Years, Vol. 2
The Willow Files, Vol. 1
The Willow Files, Vol. 2
How I Survived My Summer Vacation,
  Vol. 1
The Faith Trials, Vol.1
Tales of the Slayer, Vol. 1
The Lost Slayer serial novel
  Part 1: Prophecies
  Part 2: Dark Times
  Part 3: King of the Dead

Child of the Hunt
Return to Chaos
The Gatekeeper Trilogy
  Book 1: Out of the Madhouse
  Book 2: Ghost Roads
  Book 3: Sons of Entropy
Obsidian Fate
Immortal
Sins of the Father
Resurrecting Ravana
Prime Evil

The Evil That Men Do
Paleo
Spike and Dru: Pretty Maids
  All in a Row
Revenant
The Book of Fours
The Unseen Trilogy (Buffy/Angel)
  Book 1: The Burning
  Book 2: Door to Alternity
  Book 3: Long Way Home

The Watcher's Guide, Vol. 1: The Official Companion to the Hit Show
The Watcher's Guide, Vol. 2: The Official Companion to the Hit Show
The Postcards
The Essential Angel
The Sunnydale High Yearbook

Pop Quiz: Buffy the Vampire Slayer
The Monster Book
The Script Book, Season One, Vol. 1
The Script Book, Season One, Vol. 2

SIMON PULSE

NEW YORK LONDON TORONTO SYDNEY SINGAPORE

This book is a work of fiction. Any references to historical events, real people, or real locales are used fictitiously. Other names, characters, places, and incidents are the product of the author's imagination and any resemblance to actual events or locales or persons, living or dead, is entirely coincidental.

First Pocket Pulse trade paperback edition October 2001
First Simon Pulse edition May 2002

SIMON PULSE
An imprint of Simon & Schuster
Children's Publishing Division
1230 Avenue of the Americas
New York, NY 10020

Printed in USA
4 6 8 10 9 7 5

Library of Congress Cataloging-in-Publication Data

Tales of the slayer.
p. cm.—(Buffy, the vampire slayer)
ISBN 0-7434-0045-3
1. Vampires—Fiction. 2. Horror tales, American. 3. Buffy the Vampire Slayer (Fictitious character)—Fiction. I. Buffy, the vampire slayer (Series)

PS648.V35 T35 2001
813'.0873808375—dc21

2001133046

Contents

A Good Run

Greg Rucka

The Slayer Thessily Thessilonikki
The Battle of Marathon

Greece, 490 B.C.E.

She runs.

The ground is hard and dry, littered with stones and the bodies of the fallen, Athenian and Persian alike. She runs barefoot and avoids the bodies, but cannot avoid the stones. They bite at her soles, digging into her skin, and she can barely feel it, but she knows her feet are raw and blistered, and that with each stride she leaves a trail of bloody footprints across the plain. She barely feels anything but a distant and crackling pain from her lungs and a dull hot throbbing from the wound in her side, where the poison entered her body almost four days ago. Her chiton, once white, is now almost black in places, stained with days of dirt and sweat and blood, and linen has torn at her shoulder where a vampire grabbed her while trying to take her throat.

That vampire is dead, as are a hundred others, and she is dying, too, but she keeps running.

She has run nearly three hundred miles in four days, and she is almost finished.

In her right hand she carries her labrys. Perspiration from her hand has soaked the leather-wrapped grip, turning it blacker than her filthy tunic, and fine dust clings to the point of sharpened wood opposite the ax head, the part she uses as a stake when a stake is better than a blade. The handle is scored in several places, where she has used it to block blades or blows or teeth, and the head is chipped. The staking end, however, is still sharp. This is her favorite weapon, the one she has used again and again for almost eighteen years.

But now, and for the first time in her life, the labrys is heavy. The poison riding through her veins makes her hallucinate, and when she hallucinates, she loses her grip. Twice already she's come back to the present from her dreams to find the labrys dropped and retraced her steps to retrieve it. It matters that much to her.

She runs.

Her name is Thessily, sometimes called Thessily of Thessilonikki, though no one she has ever known has ever been as far north as Thessilonikki. It is simply a name, given to the woman who was once a girl who was once a slave and who is now the Slayer.

For a little longer, she thinks. *The Slayer a little longer.*

She is twenty-nine years old, and ready to die.

She is twelve years old, and has been a slave all her life.

Her mother is a dream memory who died before she could talk, and Thessily has been raised in the household of Meltinias of Athens, a fabric merchant. She has been well treated, or at least never abused, because only a fool abuses a slave; they're just too expensive to replace. She has never argued or been difficult, but Meltinias has seen it in her eyes.

Defiance exists in Thessily, and she is biding her time.

Meltinias thinks she is trouble. Smart for a slave, perhaps too smart, and growing dangerously attractive. The girl has hair blacker than the night sky, cold blue eyes that seem to judge everything, and skin that is pale like the skin on the statue of Pallas.

Thessily is exotic, and Meltinias has already pocketed several coins by charging other men for the simple pleasure of looking on her. Now that she is getting to be old enough, he is considering other ways he could make more money off of his prized slave.

In truth, he might have done so already were it not for the unblinking stare Thessily so often turns his way. The look is unnerving. He thinks, perhaps, it is a look from Hades. It is a look that will certainly lead to trouble.

But not anymore, because today Meltinias has sold his exotic, Hades-in-her-eyes slave to Thoas, the high priest of the Eleusinian mysteries. Thoas is the hierophant, and if anyone knows how to deal with Hades, it is he. The hierophant, after all, is the one person in all of Greece who can guarantee safe passage into the afterlife.

Meltinias watches them go, the tall, middle-aged priest and the pale-skinned girl. Thoas was almost desperate to purchase the girl, and Meltinias will live well on the sale for months to come. Meltinias breathes a sigh of relief.

And he catches his breath, because Thessily, now outside the door, has turned and looked back at him, and smiled.

And the smile is from Hades, too.

She is seventeen and Thoas, her Watcher, is at his table in their home, pretending to be at work with his scrolls. It is only an hour before dawn, and Thessily is happy and tired and sore, and when she comes inside, Thoas looks up as if surprised to see her. She knows he isn't; this is his game, and has been since they started. Every evening she goes out with labrys in hand, to patrol and to slay, and always before dawn she returns, and when she crests the rise above the amphitheater, she can see his silhouette in the doorway of their house, watching for her. Then Thoas ducks back inside, and when she arrives only minutes later, he is always at the table, always pretending that he was not worried.

She loves him for this, because it is how she knows that he loves her.

Thoas looks her over quickly, assuring himself that his Slayer is uninjured. If she were, he would hurry to bind her wounds and ease her pain. But tonight she is not, and so Thoas proceeds as he always does, and asks her the same question he always asks.

"How many?"

"Seven," she tells him. "Including that one who has been haunting the agora, Pindar."

"Seven. Good."

Thessily smiles and sets her labrys by the door, then pours herself a glass of wine from the amphora on the table. "There was something new, a man with orange skin and an eye where his mouth should be."

"Orange skin or red skin?"

"Orange skin. And silver hair, in a braid."

"How long was his braid?"

"As long as my arm."

Thoas nods and scratches new notations on his scroll. "Jur'lurk. They are very dangerous, but always travel alone. You did well."

Thessily finishes her wine and nods and says, "I am to bed."

"Rest well, and the gods watch you as you sleep."

She goes into her room and draws the curtain, then sits on her bed and removes her sandals. Before, in Meltinias's house, she was simply a slave, and not a very good one. Here, living with Thoas, pretending to be his aide, she is the Slayer.

She is damn good at being the Slayer.

She smiles.

She frowns.

It is three nights ago, and she is running through olive groves and down hillsides, trying to protect a man Thoas has told her must not die. The Persians, led by their king, Darius, are coming. They will land their ships at the coast in only three days. Athens has no standing army, and the Persians have never been defeated. It is already assumed that the glory of Athens will fall, that the city will be looted, the men murdered, the women raped, the children taken as slaves. The greatest civilization the world has ever known is only seventy-two hours from total annihilation.

But there is a thin hope, and it lives in the man Thessily follows, a man named Phidippides, who is running to the Spartans with a plea for help. It is 140 miles from Athens to Sparta, through some of the roughest terrain Greece can offer, over rugged hills and through cracked and craggy ravines. Phidippides is a herald, a professional messenger, known for his stamina and his speed, and rumored to have the blessing of Pan. He runs with all his heart, trying to pace himself, yet knowing that time is against him, and Thessily admires him for this, if not for the errand itself.

She understands the wisdom of appealing to the Spartans. They are the greatest warriors in Greece, their whole culture is built around war and honor and service and dying. She knows how fierce they can be in battle, because even though the Slayer is forbidden to kill Men, she has battled the Spartans before.

The Spartans are lycanthropes, werewolves, and though they control their bestial nature, Thessily does not trust them. But because they are werewolves, they can save Athens.

Athens knows only that Sparta is great in the arts of war, not the truth behind that fact. That is why Phidippides runs 140 miles to ask for their help.

Thessily runs because with the Persian soldiers there also travel Persian vampires, and the vampires fear the Spartans.

Thoas has told her that the vampires will do everything they can to stop Phidippides from reaching his goal.

Thoas is correct.

The first assault comes only hours into the run, as Thessily parallels Phidippides's route, staying hidden from the herald's sight, as the terrain turns mercifully flat for a brief while. She leaps across a small creek, starlight reflected on its flowing surface, trying to stay ahead of the herald, and she sees three of them up ahead, using the edge of an olive grove for cover. The vampires aren't even bothering to hide their true faces, and without a pause Thessily frees her labrys from where it is strapped to her back, and she flies into them.

She has done this easily a thousand times before, possibly even more than that. Thoas has never found a record of a Slayer who has lived as long as Thessily, who has survived and fought for so many years without falling for the final time. She has been the Slayer for seventeen years now, she has grown up and is growing old, and though her body is not as fast or as strong as it once was, she is still the Slayer, and there are no mortals alive who can challenge her.

She takes the vampires by surprise, and has felled one of them with the labrys before they've begun to react. On her follow-through swing, Thessily ducks and spins, bringing the ax up and ideally through another of the vampires, but she is surprised to find she has missed. It is a female, dressed in rags and patches of armor, and the vampire hisses and flips away, and Thessily has enough time to think that perhaps these Persian vampires are a little more dangerous than the ones she is used to when she feels the arrow punch into her side.

It feels like she's been hit with a stone, and it rattles her insides and pushes her breath out in a rush, and she turns to see the archer, the third vampire, perched in the low branches twenty feet away. Without thinking she drops the labrys and takes the stake tucked on her belt, snapping it side-armed, and the point finds the heart, and the vampire's scream turns to dust as fast as his body.

Then the other one, the female, falls on her from behind, and Thessily tries to roll with it, to flip her opponent. She feels a tearing of her skin and muscle and the awful pain of something sharp scraping along bone, and she stifles a scream. The vampire has grabbed the arrow sticking in her side, twisting it and laughing. Through sudden tears, Thessily strikes the vampire in the throat with the knuckles of a fist, forcing the once-a-woman back, and it buys her time.

Thessily is out of stakes. Her labrys is out of reach. With one hand, she holds the arrow against her body. With her other, she snaps the shaft in two, turning the wood in her hand even as the vampire leaps at her throat again. Thessily drops onto her back, bringing the splinter up and letting the vampire's own motion drive the stake home. There is an explosion of dust and the all-too-familiar odor of an old grave, and then the night is quiet again.

Thessily lies on her back, catching her breath. After a second she hears the sound of Phidippides's sandals hitting the soil in a steady rhythm, the shift of the noise as he comes closer, then passes the grove, then continues on his run. There is no pause or break in his stride, and she believes he has noticed nothing, that she is still his secret guardian, and she is grateful.

She tries to sit up and the pain blossoms across her chest, moving around and through it, and she gasps in surprise. In all the years she has been wounded, she's never felt a pain like this. She looks down at the remaining shaft of arrow jutting from her chiton, the spreading oval of blood running down her side, and gritting her teeth, she yanks the arrowhead free. Her head swims, and she sees spots as bright as sunlight. She raises the arrowhead and tries to examine it in the starlight, sees only the metal glistening with her own blood. She sniffs at the tip, and recoils, dropping it.

The odor burns her nostrils as she gets to her feet and retrieves her labrys. The straps on one of her sandals have torn, and she discards the other rather than try to run in only one shoe. She turns and follows after Phidippides, and has only gone three strides when she feels the first distant wash of nausea and giddiness stirring.

And she knows that she has been poisoned.

It is hours later that same night, and she has fought eight more vampires, each time keeping them from Phidippides. The vampires are savage and fast, and she is already tired and hurt, and slowing.

She wins each fight.

She runs.

It is today, and now she runs with Phidippides following, not caring if he spots her, because it is finished and because she is going home. Behind her lie the remains of the battle, where Athens met its enemy that morning. Six thousand, four hundred dead Persian soldiers litter the field, lying together with the bodies of one hundred and ninety-two Athenian men who have given their life for their city.

The sunlight is fierce above, and Thessily trips as she comes off the plain called Marathon. She tumbles through dirt and scrub before she can find her feet once more. She has lost the labrys, and loses precious seconds of her life trying to find it again.

Athens is only ten miles away, now, she can see it in the distance to the south, shimmering with color. Sunlight glints gold off the statue of Pallas Athena, off the tip of the mighty goddesses' spear.

She continues to run. Thoas is there, waiting, and she has to tell him that they won.

She has to tell him that she is ready to die.

She is nineteen, and full of herself, and is fighting a mob of vampires called the Horde, who have taken up residence at Delphi. She attacks with flaming oil and her bone bow, then with her labrys, then with her stakes, and she kills dozens, and still there are more, because they are, after all, a horde.

One gets behind her and puts her in a headlock, yanking her off her feet, and she can feel his breath burning her neck. His breath smells like rotten meat. Another is charging at her from the front, either not caring that she is already pinned, or hoping to capitalize on the moment, and he has a sword in his hand.

Thessily tries to go up, to flip herself out of the headlock and out of the way, so that the one vampire will stab the other. But as she tries to move, she feels the fangs tear at her neck and then the sword punching through her side, and it is the sword that saves her, because after it goes through her, it goes into the vampire behind her, and his teeth leave before he can take her blood.

She screams with rage, and as the vampire with the sword pulls it free, she reaches blindly for his head and snaps his neck, taking the sword from his hands as he dies. She spins with the blade and takes the head of the one who had bitten her, shouting hatred at him as he dissolves.

Thessily staggers out of the caverns beneath the temple, one hand across her belly, trying to keep her insides inside. Dawn is breaking, and she hears the sea and smells the salt, and then the sound of the waves grows louder and louder, and instead of the world growing lighter it grows darker, and she collapses on the road.

She nearly dies. She survives only because someone brings her to the Oracle, and the Oracle knows of the Slayer. The Oracle sends for Thoas and tends to Thessily, and for three days Thessily is unconscious, until finally she awakens, and her Watcher is there, and he looks concerned.

"I'm fine," Thessily says.

Thoas shakes his head.

"Truly, Thoas, I'm fine."

Thoas rubs the crow's feet at his left eye, the way he does when he is trying to find the right words. Thessily smells the camphor and lime on the bandages around her middle, and fights the urge to scratch the wound. In three days it will be healed, and there will not even be a scar. She hears voices singing praises through halls far away.

"You should have died," Thoas says.

Thessily looks at him and blinks, then laughs. It hurts her middle, but she laughs all the same. "When did you learn to joke?"

"It is no joke," Thoas says. "The Oracle tells me that the Horde was to kill you. It had been foretold."

Thessily thinks about this for several seconds. The singing continues, a praise to Apollo.

"Perhaps the Oracle is wrong."

"Perhaps," Thoas says.

The two of them are silent.

"I want to go home," Thessily says.

"I'll get your things," Thoas says.

It is dawn, a day and a half ago, and Thessily is hiding in the shadows of Sparta, listening to Phidippides plead Athens's case. She aches all over, the muscles in her calves and thighs and back drawn taut like sun-baked fishing nets. The wound from the arrow seeps steadily, and occasionally she begins to shiver and cannot stop for a time.

Phidippides is saying, "Men of Lacedaemon, the Athenians beseech you to hasten to their aid, and not allow that state, which is the most ancient in all Greece, to be enslaved by the barbarians. . . ."

She already knows the answer will be no, that the Spartans will not come—or at least, not come yet, though she did not realize this until just hours before, running in the darkness. She wonders why Thoas did not realize this as well.

The Spartans will not march until the full moon, when they are at their most powerful, and of course, that is what their king is telling Phidippides now. Our religion forbids marching sooner, he is saying, it would earn the wrath of our gods. We cannot march until the full moon. If the men of Athens can hold out until then. . . .

Phidippides offers the king formal thanks, bows, and departs, saying only that he doubts Athens has that much time. Thessily admires his diplomatic skill; she has never been good with words, and even though Thoas has spent the last several years trying to teach her manners, Thessily knows she would only make matters worse if she tried to plead the case. Women in Sparta have less standing even than women in Athens, and while she can claim to be the hierophant's aide, that will not grant her respect, only privacy.

She moves from the shadows to the edges of the fortress-city, waiting for Phidippides to emerge, and another bout of shaking strikes her. Her mouth feels full of wet wool, and her vision blurs.

She thinks about her life, and tries not to be angry. She tries not to hate the Oracle at Delphi, who ruined everything.

Sometimes she wishes she had died with the Horde.

Phidippides comes through the city gates, and immediately begins running.

Thessily fights to control her limbs and her thoughts, and follows.

She is twenty-three, four years after the Horde, and she has killed more vampires and more demons than she can possibly remember. She considers asking Thoas what the running total is, but decides against it; the knowledge would be too depressing.

But she is depressed anyway, and Thoas spots this quickly, and asks what is troubling her.

"There is no point," she tells him.

"You are mistaken. You have saved countless lives—"

"But the vampires are legion, Thoas, and they never stop coming! If I had died at Delphi, would anything be different? Would there truly be fewer vampires in Attica? Would there be anything to mark my passing?"

"If you had fallen, another would have been Chosen—"

"Exactly. I have slain for over ten years! *Ten years,* Thoas, and for what? A list of numbers you record each and every night, and nothing more? And so I will die and another will be Chosen, and another, and another. . . ."

Her voice cracks, and it both surprises and embarrasses her. She did not mean to be so emotional, so angry.

Thoas looks at her with concern and compassion. "Thessily," he says. "There are Slayers in the annals who have been Chosen only to fight for a fraction of the time you've had. You are remarkable, you are blessed, to have battled so well for so long. Your survival is a gift."

She shakes her head, and feels tears rushing up in her eyes, and the frustration is so intense that for a moment she can't speak. Thoas rises from his chair and moves to where she sits on the bench beneath the window. He is old, now, and moves slowly. He puts his arm around her shoulders, and holds her the way every father holds a daughter.

"I just want to be remembered for more than numbers," she says through her tears, and though she is a woman, to her own ears she sounds like a girl. "I want to be remembered because I did something great. Just one great thing."

Thoas says nothing, just holds her and rocks her, and eventually the tears stop.

But the question and the desire remain.

Just one Great Thing.

It is yesterday, and they are returning to Athens from Sparta, running in daylight, and now she is suffering brief hallucinations because of the fatigue and the poison. She lets Phidippides stay ahead of her, afraid of losing sight of him, but no longer worried for his immediate safety.

She sees the Horde and the way they slaughtered families, and she remembers the feeling of the sword slicing through her body.

She sees Meltinias and his thin fingers counting the coins that men have given him to just look at her.

She sees Thoas, at once old like he is now and young like he was then, and she sees herself, and she is old, too, she knows.

She sees ships, seven of them, moving along the coast, galleys with their sails out, Persian soldiers on the decks, and hatches leading below chained shut.

Then she sees the world as it really is, she is still running back to Athens, and it has grown late and the night has fallen. She moves to a side and sprints, skirting Phidippides's position, taking the lead. Again, he seems to not know she is there. Her feet burn.

She sees no vampires, and wonders.

She sees the galleys in her mind, moving along the coast toward Athens. She sees the hatches again. She sees the chains and knows that they are there not to keep what is below in, but to keep what is above out.

She knows what is behind the hatches.

It is almost dawn, and Thessily is searching frantically for Thoas in the near-empty streets of Athens, finding him where the men are donning their armor, preparing to march out to Marathon to meet the Persians. Phidippides has arrived only minutes after her, bearing the bad news, and the decision has been made to fight despite the odds.

Thoas sees her and his eyes go wide and the lines in his face run deeper as he says her name. Breathless, she tries to explain what she knows, but Thoas won't listen, forcing her to sit down, searching frantically for water.

"You've been poisoned!" he says.

She nods, gasping for air, taking the skin of water gratefully and pouring half its contents down her throat. "It's not important," she manages to say.

"It is—"

"It isn't," she says, and she grabs at his robe and pulls him in close, forcing him to listen. "I can't—my mind is, it wanders, but I know . . . I know *why*, Thoas."

He searches her face, concerned, afraid. She can only imagine how she looks to him, dusty and sweat stained, even paler than normal. She thinks her hair must be matted with dirt and grass and mud.

"I'm not delirious," Thessily manages. "I'm *not,* I *know.* The Persians, Thoas. The galleys."

"They will attack from the water?"

"Yes, but—but—" She shakes her head, desperate. Why can't she make the words come out? Why can't she say it right? *Please understand me,* she is thinking.

"In the ships," she says, the plea in her eyes. "They must be in the ships. It's the only way they can move in the sun."

Thoas's expression smoothes, and he takes her hands in his and nods, telling her to please let go, that she has forgotten how strong she is. She forces her fingers to loosen, and as she does another bout of shaking strikes her, so violently that she is left shivering, curled on her side, with Thoas trying to wrap his cloak around her.

In the streets, the Athenian men are beginning to march down the wide promenade, past the agora, to meet the Persians.

Thessily sees Phidippides, exhausted, joining the back of the line. He is donning his armor as he goes, carrying his spear.

She forces herself to be still again. To Thoas, she says, "I'll need oil."

"How many ships?"

"Seven."

"You're certain?"

"I . . . I saw it in my mind."

Thoas considers this. "I will get oil. And we will pray that you are right."

The sun is blazing and it is still well before noon, and the Athenian men are formed in their lines on the field of Marathon, and the Persian soldiers—the human soldiers—are thundering toward them. Thessily sees the flare of sunlight off metal from the corner of her eye, and she stops for a moment to watch the battle as it is joined. Her shoulders ache, and her side still bleeds. Her labrys is heavy against her back. On ropes slung over each shoulder she carries skins of lamp oil, and the weight of it would not bother her if she hadn't already run over three hundred miles in the last three days.

She knows she doesn't have time to stare, but she does all the same, and a pressure builds against her heart that, at first, she fears is the poison and her death, but isn't. She cannot describe the feeling, but it brings tears to her eyes.

She sees Phidippides, spear low, set against a charge, standing shoulder to shoulder with his fellow citizens, free men, civilized men. Men who have walked of their own free will to a barren plain twenty-six miles north of Athens to fight a battle they believe they are certain to lose. Fighting for their homes and their loved ones and their lives.

She realizes she is watching history.

The sounds of the fighting drift across the plain to her, and then the screams of the dying men. The Persians are desperate in battle and savage, and the Athenians hold their line, and then it breaks, and she understands what she is seeing. One of the Athenian generals—she thinks it is Miltiades, he's the smartest— is trying to flank the Persians. As she watches, the Athenian line breaks into three sections, and the outer two move to the sides, and the Persians are caught by surprise. They cannot go forward without dying. They cannot go to either side without dying.

They can only retreat.

Thessily runs, as fast as she can, for the coast.

If they can only retreat, they will retreat to their ships.

She has to get to them first.

It is noon and the fires on the water are so intense she cannot breathe and has to retreat. The galleys burn slowly, but the vampires inside them burn much faster, and she can hear their screams behind her as she works from ship to ship, the torch in one hand and a skin in the other, dumping oil all over the decks. When she touches the torch to the puddles, the flame races along the cracks in the wood, sucking the air from below.

She leaps from the prow of the sixth galley to the back of the seventh, and douses the nearest hatch with the last of her oil. She drops the torch in the pool, and feels the heat rise around her so suddenly her eyelashes curl.

The hatch ahead of her bursts open, and the vampire who has broken the chains bursts into flames and falls back into the hold. She hears more hissing, and then screams, and she spares a look

down as she passes, seeing them crowded together in the shadows, trying to avoid the sun, trying to avoid flames.

For a moment, she almost pities them.

Then she leaps from the last galley to the water, and swims to
the shore.

With the last of her strength, she runs.

It is dusk and Thoas is at the gates along with a thousand other
Athenians, old men and children and women of all ages, and
Thessily tries to keep running, but her legs no longer listen, and
in truth, she feels they have earned that right. Her vision is so
blurred by tears and sweat and poison that she does not recognize Thoas until he has come out to meet her, calling her name.

She hears tears in his voice.

She falls into his arms, and he cradles her to the ground, her
head in his lap.

He kisses her brow and speaks a prayer to Dionysus, to
Demeter, and to Kore.

Through lips that are parched and cracked, she whispers to him.

"We won," she says, and though she can barely hear herself
speak, a cheer comes from the crowd at the gate. She tries to turn
her head to see what has roused them, and Thoas brushes hair
from her cheek and shakes his head.

"Phidippides has arrived," he tells her softly. "He brings the
same news."

"He can run," Thessily says. It hurts to smile, but she finds one
anyway.

"Yes, he surely can."

She shivers, but not so badly as before, and tries again to turn
her head. This time, Thoas relents, and she sees that Phidippides
is before the crowd, his helmet in his hand. She sees the fatigue
take him as he turns toward her, watches as he falters and drops

his helmet. He staggers another step, falling to his knees. The crowd behind him surges, then stops.

Phidippides reaches them on his knees, and holds out a hand. Thoas has to take it and put it in Thessily's own. Phidippides' hand is dry, too dry, and there is no heat in it any longer.

"I've seen you before," Phidippides says. His voice is ragged and hoarse. "Running with me at night."

"Yes." The word passes her throat more air than sound.

"What is your name?" he asks.

"Thessily."

He smiles a broken smile, through lips as damaged as her own, and he puts his head on the ground near hers.

"It was a good run," he says.

"Yes," Thessily says, the last of her air slipping away. "It was."

The White Doe

Christie Golden

LONDON, 1586

She ran like the deer for whom she had been named, long legs carrying her swiftly over the sandy soil, her long yellow hair flying behind her. The prey had fought and fled, but it would not escape. Her soft mouth set in a hard line, the Slayer followed it. She could smell it, could still feel its dead flesh twist beneath her fingers. No, it would not escape. It was too close to the village for her to let it do so.

Moonlight silvered the beach. She could see it now, splashing into the water a few steps and then halting. Caught between the Slayer and the ocean, the dead thing turned, and even as its hideous features betrayed its demon origin, they also betrayed its terror.

The Slayer sprang.

JANUARY 1586

Durham House, the London home of Sir Walter Raleigh, had played host to many notables of the era. John White knew that his face would not cause any stir if glimpsed by Raleigh's neighbors. He was a comparative nobody, merely an artist, when illustrious figures such as Sir Francis Drake and the queen's astrologer John Dee were regular visitors.

Nonetheless, the meeting tonight, of some famous figures and some nobodies such as he, might hold the fate of the world in balance. White always felt the weight on his shoulders every time he attended. He stepped out of the carriage and drew his cloak about himself more closely. The servants opened the door for him and took his cape, hat, and stick, silent as ever, averting their gazes. *Excellent men, all of Raleigh's servants. They may be trusted to keep silent.*

The harsh sound of arguments greeted White as he entered the private back room. Twenty-two men were crowded into it, and they sounded as if all were talking at once.

". . . don't care what Dee's bauble shows, the Spanish . . ."

". . . we've missed too many of them, if Dee says it's the New World, then . . ."

". . . take care of the ones we know about before we . . ."

"John, just the man I wanted," came a sharp, strong voice in White's ear. "I've got a proposition for you." It was Raleigh himself, grasping White by the elbow and threading his way into the close-packed room. White felt calmer at once, despite the discord in the room. Raleigh was such a powerful, imposing figure. Slim and elegant, at over six foot tall he towered over the other men. He was dressed with his usual flamboyant elegance, and large jewels winked in his ears and on his fingers. His dark, curly hair seemed black in the dim light.

In the center of the room, sitting expressionless at a table in front of a large black orb, was John Dee. His eyes glittered in the flickering illumination of candles and lamps. Before him, his Show Stone, upon which the Watchers relied heavily, also caught the gleam of candlelight, but nothing more.

"Gentlemen, please." Raleigh's voice, with its heavy Devonshire accent, sliced through the hubbub. "One of the principals in the drama about to unfold has now arrived. Pray you silence, and let me tell you where we stand.

"We have a Watcher taking care of the present Slayer, and all seems well in that quarter. Masters Peyton and Dutton assure me that the seventeen possible Slayers-in-training are progressing admirably. We are here tonight to discuss the next generation of Slayer, and where she might be found. Dr. Dee?"

The seeming statue moved to life. John Dee sat straighter in his chair. When he spoke, his long beard trembled. "My Show Stone has told me that very soon, the Slayer for whom we wait shall be born. Her birthplace is the New World. It is entirely possible that she could be a savage, such as our Croatoan Indian friends, Manteo, Wanchese, and Towaye."

John White frowned slightly. He knew the three well. It was he who had suggested that they accompany him from the ill-fated colony at Roanoke Island, in the New World, to meet the queen and who were presently staying at Durham House. He disliked the term "savage"; while they were, of course, not civilized in the same manner as the English were, they were gentle, strong, intelligent representatives of their people.

"Or," Dee continued, looking at the men who stood crowded around him, "it could be a European child, born on American soil."

Sir Francis Drake grimaced. "Bloody Spaniards," he muttered. "We're about to go to war with them, and it sounds like we'll have to start sniffing about for the Slayer in their colonies. A fine situation."

"Could be the French," someone else put in.

"Even worse."

"Or," said Raleigh, his voice ringing, "it could be an English child."

"We've no colonies, Walter," said Drake. "No offense, my

friend, but your last attempt at Roanoke was disastrous. Your cousin Grenville did a fine job of alienating the savages, and Lane practically wept like a girl in order to accompany us home."

"Our first attempts failed because we stranded soldiers and expected them to be diplomats and farmers," said Raleigh. "And Roanoke was a poor place, I know that now. But I've been able to procure backing for another attempt. This time, I want families. Women are a civilizing influence, and men are less likely to grow bored and quarrel with the natives if their wives and children are at risk. And," he added, arching a black eyebrow, "we will not settle at Roanoke. We will create the City of Raleigh on the mainland, at Chesapeake. This way, if Dee is right—"

"I am," said Dee, his voice revealing his offense.

"—then we English have at least a chance of having this Slayer born to a godly Protestant Englishwoman. John," Raleigh continued, turning to White, "you've been to the New World before. It'll be a different site, but you have at least some experience. And we'll need a Watcher, just in case a girl-child born there does turn out to be the Chosen One. We'll miss your fine drawings, but you'll be of more use to the Council and the Slayer there than here."

White didn't know how to respond. He was chagrined at the thought of leaving England again for so long, possibly for the rest of his life. He had enjoyed sketching the Indians and flora and fauna of Virginia, but he had looked forward to returning to the Council, to helping fight demons, and recording their images to aid future Watchers in their own quests. He was not a natural leader of men, not like Raleigh and Drake. And yet, the thought that he might be the Watcher of the coming Slayer—

"You honor me, Sir Walter. My own family shall be among those who settle. When do we depart?"

JULY 1587

The journey had begun ill, and continued so. The three ships, led by the *Lion* under expatriate Portuguese sailor Simon Fernandez, had gotten off to a late start. The long journey over the open ocean to the West Indies and thence to Virginia had been dreadful at best, indescribably horrific during the frequent storms. The 116 colonists had endured vile food, poisoned fruits, and noxious water. Throughout it all, Fernandez had played the part of a villain. He had put privateering and profit over the good of the colonists, despite the fact that Raleigh's gold was paying for the venture, and had continually made and broken so many promises that White had lost count. He would not be sorry to see Fernandez depart once he had deposited them at Chesapeake.

Finally, in late July, the little fleet anchored off Roanoke Island. White and a few men went ashore in the small pinnace. White felt a stirring of fond familiarity. He'd liked this place. But it would not be home. He was here to look for fifteen men left behind when Governor Lane departed last year, and then proceed on to the permanent site at Chesapeake.

"Governor!" It was one of Fernandez's men, calling from the *Lion*. "Leave your men on the shore. Only you and three men may reboard to gather your supplies and assist the rest off this vessel."

"What?" Surely White had been mistaken, but the man leered.

"You're all staying here. Captain says the summer is too far gone—he won't go on to Chesapeake!"

Even as White gaped, searching for words of protest, the swarthy Portuguese appeared on the deck. His eyes met White's, and he grinned. Sick, White realized he had no options. The deed was done. There would be no lush Chesapeake, only the harsh reality of Roanoke, which had already failed before, all because a greedy captain wished to continue to plunder.

"Don't look so sad, White!" bellowed Fernandez. "I'll be back by the end of summer, to see if any of you are tired of this New World!"

He felt a hand on his shoulder. His son-in-law, Ananias Dare. White looked into the younger man's face, knowing his impotence and fear was reflected on his features.

"You and Eleanor should have stayed in England," he said, his voice breaking. "Roanoke is no place to give birth."

"Perhaps better here than onboard the ship. We are all in God's hands. This must be our destiny," said Ananias. "And the baby will come regardless."

There was nothing more to say. They continued on toward the beach, and White felt the eyes of some who were not as kind as Ananias boring into him.

"God's teeth," swore Christopher Cooper, one of White's ten assistants. "Look."

It had been hard to see the sun-bleached bones against the paleness of the sand, but now that the eye had picked it out, it was impossible not to see it. The skeleton was naked, flesh and clothing both stripped away by the harsh environment. As they approached, silent and horrified, they saw several arrowheads lying on the sand inside the rib cage.

"Shot to death," said Cooper, softly and angrily.

"No," said George Howe, another of White's assistants who had gone around to the other side of the corpse. "Bludgeoned. Look." He indicated a massive hole in the skull.

White swallowed hard and, despite the heat of the summer's day, felt cold. In many cultures plagued by demons and vampires, it was common to enact a "second death." The brain was often seen as the site of the demon's power. Once the creature had been slain by conventional means, its skull was often smashed to pieces to ensure it did not rise again. The same could be accomplished by cutting off the head, a slightly—but only slightly—more civilized method. It seemed this glorious New World was not free of the Old World's demons. If this man's skull had been crushed, it could be assumed that someone feared he would rise again . . . as a monster.

Yet he could not tell these men this, not yet. Not until he was certain that the danger was real, and not just an ancient tradition the Indians had kept alive throughout God-alone-knew how many centuries. He'd have to speak with his friend Manteo, whom he trusted to tell him the truth.

"Butchers," said Roger Pratt, practically spitting the word. "Not enough to kill a man with an arrow, eh?"

"It is probably part of their primitive religion," said White, trying to sound as though he meant the words he said.

Reverently, they gathered the bones. They would give the man a decent burial. There was no way to tell if this had been an innocent man slain by the Indians, or was being drained and about to be Turned and then, once dead, would rise to walk as one of the undead. Even if he had been well on his way to becoming a vampire, these old bones were no threat and deserved at least that much.

With this grim discovery, the men settled in for the night. They ate their cold, moldy provisions and talked in low voices about the fifteen men who had been left behind.

White's mood improved when he took stock of the remaining buildings as he led the company to the site three days later. The fort itself had been razed. While the houses were damaged and overgrown with melon vines, on which deer were happily grazing, they needed only minor repairs. In fact, his old dwelling, in which he had sketched so often, was still intact. In Chesapeake, they'd have had to start from scratch. Here, he knew the land, at least; he knew the Indians. And the Croatoan Indians Manteo and Towaye, who had lived with Raleigh for the last few years, had traveled back with them; it would be good to have allies to consult. Perhaps this was the better way after all.

"We will be fine, Father," said Eleanor. She rubbed her enormous stomach. "At least my son will be born in a proper English house!"

The climate and labor did not seem to agree with one of the assistants, a hitherto jovial fellow named George Howe. With each passing day, Howe seemed to grow paler and weaker. He tired easily, and White worried about him. *Does this place have new diseases of which we are not aware?*

Six days later, he would learn the truth.

White had been peacefully sketching when young Thomas Archard hastened up to him, his face flushed with exertion.

"It's Master Howe!" he cried, almost sobbing. "He's dead, he's dead!"

The boy's hysterical cries had caught the attention of everyone in the encampment. Husbands looked to wives, mothers reached for their children. White cursed inwardly, for Tom had blurted out the news right in front of young Georgie, Howe's eleven-year-old son. Georgie went pale as a sheet, but White could spare no time to comfort the orphan.

Wordlessly, he put down his pen. He, Cooper, and Ananias followed where the boy led. White's first thought was that poor George Howe, with his increasing weakness, had died of exhaustion, even though White had ordered him to stop the hard labor and to try to catch crabs for their supper instead. The site Howe had selected was two miles away, on the shoreline again, and the image was all too familiar, if the more grotesque for its freshness.

George Howe had not died from exhaustion. In order to better reach the crabs, he had stripped to next to nothing. Now, he lay facedown in bloody sand. Sixteen arrows pierced his body like a pincushion. Worse, though, was the dreadful mess the

Indians had made of Howe's head. Brain and bits of bone were spattered about.

Tom lost control now and began to cry, turning toward Ananias and burying his head in the older' man's chest. Ananias patted him awkwardly. His eyes met White's, and White nodded.

Ananias had seen what he had seen; two small holes in Howe's throat. They could have been mistaken for insect bites, but both Ananias and White had seen this before. No wonder Howe had been weakening by the day. They would all need to take the utmost care. During the balmy nights, the open air was more pleasant than the unfinished buildings, and most of the men had taken advantage of that. They would need to rebuild the fort, and quickly, sleeping on the pinnace in the meantime. They—

"We've got to find them," said Cooper. His face glowed with a thirst for revenge. "We've got to find the savages and kill them. Look at him! Poor Georgie!"

"We'll take care of Georgie," said Ananias before White could speak.

"We must be certain who did this," said White, keeping up appearances even though he knew that, though the Indians had killed George Howe, they were not the most dangerous enemy. And he could not speak what was uppermost in his mind: *If Howe was gradually being drained and about to be Turned, then they were right to kill him.* "I'll speak with Manteo."

AUGUST 18, 1587

I sent a small group to Croatoan Sound, where Manteo's people told Edward Stafford that Howe had been slain by the hostile Roanoacs. I desired strongly to establish friendly relations with various other tribes on the mainland as well as the Croatoan, and, if possible, even the Roanoac. To that end, the Croatoans agreed to pass along an invitation to the Roanoac werowances to speak with me within seven days. When that time had elapsed and none of the chiefs showed, I yielded to pressure from the hawks in our midst to exact revenge against the Roanoacs.

White paused, the candle beside him flickering. He didn't want to write this down, but he had to. Sighing, he continued.

We made a terrible error. When we reached the Roanoac village of Dasemunkepeuc, creeping in the night, we surprised several Indians—but they were innocent Croatoans, come to gather what supplies the Roanoacs had left behind when they fled. We thus inadvertently killed our allies, including a woman with a child.

At least Manteo had understood it was the most unfortunate of accidents. It was hard for English eyes to distinguish among the tribes, and at night, in the heart of the Roanoac camp—what else was one to expect but Roanoacs? Thank God Manteo and the Croatoans were still their friends. Manteo had even been baptized in the Christian faith just four days ago. He'd been dubbed the Lord of Roanoke.

"Father," came Eleanor's soft voice.

"Not now, my dear, I'll lose my thoughts," he replied.

"Father!" The word was now a shout, and as he turned, he saw her sink slowly down to the earth, leaning against the doorframe and clutching her belly.

* * *

For the next seven hours, Ananias Dare and John White listened to Eleanor Dare's screams, moans, and whimpers as she labored to bring forth the first English child born on American soil. They heard the doctor and the midwife's soothing murmurs, but it was of little comfort. Ananias looked awful.

"I would I could be there," he muttered as he paced outside the small house.

"Nonsense," said White. "It isn't proper. The babe will be a fine, healthy son, Ananias. You'll see."

At that precise moment, a lusty wail filled the air. Both men whirled and stared at the door. Dr. Stevens, wiping blood and other fluids from his hands, opened the door and motioned that they could enter.

White thought his beloved daughter looked like the Madonna with the Christ Child as she sat, propped up on pillows, suckling the babe.

"How is he?" asked Ananias.

"*She* is a miracle," Eleanor breathed softly, looking down at the tiny child. "We'll name her Virginia, after our good queen."

White trembled. A girl. John Dee's words floated back to him: *My Show Stone has told me that very soon, the Slayer for whom we wait shall be born. Her birthplace is the New World.* And Raleigh's comment: *It could be an English child.*

Dear God, White half-thought, half-prayed, *do I behold the next Slayer?*

After George Howe's death, those who knew about such things took great care to protect the colony from vampire attack. Reverend John Bright, the minister, blessed each house as it went up. Salt was spread over the entrances, supposedly a simple tradition, but much more than that. White pushed hard for all the houses to be built quickly and for a protective wall to be ringed about them. Some argued that this would send the wrong message to the friendly Croatoans. White did not worry. He had spoken in private to Manteo, and had learned much.

"We call them the Night Walkers," said Manteo. "They are those who refuse to stay buried. After death, those who have the marks"—he touched the side of his neck—"if their skull is not smashed, they can Walk again. It is a second killing."

"You can also put a stake of wood through their hearts or cut off their heads," White had said. "In our land, we have Walkers, too. Although most people do not believe they exist."

"They are very real," Manteo had said. And White believed him. No, the Croatoans would understand the precautions. They knew what the danger was from those who Walked in the night. He had finally decided to tell Manteo his greatest secret. The Indian had proved himself a loyal friend, and if the danger was as great as White feared, they would need his support.

"Where I come from," White had said, "there is a mighty warrior we call the Slayer. She is born to each generation, and her role is to destroy Walkers and other demons. Our God has gifted her with many talents—great strength, swift healing, superior senses, so that she may fight for us and protect us."

Manteo laughed, showing white teeth against brown skin. "You play with me, John White. A girl cannot do such things."

"The Slayer can. I tell you this because I have reason to believe that she will be born here, soon. In our colony, or perhaps in your tribe. We do not know. I wished you to know of her, so that if she is born to your people, you can tell me. I am a Watcher—someone who trains the Slayer. It is vital that she be trained, or else she won't be prepared for the trials to come. Will you tell me if such a girl is born to you, Manteo?"

"If a girl-child who has these skills is born to the Croatoan, White, then you will hear us shouting aloud."

Yes, I have made the right decision. He was so lost in recollecting the conversation that the ink had dried on his quill. He scarce noticed when Ananias approached him. "Governor," said his son-in-law, "we must talk."

The other six assistants entered the small house, somber and determined. White knew immediately this was not going to be a pleasant conversation.

"What is it, gentlemen? How may I be of service?"

"That's just what we've come for," said Cooper, shifting his weight from one foot to the other uneasily. "We need you to help us."

"Because of the savages and the delays that cursed Portuguese captain put us through, we are dangerously low on supplies," Roger Bailie continued. "According to the Croatoans, it's going to be a bad winter. We'll use up the rest then and have nothing left to plant in the spring."

White nodded, seeing where the conversation was going. "When Fernandez returns—if indeed he does, the blackguard— I'll send someone back to England with a request for supplies. Who would like to volunteer?"

Silence greeted his question. "We were thinking, sir, that maybe it ought to be you," said Pratt.

"Out of the question." He was the Watcher, and he was beginning to believe that his little granddaughter might be the One he was supposed to be Watching. Of course, no one but his daughter and Ananias knew of that particular complication. "Someone else must go."

"Begging your pardon, sir," stammered Dyonis Harvie, "but

we've made up our minds. You're the only one with enough influence in London to get us a ship back soon enough to do us any good."

Sickened, White glanced from face to face, looking for someone, anyone, to raise a protest. Even Ananias looked at the floor. Ananias *knew* how important White's secondary mission was. He *knew* about the Watchers Council, and Dee's prophecy. He also knew about the Walkers. And yet he was willing to see White return to England.

For days, they argued. Finally the assistants produced a paper that they had all signed, assuring anyone who might accuse White of leaving his people like a coward that he was going for their sakes. The Slayer, if such little Virginia was, was hardly going to need Watcher guidance for the few months it would take White to return with supplies. Ananias and Eleanor had helped him in attacking demons and vampires ere now; surely they would know how to defend themselves.

Fernandez did return, but he was impatient to resume his privateering. On August 27, with the heaviest of hearts and praying that he was doing the right thing, White kissed his daughter and granddaughter good-bye, embraced his son-in-law, and departed for England.

The time passed. Summer's heat gave way to autumn, then to winter. The colony continued to work hard, finishing the needed repairs to the fort, erecting houses for each family, and making sure that the gate was well barred at night. If it had not been for the kindness of Manteo and the Croatoans, they would have died during that bitter winter. But Manteo and the sharp-eyed medicine man named Okisko, whom Manteo called "the flyer" and who wore a flattened woodpecker on his head and the head of a fox on his breechclout, kept bringing the hungry Englishmen food, even though this depleted their own stores. The colonists gratefully responded by sharing the few deer that they were able to catch on their own as well as tools and skills they had brought from England. More and more, the two very different peoples turned to one another, until at last, merging seemed the only logical thing to do.

"What do you mean, I'm not allowed to leave?" sputtered John White. "I've got Grenville and eight ships loaded with food and supplies ready to sail tomorrow! My God, man. We know she's the Slayer. Dee's confirmed it—you know what's at stake! She has to have supervision!"

The usually unflappable Sir Walter Raleigh looked as pained as White had ever seen him. "No one knows better than I, John. But I can't go against the Privy Council and Her Majesty. If they want to confiscate your vessels for use against the Spanish Armada, there's nothing any of us can do."

"But . . . she's the Slayer, Walter! And my granddaughter . . ."

Raleigh put a sympathetic hand on the man he had chosen to be governor of his newest colonization attempt. "Take heart, John. This war can't last forever."

But to the anguished John White, a father who had left behind a daughter and granddaughter, and a Watcher who had, need be damned, forsaken his Slayer, the war did indeed seem to last forever.

July 1588

It had taken many months and many trips from Roanoke to Croatoan, but the task was almost complete. All the housing had already been broken down and transported by canoe and pinnace. The last of the supplies were going over the next day or two, and then the colonists would move. Two more nights in this place, and then it would be a new beginning. Eleanor hummed to herself as she finished packing her father's prized possessions. They would be buried, kept safe from the ravages of nature and beasts, and when he returned, he would be overjoyed to see how well the colonists had taken care of his things.

She turned to packing the few items her own family would be taking to Roanoke. Little enough—blankets, a few precious books, tools. Virginia's cradle. Eleanor paused for a moment to regard her sleeping child with love.

Ananias bent to pick up the chest containing the governor's personal items. "Find another to help you," Eleanor warned. "Armor isn't light."

"You shouldn't be packing that. We could use it," he replied.

"Our real enemies don't care about physical armor," she reminded him, lowering her voice. The Night Walkers had done their share, more than the fearsome Roanoacs, to diminish the ranks of the colonists. Several hunting parties had failed to return, and when their bodies were eventually found, according to Ananias they had had their skulls literally pulverized and sported two marks on their throats. Yet she and Ananias had refrained from informing the others, and soon, the threat would be gone.

She shivered, though the night air was balmy. Yes, it would be good to be safely with their friends the Croatoans. Manteo had said there were no Walkers on Croatoan Island.

"Lest I forget in the excitement of leaving, I'm going to go leave the message John told us to," said Ananias.

Eleanor looked up at him. "Can it not wait until morning? The Walkers . . ."

"We've never seen a trace of them this close to the camp. I'll be careful." He kissed her quickly, and then stepped into the night. The two men whose job it was to guard the gate bolted the door behind his back. Eleanor stood and stared at the door, whispering a prayer for her husband's safety.

Before he left, White had taken Ananias aside and told him, "If you must leave, for whatever reason, carve the name of your destination in a conspicuous place. Then I shall know how to find you. If there is danger, carve a cross beside the name."

Ananias glanced about, but the night was still. He turned his attention to carefully carving the word CROATOAN in one of the fort's stout posts. He nodded to himself, pleased that there was no need to carve the cross. It was a good departure. On an impulse, he decided to also place the word on a tree near where it was likely White would come ashore, just to be certain.

Briskly he strode to the shore, found the tree, and began to carve.

When dawn came, Eleanor reached for her husband. He was not there. She bolted upright and hastened toward the men who had stood watch all night.

"Has Ananias come and gone, then?"

Roger Bailie exchanged glances with Chris Cooper. "Nay, Mistress Dare. He has not returned. Perchance he got lost in the dark, and will return soon."

She felt the blood drain from her face, but she forced a smile. These men did not know of the Walkers. But she did. She knew she was now a widow, and yet could not shed a tear. She kept up the facade through the day and into the evening. When a search party failed to find Dare, others grew concerned as well, but it was decided that they would leave as scheduled.

"We'll leave him a canoe," said Bailie with exaggerated heartiness. "He'll join us soon, I'm certain."

"Yes," managed Eleanor, raw with grief and with a false smile on her face. "You are probably right."

That night, as the colonists finished packing and lay down in small clusters of family groups around the bonfire in the center of the encampment, a familiar voice was raised outside the palisade.

"Ho, good folks of the City of Raleigh! A lost lamb has wandered home!"

The hairs on Eleanor's arm stood up. She had been lying beside the fire, Virginia asleep in her cradle, and she turned at the sound of her husband's voice. Fear gripped her heart, and for a moment she couldn't breathe. Then air rushed into her lungs and she lurched to her feet, screaming, "Master Bailie! No! Don't let him—"

The gate swung open. Ananias stood there, grinning. Blood covered his neck and stained his shirt black in the flickering firelight. His teeth were sharp, and as his eyes met hers, they lit up as with an inner fire of their own.

He had not come alone. Behind him stood several dozen Walkers, and like a tidal wave, they poured into the encampment.

Though her heart was breaking, Eleanor Dare was the daughter of a Watcher, and she knew what she had to do. She dove for the fire and snatched a stick from its heart. It burned her hand. She reached for her child and, steeling herself against her daughter's scream of pain, branded the girl with a cross on her perfect, pale forehead. Tears in her eyes, Eleanor whirled to face the thing that had been her husband. She stabbed forward with the sharp piece of wood, but the Walker was quicker.

His hands grabbed her wrists and squeezed. Eleanor cried out as the bones snapped, and the stick fell from her hands.

"It's not so bad, my love," Ananias whispered, lowering his mouth to her neck. "It's sweet . . . so hot and sweet. . . ."

Amid the shrieks of the dying and the victory cries of the killers, one sound rose up into the night sky more piercing than any other: the treble, thin cry of a wounded and terrified infant.

When the colonists did not arrive on the shores of Croatoan as planned, Manteo feared the worst. Mindful of the approaching night, he and Okisko, Ceremonial Fox, took a canoe to Roanoke. They heard no sounds of talk. All the canoes and the pinnace were on the shore, laden with supplies.

"Ananias!" Manteo called. No answer, save the cry of a lone hawk.

"Takes From Eagle," Ceremonial Fox called to him. "Look at this." Takes From Eagle, called "Manteo" by the English, looked to where the conjurer pointed. On a tree were carved what the English called letters. Takes From Eagle had learned how to read when he lived with Raleigh in England. He sounded the letters out: "C. R. O."

He turned to Ceremonial Fox. "It seems as though someone was trying to leave a message. These symbols are the first three letters of our island's name in English."

Ceremonial Fox frowned, then reached into his medicine pouch and withdrew a handful of uppowok, which the English called "tobacco." He sprinkled Takes From Eagle with it, then himself. It was an appeal to the *mantoac,* the gods, and it would help keep them safe. "We must hurry," he said, glancing at the sky. "Night comes."

The fort's massive door stood wide open. When they entered, the carnage that met their eyes was almost beyond belief. Both of them had seen Walker victims before, but never so many. Takes From Eagle's eyes filled and he couldn't see.

The more practical Ceremonial Fox said, "They are not all here. The Walkers have taken many of them."

Takes From Eagle rubbed his eyes, and with fresh horror saw that Ceremonial Fox was right. While the number of bodies was staggering, it was nowhere near the hundred that they should have seen.

"We need to take all the vessels away from here," Takes From Eagle said. "So many Walkers . . ."

Steeling themselves against the gore, they completed the grim task of pulverizing the skulls of the dead men, women, and children. They carried the bodies down to the shore aboard the pinnace, then set the ship aflame and cut the rope. The tide would take it away. As they turned to their own, they heard a faint sound from inside the fort. Takes From Eagle froze. It came again—the whimpering of an infant. Against all odds, someone had survived. He walked back to the English encampment. Slowly, almost reverently, Takes From Eagle picked up the baby from her cradle.

"What is that on her head?" cried Ceremonial Fox. "Do these white men mutilate their own?"

"It is a cross," said Takes From Eagle. "A holy symbol. Eleanor no doubt marked her, to keep her alive. At the cost of her mother's life, Virginia Dare yet lives." He brought the infant close to his chest. The exhausted baby turned her head, seeking nourishment. "We will take her with us," said Takes From Eagle. "She will be raised as my daughter. She will not fall to the Walkers as her parents did."

AUGUST 18, 1590

It had been with a mixture of apprehension and anticipation that John White had finally returned to Roanoke. The trip, as seemingly every sea voyage he had undertaken with regard to the colony, had been wretched and fraught with near disaster. He had fought steadily for permission to bring ships back to Virginia, and after three long years, he was finally honoring his promise to return.

The day before yesterday, they had wasted precious time exploring a fire on the mainland, which had turned out to have been sparked by lightning, not by man. Yesterday, the expedition had gotten off to a very late start, and the weather had been horrible. The violent waves nearly sank White's small vessel, and though there was no loss of life aboard, food, furniture, and gunpowder were swept overboard. Captain Spicer's vessel fared more tragically. Seven men, including the captain himself and the surgeon who had come to join the colony, drowned. It had taken every ounce of persuasion White possessed to entice the disheartened men to put ashore. They headed for a second fire. They called aloud, sang English songs, and blew trumpets. Nothing. They had been duped a second time by nature into thinking the fire man-made.

Finally, the party came to the site where the colony had been. On the beach was a tree that bore the letters *CRO*. White smiled to himself. *They remembered.* Then the smile faded. *Why was not the word completed?*

As they made for the fort White's eager footsteps slowed. All the houses had been taken down, and there were charred remains of what had once been a wooden palisade. Again, there was something carved on one of the remaining posts: CROATOAN. He felt a wave of relief. There was no cross, no sign that they had left for any reason other than their own free will. The Slayer was safe.

Further exploration located White's personal items, buried but since dug up and their contents ruined. His books were torn from the covers, the maps rotten and spoiled with rain.

"My armor," he sighed, gazing at the once-beautiful breastplate now nearly eaten through with rust. *Ah, well. If my family is safe with Manteo's people, it is little enough to pay.* Tomorrow, he would see them at Croatoan.

But evening brought more foul weather, such that they barely made it to the *Hopewell.* The storm raged through the night and into the next day. While Captain Cocke could make it to Croatoan, landing was impossible. Cocke made his decision. They would not land at all.

Despite White's pleas and protests, Cocke turned the fleet toward Puerto Rico. Yes, of course, they would return in the spring, he assured White. But even as he looked on Cocke's face, White knew the truth, and it was a bitter draft.

He could, and would, continue to try to get a relief fleet to the colonists. But in his heart, he knew that, despite his efforts, he would never see his family again.

They gave Virginia Dare the name White Doe, and she grew up as one of the other Croatoan children. Takes From Eagle doted on her but strove to show no favoritism. Even those who disliked the white man, among them Wanchese—He Who Flies Out, who had traveled to England with Takes From Eagle, had no dislike of this innocent little girl.

Takes From Eagle decided that it would be best if the girl did not know her horrific origins. She would be a gift from the *man-toac* to the tribe, nothing less.

But destiny would not permit White Doe to grow up as just another Croatoan, albeit a pale-complexioned, yellow-haired one. No child in the tribe was more agile in climbing trees or catching fish with the spear than White Doe. No child could run as fast, or as far, and no child survived the bumps and scrapes of play with as little injury as the English child. At first, Takes From Eagle attributed it to her race. Perhaps the white man was hardier than the Croatoan. But when White Doe was six and a broken bone healed within days, everyone took notice. This was more than good heritage. This smacked of spirit intervention.

The werowances met one night after the children had gone to bed. They talked about White Doe in soft voices until finally Takes From Eagle had to speak the truth that was in his heart.

"She is no demon," he said, sorrow tingeing his voice. He had not realized until now how much he had wanted his adopted daughter to just be herself, not something as magical as. . . .

"Before he left, John White told me of a heroic Walker-killer who is born to each generation. She has miraculous healing power, sharp senses, and strength beyond even the most powerful warrior. Her destiny is to stand against evil, be it demons or Walkers. It is always a girl, and the name White gave me to call her, should she be born into our tribe, is the Slayer."

He studied their surprised reactions, but no one doubted him. Takes From Eagle did not lie. "White Doe was not born into our tribe, but she has been Croatoan since she was but a few months old. I could not love her more if she were my own flesh. I believe that she is this Slayer of whom White told me, and it is imperative that we protect and train her, that she will later protect us."

"I think Takes From Eagle is correct," said Ceremonial Fox. "We should begin training White Doe immediately, lest these powers get out of hand."

"A few more years," pleaded Manteo. "Let her be a child a little while longer."

They surrendered to his plea, but when the day came that Manteo's wife told him that their pale child had experienced her first bleeding, Manteo knew the time had come. With the moon blood came womanhood, and White Doe was no longer a child. After her flow had run its five-day course, he called her to him. She came at once, as always, eager to please her beloved father.

"You sent for me, Father?"

He nodded sadly and indicated that she sit on the floor of their large house. She did so.

"Your mother tells me you have become a woman."

By the firelight, he saw that her face reddened. It was a reaction unique to her; Croatan skin was so dark that the rush of blood could not usually be seen.

"Yes," she whispered. "I am now a woman."

"You are more than a woman, daughter, and the time has come for you to accept your duties. Surely you have noticed that you are different from the others?"

"My skin—"

He waved the words aside. "Nothing so trivial as that. Your healing. Your skill. Your strength, your agility . . ." He took a branch that would soon be used to feed the fire. "Squeeze this as tightly as you can."

She obeyed, and he felt a shiver run through him as the branch, thick as his arm, shattered. Calmly he took a sharp splinter the width of his hand from the shattered branch, and he jabbed it deep into the soft flesh of her left arm. She cried out and pulled the stick free. But once she had wiped off the blood, she saw that the wound was already beginning to close.

"Do you see? You are a gift from the gods, more than we had dreamed. You are born to protect your people from darkness, White Doe. You are the Slayer, and whether you will it or no, you must be trained. It is a brave and noble calling. Do you accept?"

She lowered her eyes. "I didn't want to be different . . . but I suppose I have always known." She looked up at him, and her gaze was steady. "I will be the Slayer, Father, if you will teach me how."

And so for the first time in the history of the Croatan people, a woman was trained in the arts of war. Evergreen Thunder, her instructor, was shocked at how quickly and well White Doe learned, even though glimpses of her uncanny powers had manifested to one degree or another all her life. Her aim with the bow was deadly. She handled the knife well in hand-to-hand combat, executing staggering flips and dives that caught him off guard time after time, even when he knew to expect them. For the specific training she would need to slay Walkers, they used the bodies and skeletons of their enemies. Soon a young maiden barely into her womanhood was smashing skulls and stabbing chests without a qualm.

"You are ready," said Evergreen Thunder a few months into her training. "We can go to the mainland."

They went to the village of Dasemunkepeuc, where, unbeknownst to White Doe, her grandfather had accidentally killed many of the Croatoans, believing them to be Roanoacs. The village was deserted by the living. The Roanoacs had abandoned it long ago, and the Croatoans, remembering the tragedy, had also left it alone, despite the supplies that they could have used. According to Ceremonial Fox, whose magics enabled him to see far beyond what mortal eyes could, it was a veritable nest of Walkers.

Evergreen Thunder, Takes From Eagle, Ceremonial Fox, and White Doe landed there midmorning. White Doe was nervous and awkward, and in her eagerness she ran the canoe over Ceremonial Fox's foot while hauling it ashore.

"Ai!" he cried, hopping and clutching his injured foot.

"I am so sorry!" said White Doe, feeling her face grow hot. She was turning that odd shade of red, that shade that none of the others turned, and she hated it.

"A new war dance, Ceremonial Fox?" teased Evergreen Thunder. Ceremonial Fox glared, then gingerly tested his foot.

It was a brief walk to Dasemunkepeuc, and some of White Doe's enthusiasm faded. The few buildings still standing were overgrown with vines and wild melons. What had once been high stocks of fresh corn was now little more than dried, picked-over cobs. It was a bad place, with a tense feel to it.

"There is little here to salvage," said Takes From Eagle. "But that is not the reason we came. White Doe, we can return if you so wish it."

She wanted to cry out, *yes, let us return, I shall fight Walkers soon enough, there is no need to sit and wait for them to come!* Instead she said, with a calmness that surprised her, "We have come to kill Walkers. Let us do so."

They scouted about, hoping to surprise a Walker or two asleep, but luck was not with them. They started a fire and ate their evening meal of stewed meat, fish, fruits, and vegetables early, before the sun set. When they had finished, Ceremonial Fox removed the small pots of paint, blessed them, and carefully painted the warriors in preparation for the battle. The others took naps, but White Doe could not sleep. All she saw when she closed her eyes was the shuffling Walkers, rotting flesh dripping from their faces, approaching with slow, implacable purpose.

The sun began to set. Takes From Eagle added more wood to the fire. White Doe noticed he kept looking at her. The irritation she felt drove out the fear, and she was grateful.

Ceremonial Fox tensed, his alert pose mimicking that of the fox for which he was named. "They come," he said, softly. White Doe tensed. In the bag slung across her shoulder were the tools she would need: several sharp stakes of wood and a small toma-hawk, to bash in the Walkers' skulls. Now she withdrew a stake, and clutched it, ready to strike as she had been trained. As one, the warriors got to their feet, their backs to the fire, and waited.

The Walkers—seven of them—emerged from the shadows, and White Doe blinked. These did not look like monsters. They looked human. She even saw the familiar face of Careful Listener, who had disappeared a few months ago.

"Father," she said, "these are not Walkers." She lowered the hand that held the stake and looked at her father. And that was when the Walker sprang.

Careful Listener's face contorted before her eyes. His brown eyes went yellow, his face angular and bestial. Hot breath that smelled of old blood assaulted her as he opened his mouth, crammed full of impossibly sharp teeth. Instinct and training kicked in, and White Doe fought back, getting her hand under his chin and shoving upward with her full strength. She saw surprise flit over his obscene features, but he rallied. Twisting, she managed to flip the Walker onto his back. She saw an opening and took it, jabbing the sharp stick into the center of his chest. Careful Listener cried out, sharply, then the next thing White Doe knew she was kneeling on the earth, covered with fine dust.

She sprang to her feet and seized another stake in a single smooth motion. Shouting, she leaped onto the Walker who clutched Takes From Eagle. A fluid motion, and the Walker was destroyed.

White Doe whirled to catch the next one, and the next. *Dear gods, there are so many. . . .* She was dimly aware that she was not alone in this fight. Ceremonial's chanting voice rose above the furor, and Takes From Eagle swung his club fiercely.

And as quickly as it had begun, it was over. White Doe stood panting, her body slick with sweat, her fine golden hair matted to her brow. They were gone, save the three that lay with smashed skulls at their feet.

A hand fell on her shoulder. She whirled, and was only just able to stop in time to prevent herself from injuring Takes From Eagle. She stared at him, then wordlessly let herself be folded into an embrace. She began to sob. She had not expected it to be so horrible.

"You are very brave. I have never seen anyone fight as you

have, little White Doe. We shall call you the Slayer, for you slay with the strength of many men."

As she recovered and pulled away from her father, she saw Ceremonial Fox regarding her with an odd expression. She did not like that look. Something about it frightened her.

As the years passed, White Doe became a fixture in all the hunting parties and war parties, and whenever the Walkers were sighted, she would destroy them. Despite her age, she was soon a high-ranking wereowance, included in all councils and consulted in all things. Some muttered against her, jealous of her ability and rank. But most loved her, and chief among those was the son of He Who Flies Out, the handsome, fiery-eyed Seal of the Ocean. Yet he did not speak. Who was he to claim White Doe, the Slayer? Surely she would be the mate of another, more powerful man, and not a youth.

Yet he watched her, with an aching, hungry look on his fine features that spoke more loudly than any words.

Ceremonial Fox was engrossed in blessing his latest batch of gathered herbs when he heard White Doe calling. Since her first battle against the Walkers, she was almost his equal, and had no qualms about lifting the door and peeking in.

"Oh, I am sorry. I will return later, when I won't disturb you."

"No, come in. These can wait. What is it, White Doe?" He had a sudden image of her four years ago at Dasemunkepeuc, when she had put on such a brave face to cover her understandable terror at facing Walkers.

But she was a girl no longer. She had proved it with that first battle. Ceremonial Fox let his eyes roam over White Doe and saw not the happy, pretty child she had been, but the striking woman she had become. Her legs were long and lean as she crossed them to sit in front of him, her body taut and strong from fighting. Her breasts, uncovered in the manner of Croatan dress, were full and soft, and would fit just so into the cup of his hands. Her pale hair was long, and although she bound it, unruly, wild tendrils escaped, as if they, like the woman they adorned, could not be tamed. Even the scar on her forehead seemed beautiful to him, a symbol of her uniqueness. A white doe she was, pale and exquisite, with eyes that, like the sea, could drown a man. . . .

"I'm sorry, I did not hear," he said, realizing she had spoken.

White Doe smiled, and her cheeks flamed red. "A love potion," she repeated. "There is . . . someone I would have notice me."

Did he dare hope? Why else would she speak so boldly to him? Ceremonial Fox leaned forward. Unable to help himself, he reached and pulled loose a lock of that amazing, corn silk hair. "You do not need a love potion to attract him," he said, his voice husky with desire.

She brightened, and his heart soared. "You are certain?"

"Oh, yes," Ceremonial Fox said. "I am certain."

"It is only . . . I believe he thinks of me as a sister. . . . I will go to Seal of the Ocean right now! Thank you!"

She scrambled to her feet, all graceless fawn in her excited movements, and hasted out. Ceremonial Fox stared after her. Pain such as he had never known seared through him. *Foolish, foolish man! You are thirty years her elder! She wants young, hot blood like her own, not your wrinkled old man's touch. . . .*

He could not bear it. Could not bear to see her face light up when she looked at Seal of the Ocean, see the young man's intent gaze, watch them touch and kiss, see them wed, bless their children. He could not.

If Ceremonial Fox could not have White Doe, then no one would.

* * *

As Ceremonial Fox had known he would, Seal of the Ocean delightedly accepted the unusual courtship initiated by White Doe, and within a day they were formally betrothed. Ceremonial Fox did not participate in the celebration; there was much he needed to plan. The next day, after making the necessary preparations, he took White Doe aside and asked her to come to his house after nightfall. Obedient, she did so, sitting in front of him and looking at him expectantly.

"White Doe, we need you to go to Roanoke."

White Doe looked at Ceremonial Fox askance. "We're not permitted to go there. You yourself have forbidden it, because of the spirits who—"

"There are no spirits," said Ceremonial Fox. He leaned forward intently. His dark eyes were deep pools in his face. "That was a lie we had contrived to tell you, White Doe. For your own good."

"Why would you need to tell me a lie about Roanoke?"

"Because you came from there," the conjurer said intently. "You were not found in the wild, a gift from the *mantoac*. You are the daughter of men like us. Pale men, with hair the color of sunlight." He reached, as if to touch her long yellow hair, then curled his fingers into a fist and brought it back to his lap. "They came from across the sea. When you were but a few months old, the Walkers came for them. They slew your family, White Doe. Killed, feasted upon, and perhaps even Turned them. The only reason you survived was because your mother made the holy mark on your forehead. When Takes From Eagle and I came the next morning, we found only you alive. We took all the canoes, filled their ship with bodies, and set it afire, and stranded the Walkers on Roanoke. I commanded the water spirits to prevent them even trying to leave. There they have remained, feasting upon the wild beasts and hungering for human blood."

White Doe stared. She didn't want to believe him. She

couldn't believe him. It would mean that everything Takes From Eagle, her beloved father, had told her was a lie. She began to breathe shallowly, her fertile imagination racing with images of people who looked more like her than Ceremonial Fox or Takes From Eagle or even Seal of the Ocean, people with pale skin and sea blue eyes and corn yellow hair.

Her parents. Her true parents, slain by the Walkers. Left to rot on the beaches of the Forbidden Island—

—or else Walking the beaches themselves—

Gorge rose in her throat, and she choked it down. Tears burned in her eyes, her eyes that were not brown like those of the Croatoan, but sea blue.

"Why do you tell me this?" she whispered, and she could feel her heart breaking inside her chest.

"Because you are the Slayer," Ceremonial Fox replied, whispering the word fiercely. "It is time you freed us from the fear that somehow, someday, the Walkers of the Forbidden Island will be able to cross to our home. For now, the water spirits accept my commands. But someday I will be gone, and I do not know that the water spirits will obey my successor. And, someday, the people across the sea might return to Roanoke, bringing canoes with which the Walkers could cross. These Walkers will be worse, far worse, than the others."

"Because . . . because they are the Walkers from across the sea. Because they are . . . they were . . . like me?" She lifted her tear-stained face to his, silently pleading for a denial.

"Yes. And because for many years, they have hungered and been denied. You are the Slayer, and they were your people. It is only right that you destroy them." The conjurer paused, then added, "Takes From Eagle thought you too weak to know. He feared you would go soft inside, knowing that they were your family. He would not approve of my telling you this, of asking this of you."

Anger rose inside White Doe, chasing out the crippling sense of betrayal. "He would rather put our people in danger than let me do what I was born to do? He *lied* to me for that?" When Ceremonial Fox nodded, she squatted back on her heels, thinking. Finally, she looked at him and knew by his expression that her eyes were as stormy as the sea could become.

"I will go to Roanoke. I will slay the Walkers. And when I return, I will speak with Takes From Eagle."

"When you return," Ceremonial Fox agreed silkily, "then Takes From Eagle will be shamed by your bravery."

Roanoke was two days' journey to the north. In the predawn stillness, before anyone had risen, White Doe took a canoe and filled it with the tools she would need. Without even a backward glance at the place she had called home all her life, she slid the canoe into the water.

She stayed close to the shoals, and when night came, she pulled the canoe up onto a sand bar, stretched out a mat, and fell into a fitful sleep. On the evening of the second day, she saw Roanoke.

Despite Ceremonial Fox's words that these were Walkers, something she understood, and not spirits, she felt a chill fall over her. Once night came, her unnaturally sharp vision could see figures moving about. Could it really be that her blood parents were on the island? *Am I watching them even now?*

She stayed awake all night in the gently pitching canoe, watching them move. At last, dawn came, and she paddled ashore. Sand crunched as she hauled the canoe safely onto the beach. Her eye caught some strange carvings on a nearby tree—*CRO.* They meant nothing to her. She took a deep breath, calmed herself, and began.

First, she would seek out likely hiding places and slay as many as she could in the daylight, when they were most vulnerable.

When night fell, they would come at her full strength. Fortunately, the Walkers had probably waxed lazy in the intervening years. Nothing was hunting them here on Roanoke.

Until now.

She surprised a few dozen sleeping in the remains of houses inside the circle of wood. Such protection was not unknown to White Doe; the Croatoans sometimes erected wooden barriers. They wore tattered, filthy remnants of strange clothing, and as Ceremonial Fox had predicted, they all were as pale as she. She moved as silently as death itself, with a steady, burning purpose, and dispatched the Walkers before they were even fully roused.

White Doe then scouted out every overhang, looking for caves; every cluster of trees, searching for anything that might serve as shelter for the vile, not-dead Walkers. Several dozen more she found and slew methodically, with a detachment that would have surprised and grieved her adopted father.

Ceremonial Fox told her that he and Takes From Eagle had destroyed only a few. That meant, despite the many she had already killed, more had escaped. They would come for her at nightfall. She would be ready for them.

She built a fire, protection and weapon both. She gathered up the stakes and arrows—special arrows, with no stone arrowheads, only sharpened wooden ends—and resharpened them to fine points.

The sun had only just set when they appeared. Coolly, White Doe nocked an arrow and let fly. Her aim was unerring, and in the space of a few heartbeats she had managed to slay ten of them. Abandoning the bow, she took a stake in each arm.

"Virginia," came a woman's voice. White Doe started and looked for the speaker. It was a tall woman, with a face and hair as fair as her own. She had a sad, resigned look on her face. A male Walker stepped up to join her.

"Daughter," he said in the Croatoan tongue. "We never thought we would see you again."

Sudden weakness flooded White Doe. She had hoped that these two in particular were already among the truly dead. They looked kind, friendly. They would have been good parents had they not—

Had they not been Turned to Walkers. Resolve flooded her, and she straightened, again clutching the stakes in a defensive posture.

"Join us, and let us be a family again," pleaded the woman. Smiling, she stepped forward, hands raised as if to enfold White Doe. For the briefest of moments, White Doe allowed herself to mourn all that could have been. Then she sprang. One stake found its mark in the woman's breast, the second in the man's.

After that horrible moment, the killing came easier. She whirled and shrieked and leaped and fought like a demon. More than once, Walker hands or teeth found her flesh. She was soon bleeding, which roused the creatures to a frenzy that made them careless and even easier to kill. They came on and on, wave after wave, until finally, White Doe found herself standing alone, her sweat-slicked body covered with fine dust that faded quickly.

Silence. She gasped for breath, the sound of her own hammering heart ringing in her ears. She could not sense any more.

In one day, White Doe had slain almost a hundred Walkers.

Then, like a wave, the recollection of the faces of her true parents crashed down on her. The stakes fell from her hands, and her knees gave way. Her mind filled with images of Walkers who had once been living, breathing people, White Doe wept piteously, her heart breaking with each racking sob.

"You live," came a familiar voice. "I am glad."

She turned her swollen eyes upon the figure of Ceremonial Fox. Yet—there was something amiss. She could almost see through him. Fear began to seep into her.

"But I cannot let you return to Croatoan and marry that mewling boy," the image of Ceremonial Fox continued. "If you will agree to marry me—"

Anger rushed through her. *How dare he demand where I give my heart? I am the Slayer!* Look at what she had done here, where he had sent her alone and thought she would die. She got to her feet and cried, "Never! I love Seal of the Ocean! I'm the Slayer, Ceremonial Fox, and there is nothing you can do to prevent me from wedding the man I love!"

His face, never handsome, was hideous in its sneer. "Oh, but there is. You have powers, yes, but so do I. White Doe you are, White Doe you shall become!"

Pain shot through her. She grit her teeth to prevent a scream from escaping. She would give him no satisfaction. Her legs gave out, and she fell to the sand. Colors bled, until her world consisted of black and white and gray. She flailed, trying to rise, and to her horror saw not human arms and legs but those of a white deer.

Now she did scream, but the sound that left her throat was the squeal of a deer. Frantically she rose, four legs scrambling for purchase in the shifting sand. Craning her head on its long neck, she looked down and saw that her fears had been confirmed.

Stretching behind her was the white torso of a deer. She had truly become a white doe.

The image of Ceremonial Fox was gone, but she did not despair. He would not triumph. Surely, someone would understand when a white doe behaving like a human entered the village of Chacandepeco! They would force Ceremonial Fox to change her back. The tribe needed her protection. It was not so far that she could not swim. Boldly, she strode into the waves on slender, long legs.

A terrible shriek assaulted her newly sensitive ears. Before White Doe's eyes, the water took on a monstrous form. Everywhere she turned, she saw blue and white demonic-looking creatures. One of them extended an arm. A wave crashed down on her so violently that she stumbled. She fought, floundering and flailing to keep her head above water, straining for air. The next wave tossed her carelessly onto the beach. Gasping, but determined, White Doe struggled to her four feet, her flanks heaving as she sought air.

The water spirits. She had forgotten that Ceremonial Fox could control them. She was a prisoner on Roanoke Island, the place where she had been born. The place, barring an unlikely rescue, where she would die.

The white doe sank to the sandy soil, lifted her large, sea blue eyes to the sky, and began to keen.

By evening that first night, White Doe was missed. Ceremonial Fox watched, satisfied, as the tribe scurried about like ants, organizing search parties and talking among one another about who had seen her last. He especially enjoyed the stricken look on Seal of the Ocean's pretty, boyish face. He was not so pleased at Takes From Eagle's raw grief, but Ceremonial Fox knew no softening of the heart.

Of course, there was no trace of White Doe. After several weeks, even Takes From Eagle resigned himself to the fact that his precious adopted child was no longer among the living. There was a great mourning ceremony, in which the aging priest Many Trees prayed to the *mantoac* to permit her to walk in paradise, not suffer in Popogusso. That night, in his scrying bowl Ceremonial Fox saw the white doe standing again on the beach, looking longingly to the south, to Croatoan Island.

The summer was an unforgiving one. No one living could remember such a scorching sun, or such a long stretch of days without even a hint of rain. Many Trees informed them that the *mantoac* were offended with the Croatoan. More prayers and ceremonies were offered in the temple to the Kiwasowac, the images of the mantoac, but the gods seemed to be unmoved. Uneasily, Ceremonial Fox wondered if they were angry with him for what he had done to White Doe.

The werowances met and decided that, since water and food were so scarce, hunting would be permitted on Roanoke Island for the first time since the massacre. Deer were plentiful on the island, and the tribe needed nourishment. Ceremonial Fox was loath to obey, but he had no choice. He reluctantly agreed to call off the water spirits for one day only. The tribe could hunt all the deer they could in that time, but they needed to leave by the time the sun began to set.

The young men began to prepare eagerly for the hunt. Ceremonial Fox stayed behind, doing what he could to magically bind the doe to the island. She struggled, and once she seemed to gaze directly into his eyes as he watched her image in the water. But she did not leap for freedom, as he had feared.

Nonetheless, so remarkable a creature did not go unnoticed. When the braves returned, they were full of stories of a marvelous white doe, which seemed to vanish before their eyes. The words made Takes From Eagle grow somber, as he thought of his own lost child. Ceremonial Fox listened, his face impassive but his heart racing, praying no one would make the connection.

"A white doe is sighted on the Forbidden Island, when our own White Doe has gone," said Many Trees in his raspy voice. "All in the midst of a terrible drought. It is ill. It could be that if we offer this white doe to the *mantoac,* they will restore both the lost child and the withheld water."

"I will slay the white doe!" cried Complacent One.

"No, I will!" declared Seal of the Ocean, his voice ringing with conviction.

"Let there be a hunt on the island," ordered the chief. "The brave who kills the white doe shall receive much honor, and the pelt to wear."

Loud whoops filled the village at the news. Honor to be won, a beautiful pelt to be fashioned into unique clothing, White Doe to be returned, and the rain to fall. Why not rejoice? Only Ceremonial Fox retreated quietly to his house, there to contemplate his next move.

Seal of the Ocean felt alive for the first time since White Doe had disappeared. He still felt she lived. Maybe she had been taken by the Roanoac, though the warrior that could best her would have to be a fearsome man indeed. He held on to hope even after her own adopted father had resigned himself to her death.

The thought that slaying this uncanny white deer might bring his own beloved White Doe back gave him renewed energy. He carefully took with him a special arrow, one given to his father by the white man's Queen Elizabeth, a powerful werowance. It had been a parting gift to One Who Flies Out. It was a beautiful thing, with a silver arrowhead instead of stone. The queen had told his father it had magical powers and would never miss its mark, so it seemed the right arrow with which to hunt the white doe.

The day passed quickly with no sign of the strange animal. Finally, at twilight, just as he was about to give up and meet the other braves back at the canoes, he saw something gleam in the near darkness. He turned.

There it stood, a ghost in the fading light, white as the snow. Were its eyes really blue-green, or was that a trick of the twilight? It did not move but regarded him steadily.

Seal of the Ocean took a deep breath, nocked his magical silver arrow, and said a prayer.

*   *   *

Miles away, Ceremonial Fox stared into the image his scrying bowl showed him. He did not want another to have White Doe, but he had never truly wished her death. Even in the heat of his pain, when he sent her to Roanoke, he had hoped she would live. And yet Seal of the Ocean had managed to find her, despite the charms Ceremonial Fox had employed to keep her hidden from human eyes. Or was it simply that among White Doe's gifts was the ability to resist, at least a little, Ceremonial Fox's magic?

He saw their eyes meet, saw the doe stand rock still. Slowly, Seal of the Ocean nocked his bow with his silver arrow.

Tears filling his eyes, Ceremonial Fox felt his hardness break. Quickly, before it was too late, he spoke the words to reverse the spell. Better to see White Doe in another's arms than lying dead on the sands of Roanoke.

Seal of the Ocean let the arrow fly.

At that instant, the form of the white doe shimmered. Before his horrified gaze, it shifted into a familiar and beloved shape. Smiling joyfully, White Doe, human and alive, lifted her arms— and stared down at the arrow protruding from between her breasts. Her face froze, and she crumpled to the earth.

Shrieking, Seal of the Ocean rushed forward and cradled the naked girl in his arms. Blood spurted from the arrow, buried almost to its fletching in her chest. One pale hand lifted, touched the shaft, then fluttered down again. Blood dripped from her mouth as she lifted her eyes to him. Her lips moved.

"No, don't speak," Seal of the Ocean whispered. Lifting his head, he cried, "We need help!"

The bloody white hand touched his own strong, brown one. White Doe smiled gently.

"Too late," she whispered. "Listen . . . I must speak. . . ."

Tears pouring down his face, Seal of the Ocean leaned down, straining to catch her words.

"I was . . . the Slayer. I let anger and hurt and pride . . . betray me, and now I pay the price. Do not mourn. I die loved. . . ."

Her soft whisper trailed off, and her head lolled back on his arm. When the other braves reached Seal of the Ocean, they found him crying over the body of White Doe. Gently, they took him away, returning a moment later for the body.

It had vanished.

Miles away, Ceremonial Fox screamed in anguish, aghast at the tragedy to which his desire had led.

An ocean away, John White, ill and feverish, stirred in his sleep. Something had awakened him from such a sweet dream, a dream in which he embraced his daughter and his daughter's daughter, a beautiful girl with long, clean limbs and her mother's golden hair. . . .

"Your pardon, sir," said his servant. "I told Sir Walter's messenger you were sick, but he insisted I give this to you." Carrying a small candle, the servant stepped into the room and handed a note to White.

White waved it away. "Read it." At the servant's hesitation, he said, "I don't care what the messenger said, I am far too sick to read it on my own."

"Very good, sir." The servant set the candle down beside the bed, broke the seal, and frowned. "I don't understand it, sir. Only five words: 'There is another Chosen One.' "

White gasped. Deep sorrow flooded him, and he turned away so that the servant would not see the hot tears escaping his eyes. "I understand. Leave me."

And alone with ghosts and nightmares, John White mourned the death of the grandchild he had never seen.

"Virginia," he whispered hoarsely. "I am so sorry."

They say that the spirit of Virginia Dare still haunts Roanoke Island. At just the right hour on just the right night, you can catch a glimpse of a ghostly white deer, a luminous, transparent figure. Some say she gazes with unspeakable sorrow eastward toward England. But others say her heart lies to the south, to the island once known as Croatoan. And it is there the shade of Virginia Dare turns; to the people she loved and protected with her life, to where she was more than the Slayer—she was beloved White Doe.

die Blutgrafin

Yvonne Navarro

HUNGARY, 1609

"What evil is it they do, my *vigyázni?*"

Standing beside Kurt Rendor in the frigid darkness, fifteen-year-old Ildikó Gellért saw him start when she said *vigyázni—guard*. It was the closest the newly called Slayer could come to the word *Watcher* in their native Hungarian, and also her first true acknowledgment of his post in her life. She knew he would take it as a huge step for their relationship, a hint that the fierce and headstrong Ildikó might finally accept Rendor's experience, if not his authority.

Rendor hunched inside his woolen cape, and Ildikó knew he was feeling the bite of the wind in every joint of his seventy-year-old body. While she and her Watcher hid in the tree shadows at the forest's edge, the moonlight was still strong enough to break through the wintery cloud cover and the swirling snow; more often than not, there was plenty of light with which to see the figures in the clearing a hundred feet away. They bent and straightened, bent and straightened, fighting with something on the frozen ground.

"They bury the evidence," Rendor said finally. He kept his voice low, knowing the treacherous wind could switch directions at any moment and carry his words to the ears of those they spied upon.

Ildikó strained to see in the darkness. "They murder?" she whispered.

When she would have started forward, Rendor stopped her with a hand on her shoulder. "Wait," he instructed. "You will do a greater good if you hear me out and plan your moves with care."

She paused and said nothing for a few moments as the figures, dressed in much sturdier clothes than she and Rendor, finished their task then hurried down a path at the other end of the small clearing. While the Carpathian Mountains rose cold and majestic behind them, Ildikó knew the path across the clearing would ultimately wind back through the foothills to Castle Csejthe. "Whose bodies did they hide?" she asked quietly. "Those who have fallen prey to vampires?"

Rendor shook his head, then steered her into the forest and back toward the village. Wolves howled somewhere on the mountainside, their cries multiplying and echoing mournfully. "Not to vampires," he told her as they picked their way through the snow. "Serving girls—the latest victims of *die Blutgrafin*."

The Bloody Countess?

Ildikó looked at him sharply. "Countess Bathory did this?"

"These are the rumors, yes." The wind had risen, driving the snow in vicious circles in the air and slapping it against their faces, making them both huddle deeper into their garments. "She—" His murmured sentence ended suddenly, the words choking off in surprise as something leaped on him from the heavy darkness of the surrounding trees.

Rendor went down. *Wolf!* Ildikó thought and surged forward, intending to grab the hide of the snarling form. Then her hands gripped flesh—*cold* flesh—and she realized it was a vampire. Desperate and cold, starving enough to try an attack even when outnumbered. Oftentimes the wintry mountainside would do her work for her, the vicious weather numbing a vampire until the creature could barely function and found itself too far from shelter come dawn. This one had clearly felt that the last of its strength was better pitted against two foes than the frigid hand of nature.

She hauled the beast backward then realized Rendor had come with it—the dreadful thing had managed to clamp its teeth into one of her Watcher's shoulders. Even as the creature grunted with short-lived satisfaction, she could hear the elderly man fighting not to cry out, knew he was afraid the noise would draw more unwanted attention in the night. He pounded on the vampire's head to no avail, the snow making his blows slide harmlessly aside.

But Ildikó's strike would not be so easily ignored. She let go of the bloodsucker's wrist and buried her left hand in its matted hair instead; her right slid under its chin and she hooked her thumb and middle finger on each side of its jaw, digging in viciously until its jaw was forced open and the hold on Rendor released. The thing's mouth gaped, but its hiss of anger died abruptly as Ildikó pushed it backward and off balance—right onto the jutting limb of a dead tree.

Ildikó ignored the dust as it died and rushed to her fallen Watcher. "Are you all right? How badly are you hurt?" she asked urgently.

"I'll survive." Rendor was gasping with pain as she helped him upright. "We must get home quickly and cover the blood smell lest it draw another attack. I fear I would not be able to fight such an encounter."

"Of course." She ducked under his arm and used her shoulder to carry a good part of his weight. "Lean on me."

He did so, and they had taken only a few short steps when the question she was already dreading came. "Ildikó, did you not sense the night beast before it attacked? Not at all?"

The Slayer was silent for a moment, but the truth had to be admitted. "No."

Rendor said nothing more about it, but Ildikó knew it weighed heavily on his mind. She had trained and tried to learn the ways of a Slayer, and in most things she felt she didn't do badly. This, however, was her biggest shortfall—her inability to perceive a creature of the dark when it was near—and it was something for which her Watcher could provide neither mentoring nor training. This lack of intuitive skill had occasionally hindered her in the past, but tonight it had nearly cost the life of her Watcher. Ildikó swallowed, feeling ashamed and small, as though she had let down the one person she most hoped not only to protect, but impress.

She decided to turn the subject back to the countess, the castle, and the burial they had seen—anything to take their minds off this nearly fatal failure.

"The countess," she said. "You said she takes young serving girls?"

"Yes." Rendor's breathing was labored. "I will tell you more when we get inside, after we have cleaned my wound, supped, and rested a bit."

Like it or not, Ildikó was left to her own thoughts, as it took them another twenty minutes to get through the trees and make it to where they lived, in Rendor's small house at the outermost edge of the village. Set apart from the others, Rendor had once been a successful farmer; now grown old, he had sold off all but the small piece of land upon which his home was built. He was a man who loved solitude, and it had pained him to see the space that ensured that dwindle; still, while the surrounding earth had been turned and tilled by its new owners, his privacy was not yet threatened. No one saw him and the young Ildikó take refuge inside against the brutal, late Hungarian night.

After Rendor washed and wrapped the puncture marks in his shoulder, he then set to preparing a simple meal, something hot to chase away the cold. He set water to boil in the iron pot above the fireplace, scooped out a bit to make tea, then added a handful of root vegetables, herbs, and a chunk of dried mutton. While he worked at that, Ildikó braved the outside wind to fetch more fuel for the fire, then she spread their outerwear to dry.

"Tell me of the countess," she said when the meager soup was ready and ladled into trenchers in front of them. Its pleasant aroma mingled with the stronger scent from the still-steaming tea. "And of these rumors."

She had slain many vampires since her calling a half year previous, and often her Watcher, despite his great age, had helped her with these endeavors, tossing her a well-timed weapon, even setting a blow or stake himself a time or two. Oddly, tonight's excursion appeared to have taken more out of him than a dozen of the others combined. This seemed to go beyond the injury he had sustained, as though what he was about to reveal were a weight nearly too great for him to carry. *If such is the case, is it not better that he should share this burden with me?* she wondered.

Now Rendor leaned forward on his chair and gripped his mug tightly, warming his hands on the rough stoneware. "The Countess Erzsébet—Elizabeth—Bathory came to us as the young bride of Ferencz Nádasdy. She has been in Castle Csejthe for nearly twenty years, and while the count himself ran about the countryside battling the Turks, his wife had free rein in his absence. It is said that she . . . grew bored with the everyday tasks of raising her family and running the royal household."

"Bored?"

Rendor nodded tiredly. "She was a beautiful but obstinate

young woman, proclaimed in her youth to be nearly uncontrol-lable." Ildikó's Watcher glanced at her and smiled faintly before gazing again at the liquid in his cup. "Now she has grown in power and will not tolerate disobedience. No matter what her orders."

Ildikó tilted her head to one side. "And what things does our lovely countess demand?"

Rendor rubbed his forehead and Ildikó was again struck by the way his age seemed to hamper him tonight. This Countess—was she truly so much to be feared? "Some say she drinks the blood of virgins," he said softly.

"*What!*"

He cut off her surprise. "Others claim she only bathes in it, that she is not truly *vampyr.*"

"Sweet Lord," Ildikó breathed. "But *why?* A vampire would be bad enough, but if she is not . . . for a human to do such things to her own kind is unspeakable!"

"It is," Rendor agreed. "And while the number of her sus-pected victims makes her crimes the more monstrous, no one can prove her wrongdoings."

Ildikó gripped the sides of the small plank table between her and Rendor. "How many?"

"Some say . . . several hundred."

It was all she could do not to throw the table aside and shake her Watcher. Splinters from the rough wood dug deep into her palms as she fought to control her temper. "Why have you waited so long to tell me of this?" she demanded. "How many more were you willing to sacrifice, and for what?"

"I am not *willing* to sacrifice anyone," Rendor shot back. "Least of all *you,* Ildikó." He paused for a moment, then inhaled deeply. "To be truthful, for some time I have sought to prepare you for exactly this—to face *die Blutgrafin.* But I do not feel that you are ready. Tonight was evidence of that."

Ildikó inhaled, willing herself to calm down even as her face flushed with embarrassment. "I am sorry you are disappointed in me. But though that one skill may be lacking, it is only a small thing—I can do much else. Why do you not acknowledge that, Rendor? I am strong, capable—"

"Because you cannot simply go rushing into Castle Csejthe," her Watcher said sharply. "It is a huge place, filled with people, darkness, and more importantly, the *unknown*. You seem apt to dismiss it, but that 'small thing' could be the very sense that saves your life! Ildikó, this is far beyond the blood beasts you have battled in the forest, or even the nest of *vampyr* you discovered in the cave at Skole. If the countess is to be your next adversary, your past foes will seem like insects by comparison, easily crushed and hardly consequential. This is no mere human with whom you must deal, nor is it a feral beast of blood with little to consider beyond its hunger. The countess is no doubt the worst of both the light and dark worlds, a human with a soul who walks in the day, but who possesses the black heart of a devil."

Ildikó lowered her gaze. "It is hard to believe such a person exists," she said in a quiet voice. "To slaughter so and be without conscience—perhaps she is in league with a vampire, or under the spell of a demon. Because to be so evil and still function beneath the eye of God in the sunlight . . ." She shook her head, then her chin lifted. "Be that as it may, she is still just a woman. I will—"

"You will what?" Rendor interrupted. "You forget that this 'woman' carries the benefits of royal blood and family. She conducts herself with impunity from within a closely guarded castle. She has relatives and servants and soldiers, likely hundreds more than you or I have seen, who inhabit that abominable fortress she claims as her home." Her Watcher brought his tea down on the tabletop so hard that the now-cooled liquid splashed out of his mug and made a sloppy wet circle on the wood. Rendor pointed at it. "She is like this cup," he told her. "The ruler of a small country surrounded by servants and a constant entourage. If you think you can simply announce yourself and request an audience, you are sorely mistaken." He ran one hand across his forehead. "No, we should wait until your skills are more fully developed, until you can feel the night beast that might surprise you from the shadows. Six months is far too soon for you to face an adversary such as this."

"We cannot wait any longer, Rendor. Perhaps we have even waited too long already. You *know* that—every week that passes marks the death of more innocents. If the countess is a night beast, it is my duty to destroy her, the very reason I exist as a Slayer; if she is a monster in woman form, then her crimes must be exposed to the king in the courts of Hungary so that he can punish her as he sees fit." Frustration made her hands ball into fists. "But *how?*"

Rendor pressed his lips together. "Those we saw tonight were no doubt several of her personal serving maids," he said. His mouth twisted downward. "Tonight they buried perhaps another half dozen unfortunate victims. I have heard that there are many more of these sad, hidden graves."

"What is she doing to them?" Ildikó asked suddenly. "You never said."

For a long while Ildikó thought he wasn't going to answer. "It is rumored that at first the countess only beat her charges," he finally replied. He pulled the collar of his coarse shirt closer about his neck, as if just to speak the words chilled him more than the November night. "Her temper ran high and quick, and quite often. As the years of her reign increased, the villagers whispered of torture and depraved acts of the flesh, and the pastors talked of young girls who perished from 'strange maladies' while under the attentions of the countess. But upon her husband's death in 1604, *die Blutgrafin* began to overshadow even her own evil. Now she believes she can retain her youth and beauty for the remainder of her life by draining and bathing in, and perhaps drinking, the blood of young virgins."

Ildikó's eyes widened. "Then she *is* a vampire!"

But Rendor shook his head. "That is not confirmed. Her servants—the ones who survive—are relentlessly loyal."

Ildikó stood and began to pace the tiny, one-room house. At one end was Rendor's small bed, at the other her pallet on the floor, and she covered the distance in only a few strides. "Then I will have to get into the castle," she decided. "The countess is always sending ladies-in-waiting to secure new servants. I've paid little mind to such matters in the past, but I will make it a point to be among the next group selected to serve."

Her repeated pacing took her past the table, and Rendor reached for her with surprising swiftness. His fingers locked around her wrist and his touch was dry and papery, stronger than she'd expected. "Listen well, Ildikó. You must use great care in this matter, perhaps even reconsider. I cannot be of assistance to you should you gain entrance to Castle Csejthe—I have had no time to prepare, no time to find and make ties with those within who might come to your aid should you need it. Hear me well when I say again that I do not believe you are ready for such a battle as this. I know not if this evil woman has turned to true vampire, but in the eyes of those of royal blood, my influence is as that of a gnat on the hide of a great beast—not even noticed. Once the doors close behind you, there is nothing I can do, and no one to whom I can turn if you need help."

Her first impulse was to shrug away his concerns, but Ildikó made herself stop and think about his words. Perhaps it was because she was finally gaining a measure of maturity, or an appreciation for Rendor's wisdom, that she realized what he said was true, frighteningly so. All her life she had been an outcast among her peers because of her lack of interest in or skills with the feminine arts. Asking her to turn a tapestry thread or prepare a boar for roasting was the same as demanding she construct a stone dwelling of her own—she had as little knowledge of the first two as she did of the last.

Three years ago she'd been a wild runaway from her parents' gypsy camp and Kurt Rendor had saved her life, taking her in and giving her shelter on just such a night as this. When her calling as Ildikó the Vampire Slayer had come six months ago, her life had changed again, even more drastically than before. Under the guise that she was the granddaughter of Kurt Rendor's deceased cousin, she'd gone from a nomadic child to the charge of a respected village elder; from there she'd ultimately been told that the safety of those within her small world, literally whether or not many would see the next dawn, rested on her young shoulders.

She'd never had much in this world, but what she did have she'd gotten these last three years. Inside the castle she would be more isolated than she had ever been, cut off not only from the outside world but also from her savior, the only person in the world who likely cared if she lived or died.

Still, in her heart Ildikó knew she had no choice. Because if she did not stop *die Blutgrafin* . . .

How many more unsuspecting girls would perish?

"From now on you will accompany me to the market each morning," her Watcher told her when they rose at the next dawn. "It is well known that the countess sends her ladies-in-waiting not only to supervise the purchases of the housekeeping staff, but also to peruse the maidens for suitable additions to her entourage."

"Shopping? With . . . money?" Ildikó looked at Rendor doubtfully. Surely he hadn't forgotten how poorly she had fared with his repeated attempts to teach her reading, writing, and addition. "My numbers aren't very good."

"Yes, shopping with money." He tapped the small money bag hanging on his belt, but his expression softened. "Don't worry— I'll be there to do that part. You just take care of positioning yourself properly when the time comes. And you must remember—absolutely no behavior unbecoming a maiden. This means no arguing with the other girls, or being disagreeable with anyone." He sounded frustrated already. "I do so wish we had more time to ready you—the spring would be better."

Ildikó scowled and shook her head in answer to his hint. She disliked the learning part as much as he, but she knew it was necessary—the countess's women were unlikely to choose her if she seemed unladylike or ill-tempered. She would not voice her doubts to her Watcher, but it might already be overly hopeful for her and Rendor to believe this plan would gain her access; unfortunately, it was the only plan either had been able to devise.

"And you must clean up a bit." Rendor's semi-irritated tone pulled her thoughts back to the present. "Bathe yourself, and keep your face and hands clean at all times. Pay particular attention to the fingernails. And you must wash the dirt from your garments regularly."

Bathing? Washing? Wastes of valuable time, but again Ildikó kept her silence, recalling the differences between her and the other girls of the village. Some of those contrasts could not be changed—her hair, for instance. The battle to destroy the nest of night beasts at Skole had been intense and brutal, her injuries extensive. It had taken Ildikó several weeks to recover, sequestered in their small home while the cuts mended and the bruises faded. The scars were easy to hide once she was well again, but Rendor had been forced to cut her hair to a boyish length, even with her chin, to eliminate the ragged chunks that had been torn out by the vanquished vampires. Once long and luxurious thanks to her gypsy heritage, her short, shiny locks would now be much more fitting on a man. Ildikó actually preferred her hair cut this way—it was easier to care for, and appearances weren't something with which she was often concerned.

Rendor pushed the frame of his bed aside with one knee, then reached into the space between it and the wall. When he straightened, he held a small, well-filled money bag that Ildikó had never seen before. "Today at market we will purchase another dress for you," her Watcher announced. "This way you will always have a clean garment to wear."

Ildikó frowned. "Surely the money would be better spent on food," she said.

Rendor lifted one eyebrow. "Sacrifices must sometimes be made in order to achieve a goal," he told her. "If we are to have a chance of getting you inside Csejthe Castle, you must be properly attired."

Ildikó pressed her lips together, then nodded. "You're right, of course."

"Come on then," he said. "It's time for us to start the process of turning you into one of the countess's serving girls."

The day was no less cold for the sun that was shining down on the village, the breezes swirling down the mountainsides no less sharp. Huddled into capes and scarves, shivering despite the deceptive brightness, people hurried about their business and spent as little time as possible in the bitter outside air. Ildikó could not have put into words how much she despised these simple, everyday tasks, nor could she have said specifically why. Perhaps she was more suited to the life she had fled, that of a wanderer with her family's gypsy camp along the borders of Hungary and Romania. Wild and free—at least to the extent that a woman was allowed to be such—she and her family had traveled with a dozen other families and lived out of their wagon.

But no, that life had not fit well with Ildikó. She had wanted something more, something . . . illusive and unnameable. Never would she have imagined the contentment she had found in Rendor's simple household, the evenings of sitting before the fire, sometimes talking and sometimes not. The lessons he tried to impress upon her were frustrating but not so much that she had ever considered abandoning the effort, and when he had told her one beautiful spring morning that she was the newly called Vampire Slayer, Ildikó had finally understood in her soul what the word *destiny* meant. She was fated to find Rendor and this small village and, perhaps, fated to face the dreaded Countess Elizabeth Bathory.

"This would suit your niece well, would it not?"

Their first stop was in a small fabric shop, and the owner, an older woman of nearly fifty years, held up a dress invitingly. Ildikó cringed when she saw the feminine cut—a gathered bodice above a high-cut waist—but at least the material seemed sturdy, and the dyed dark blue skirt would hide stains. She didn't have the buxom build that adorned the frames of most of the other girls in the village, and if nothing else, the style of this dress might conceal that shortcoming.

"Hold it against yourself," Rendor instructed. Ildikó did so, feeling self-conscious as her Watcher and the shop woman eyed her up and down. "Yes," he said. "I believe it will. How much?"

The woman named a price that made Ildikó wince, but Rendor countered with a lower offer. The two haggled for a while and finally agreed on an amount that Ildikó still believed was robbery. Be that as it may, her Watcher paid it and waited as the shop woman bundled up the dress and tied it with a bit of string.

Outside the bright sunshine had disappeared, blocked by a building cloud cover. They fought the biting wind and turned gratefully into a slightly larger shop in the village square. Ildikó wasn't sure what they were after, since they had plenty of root vegetables at home, as well as bread and cheese. Then she realized that Rendor wanted more than simple foodstuffs—he wanted to expose her to the other villagers and find out what was going on in the area. She hung back and listened to him chat with others from the village, waiting as they shopped and browsed and talked about things she basically considered worthless. What did it matter in her world if Magdolna was now betrothed to József, or if Alisz and Hajnal had just reached their fifteenth years and their seamstressing skills were remarkable?

Her impatience was running high when she felt Rendor grip her arm and pull her to his side as he spoke with an elder named Barna from the village. The well-dressed man was nearly as ancient as her Watcher, although clearly not as well preserved—his teeth were crooked and blackened, his skin creased with the ravages of age below a crown devoid of all but a wisp or two of gray hair.

"Oh, yes," Barna was saying. He turned to Ildikó and gave her a smile that made her shudder inside. "My two youngest daughters were in the market square and caught the attention of the countess's ladies-in-waiting the last time they visited the village." He nodded vigorously. "They've been at the castle for nearly two months now, so busy with their new duties they've not had time to even send us word. But we've been well paid for their services."

Two months without word—does not Barna think that strange? Has he not noticed the aura of fear that must surround talk of the countess and her entourage? Ildikó barely stopped herself from frowning; obviously his concern was more for the sums funneled into his money bag by the royal family. God help this man's children, but she had a terrible feeling that they might have been among the nameless girls buried in the various graves outside the castle walls.

Barna leaned in close to Rendor and lowered his voice, as if what he was about to say were some great secret. "It is said in the village that they will return the day after tomorrow," he said confidentially. "If your goal is to have your niece selected for service, you would do well to clean the girl up a bit and have her at the seamstress shop at midday two days hence." Barna's gaze flicked around. "Should she be chosen, they will pay you—" He finished the sentence with a whisper in Rendor's ear.

Rendor nodded, and Ildikó was gratified to see that his expression didn't change—the coins meant little to him. "We'll consider it," he said, then added, "thank you for the information."

Barna beamed, the self-purveyor of valuable advice; no doubt now he believed that Rendor owed him a favor. "My pleasure."

Finally the other man was gone and her Watcher turned to her. "Two days," he said. "It isn't much time to prepare you."

"Prepare me?" Ildikó asked. "In what way?"

"There are more things you must know," Rendor said. "Mannerisms more befitting a young lady. The absence of these may well cause you to be passed over." Ildikó had no idea what he was talking about, so she said nothing, choosing instead to follow him around the shop as he made a few purchases—a small feminine-looking satchel, a delicate comb, a pair of light-colored stockings that Ildikó thought looked incredibly uncomfortable. She wasn't so daft that she didn't realize these items were for her, but was she really going to have to don those ridiculous leggings and carry that comb in a purse? *How can a Slayer be expected to fight if she is bound in such clothing?*

"Come along," her Watcher said. He held up the dress and the items he'd just purchased. "We have the tools and we have the time. Now we must prepare the package."

*   *   *

Rubbing her arms beneath her cape, Ildikó stood with perhaps fifteen other girls outside the small shop owned by the most talented of the village's seamstresses. Despite her popularity, the woman's store was small, as was apparent by the need for them to wait for the countess's ladies outside when inside a warm fire burned on the hearth and the customers and a few employees enjoyed tea and mulled wine. There was an undercurrent to the crowd—nervousness, discomfort, *fear*—and Ildikó heard more than a few girls whisper to each other of the countess's rumored cruelties, how their families had ignored their pleas to stay home in favor of the possible compensation. *How sad,* Ildikó thought, *to have so little control over your own lives and fate that others, even your relatives, could decide, based only on their own greed, whether you might live or die.*

None of the others spoke to her, none stood by her side. The last two days had felt like the longest of her short life, Rendor's repeated lessons in proper speaking, attire, and demeanor difficult for her to comprehend. Had her Watcher's efforts succeeded? She felt no different than before, and she certainly looked the same as always save for the too-girlish dress and the stockings covering her legs, useless but for the added warmth they provided. Perhaps she would grow to find them comfortable when—*if*—she were taken into Castle Csejthe. Yes, she'd been told the right things to say and the way in which to speak, but she had no experience of such things in day-to-day living, in the real world of sewing and housekeeping and accounts. Rendor, who awaited the outcome with many of the other adults in the nearby shops, could teach her only so much—the rest of her learning would have to come from the surrounding girls, whether or not they wanted to associate with her.

Ildikó sidestepped a bit nearer to the closest three young women, pretending to study the hem of her dress. They didn't say much, murmuring now and then about the cold and their parents, talking of sewing and using terms of which Ildikó had no knowledge. She might not do well with reading and numbers, but she quickly picked up on their mannerisms and speech patterns, the way they carefully pronounced each syllable rather than running everything together like the common peasants. Fearful or not, Ildikó knew each of these girls hoped that they would be an exception to the rumors, that they possessed some special skill that might catch the attention of a royal servant and guarantee them a better, and *safe*, place within the Bathory household. *Everyone,* the Slayer thought ruefully, *holds fast to the belief that the bad things within the world would always happen to someone else.*

"Why do you crowd us?" a voice beside her suddenly demanded. Ildikó glanced sideways and saw Marika, a pretty, blonde-haired woman of sixteen summers. Her brown gaze was full of derision. "Surely you don't believe that you will be brought into the countess's service?" She laughed, and a few of the girls around her joined in while the rest simply stood and looked on miserably, stomping their feet for warmth as they waited for the royal entourage. "Perhaps you haven't recently seen your reflection in the washbowl," Marika continued. " 'Tis well known that the countess prefers her serving ladies to look like *ladies.* The mannish style of your hair will hardly draw her eye. Whatever were you thinking to trim it in such a fashion?"

Ildikó started to retort, then Rendor's warning about being disagreeable made her bite back the words. There seemed to be no one around to notice, but who knew? "It just . . . seemed like a good idea when it was done," she finally muttered. The other girls giggled among themselves, and Ildikó felt her cheeks redden and her ire rise. She might have taken the conversation a step further had not three carriages bearing the countess's coat of arms rattled to a stop in front of the shop. Steam plumed from the mouths and noses of the great black horses. Their hides were covered in ornately embroidered saddle blankets and carved headpieces were strapped to their skulls. Marika forgot Ildikó as they all stood a bit straighter and reflexively smoothed their hair into place beneath their hoods. It was a contradictory situation—being pressed to service Elizabeth Bathory might not be the goal for many, but they still didn't want to face the shame of being passed over and having to return to their families.

Waiting with the crowd of young women, Ildikó was happy to be out of Marika's attentions, since it gave her a chance to surreptitiously study the carriage and the two women who exited it. She and Rendor had heard about them, Jó Ilona and Kateline, and the rumors weren't good—it was said they were responsible for not only recruiting serving maids but also sometimes personally disposing of them when they . . . were no longer needed. Perhaps it had been them performing the late-night burial Ildikó and her Watcher had witnessed that night outside the castle.

Now, despite the bitter temperature, Ildikó and her companions tried to curtsey appropriately then stand tall during their inspection.

There was little remarkable about the countess's two main ladies, other than the obviously better quality and warmth of their garments. Jó Ilona was the older one, with a face road-mapped by time and the elements, her iron gray hair escaping her cap in frizzy tufts around a face that Ildikó immediately pegged as not to be trusted. Kateline wasn't quite so old, but she was still past the bloom of youth; she reminded Ildikó of the gypsy camp followers she'd seen in her own childhood, women who did whatever they were told so long as they were given food and shelter in return. Of course, those women had not done such things as the unspeakable deeds committed by these two.

Jó Ilona began plucking girls from the bunch huddled together and directing them toward Kateline. One here, another there, and how many would be chosen? Five? Six? Surely no more than that, and Ildikó realized that the maximum number would be reached long before the two ladies made it to her position near the end of the group. Many of the girls were trying to slip toward the back without being noticed, their fear of the countess turning to slyness—where was the shame in saying they had not been chosen because the queue had filled before they were seen? Counting on that, Ildikó pushed her way quickly toward the front of the waiting girls, ignoring the mumbled, unladylike curses sometimes directed at her when she bodily moved a girl from her path. In only a few moments she was at the front, and only three girls had been selected so far; this was the best position she could get, and now she had only to somehow sell herself to Jó Ilona.

The old woman paused and studied the girl standing beside Ildikó, then frowned and moved on. Ildikó's sensitive hearing picked up the young maiden's nearly inaudible sigh of relief, then the Slayer stood straighter as Jó Ilona stopped in front of her. For a few seconds, she was at a loss; Render had passed along the rumors that Countess Bathory preferred well-endowed blondes. What on earth could she, slender and dark-haired, do to catch the eye of the woman's recruiter?

Her gaze met and locked with that of Jó Ilona's, and more than anything, Ildikó wanted to scowl at the evil she saw in those watery brown eyes. Instead she forced herself to smile boldly, then drop into a deep curtsy. Her bow wasn't perfect, but the winter cape and the skirt of her dress hid where her feet would have made the move too awkward.

"Stand up, girl," the old woman rasped. Ildikó obeyed and

found Jó Ilona standing only inches away and peering at her. "Open your mouth."

Again, Ildikó obeyed, thinking crankily that she was being inspected as would the local mare before breeding. Jó Ilona's next words drove that impression even deeper. "Good teeth," said the countess's lady, then she reached forward and dug her thin fingers into the flesh of Ildikó's shoulders and upper arms. "Strong, too. Healthy. You'll serve us well for chores and such—go to the carriage with the others."

Rendor's plan had worked! Ildikó curtsied again then did as she'd been instructed, struggling to mask a triumphant smile. Hustled to one side by Kateline, she waited with the three others chosen so far as Jó Ilona walked the remainder of the line and pulled out two more of the young women, including Marika. Mixed as it was with the dread of their families' displeasure, the relief on the faces of those left behind was still obvious.

It felt like forever before they were moved into the carriage. Though cold, it was at least out of the brutal touch of the wind. Crowded together inside, they could at least build up a bit of warmth as they began the long and bumpy ride through the foothills. Although they knew one another, most of the girls were quiet as they contemplated what might await them at Csejthe Castle. Unfortunately, Marika seemed inclined to do little but snipe at Ildikó.

"How interesting that the countess's ladies should select you," the young woman said to the Slayer. With nothing to occupy their attention but dire thoughts of their future, the other girls seemed grateful for Marika and her words, eager for something else upon which to focus. "But then I suppose that even the countess needs workers in the kitchen, or perhaps women to clean her chamber pots."

There were a few nervous giggles from the others, but Ildikó wasn't deluded by Marika's insults. She had found herself in terror-filled situations too many times not to recognize when someone was hiding behind bravado, masking their apprehension by lashing out at whomever was closest. Poor Rendor had suffered her harsh tongue many a time over the last half year. "Yes," was all she said. "Perhaps she does."

Marika said nothing, but one of the others, a young and pretty girl whose name Ildikó didn't recall, leaned forward. Her eyes were wide, and even in the cold, a line of nervous perspiration rimmed her upper lip. "Why is it you do not seem afraid?" she demanded. "Have you not heard the stories? Do you not know what fate probably awaits us?"

Ildikó tried to think of something to respond, but before she could the words of another girl cut her off. "My mother says you're a witch," she announced. She sent a hard stare at Ildikó, then glanced meaningfully at the other girls. "Perhaps *that's* why she isn't afraid—she thinks to ally herself with those at the castle."

Now the rest of them were staring at her in horror, literally trying to push away from her in the tiny carriage. "Don't be absurd," Ildikó snapped. "I'm no such thing."

Marika sat up straighter, deciding to again join the conversation. "Then why else would you be chosen with the rest of us?" she demanded. She gestured at her golden hair and well-fed frame, then arched an eyebrow at Ildikó's more lithe build. "You must have . . . cast a spell upon the countess's ladies to make them see you as they see us."

"You heard her," Ildikó shot back. She could feel herself getting irritated despite her resolve to remain patient and understanding. "She believes I am strong and healthy enough for chores. 'Tis nothing more than that."

"So you say," muttered one of the others.

The carriage hit a particularly nasty bump and the banter

stopped as they all tried to find handholds. The roughness of the ride increased, and Ildikó was grateful for it; she was tired of defending herself against these gossipy, narrow-minded young women. How foolish that they would condemn her out of hand when in the not-so-distant future it was to Ildikó whom they might have to turn for help. Sometimes Ildikó thought that the wiles and whims of men and women ensured their own fates.

She was split from the others almost from the moment they were taken into the great hall of the castle. Ildikó watched with a feeling of foreboding as the others were ushered up the stone stairwell and into the shadowed recesses of the upper floors. Would she see them again? Would she be able to save them? Only time would provide the answer, and meanwhile the air inside the castle carried the heavy aura of fear. The servants went about their tasks quietly, sweeping, dusting, and working ceaselessly to add to or repair the heavy tapestries hung to block the dampness and drafts from the stone walls. Laughter was seldom heard here; when a few muted chuckles did escape, the sound was quickly muted, overridden by the fear of drawing unwanted attention.

As Jó Ilona and Kateline disappeared with the others, Ildikó was turned over to the housekeeper in charge of the countess's larder, a florid-faced woman named Judit who, even at this early hour, had obviously already been tasting of the castle ale. The Slayer was given an apron, then instructed to perform a multitude of mundane but physically demanding tasks—no wonder Jó Ilona had felt her muscles. The hours passed quickly, with Ildikó keeping her eyes and ears attuned to everything, learning who was who and what went where as she carted supplies back and forth and learned of necessity how to turn a knife on cooking meat and vegetables; apparently the midday meal was the big event of Csejthe Castle, and everything must be perfect. One of her first unspoken lessons was that it was best under any circumstances *not* to draw attention to oneself around the countess or her main ladies-in-waiting; the second was to never, *ever* question the whereabouts of a serving girl who suddenly no longer reported for her duties.

No matter how she tried, Ildikó was never allowed in the great hall during the meal that first day. Judit kept a hawk's-eye watch on her during that time, perhaps suspicious of all the questions Ildikó had been asking. She could hear the revelry and laughter, and they certainly went through enough food—a small army would have been well supplied for a week on what was wasted and thrown to the rather well-fed dogs and beggars. Ildikó herself enjoyed a small meal of ground meat, goat's cheese, and bread, forgoing the offered ale in favor of fresh water. By the time she did manage to slip back into the main hall, the countess had already retired to her chambers, and other servants moved around and picked up the leavings, using rush brooms to sweep the expansive floor clear of food droppings.

Ildikó was given a pallet to the side of one of the kitchen fireplaces and instructed to keep an eye on the fire during the night and make sure it didn't go out. She didn't mind; becoming a Slayer had given her an entirely new perspective on the night, and she'd never needed much sleep. Besides, there were other things she wanted to do during the dark hours here, and tending the fire would give her the excuse to be up and about when others might have expected her to bed down like a normal person.

Csejthe Castle had a . . . *smell* about it. Unpleasant and heavy, Ildikó's nose recognized the combined scents of blood and death and decay, and no amount of cooking smoke or airing could hide it. Even in its latest hours, the castle was never quiet—animal sounds filtered in from the courtyard, unintelligible voices were carried down on the tiny drafts and wind currents that worked themselves through the cracks in the heavy stonework. There were always servants and soldiers about, far too many for Ildikó to attempt exploring the darker recesses of the huge castle, the winding passageways and corridors that led to areas far larger than she could imagine.

Still, Ildikó would not give up.

Over the course of her first week, she had seen the girls with whom she had been brought here only intermittently, but those few glimpses had been enough to give her comfort that they hadn't—yet—been harmed. By the time the Sabbath had come and gone, however, fully half of them had mysteriously gone absent; no one said anything, and her inquiries were met only with dismayed glances and whispered reminders that some things were better left alone. As he had warned might happen, Ildikó had heard nothing from her Watcher, and it was obvious the worst had already befallen her peers. Ildikó could no longer bide her time and wait for opportunity—if she was to prevent the other three, and countless others, from perishing, then she must make her own way and not wait for happenstance.

A little past midnight, Ildikó slipped from her pallet in the kitchen, her path taking her within inches of another fitfully sleeping servant—it seemed no one in this castle slumbered well. Tied in the folds of the cumbersome skirts was the satchel Rendor had bought her, its only content the wooden stake that had served Ildikó well during her short time as the Vampire Slayer. She had no idea where to go, not even an inkling as to which direction marked the way to the countess's living quarters. What she did have, however, was that same Slayer-developed sense of hearing; as she moved farther away from the kitchen than she'd ever gone, she began picking up the cries of a person—female, and agonized—somewhere in this desolate structure. It was toward these muted sounds that Ildikó moved, scurrying from one shadowed corner to the next like a rat avoiding the household cat.

Up a flight of stone steps, down a nerve-wrenchingly narrow hallway, then she found another flight of stairs leading upward. The cries were clearer now, and while the average man might miss them, the faint words, over and over, of *"Mercy, I beg you!"* pierced Ildikó's heart and fed her determination. Closer then, and she took another turn, viewing the hall that stretched long and dark beyond it with dismay. There was no place to hide here, no doorway or alcove in which to slip should someone enter it from the other end. Still, the shrieks of pain were closer now, undeniable; if she wished to find and help whomever was being tormented, it seemed this would be the only avenue.

Ildikó sucked in a breath, then hastened forward.

She didn't quite make it.

"Stop right there, wench."

She would have dashed forward rather than obey had not another figure stepped into view and blocked the hallway at its farthest end. Chewing her lip, she turned back and found one of the countess's soldiers, a private guard by the looks of his dress, striding toward her; when she glanced over her shoulder, she saw that the other figure wore the same garments—she was trapped.

"Identify yourself," said the first guard. His voice was completely devoid of warmth, his eyes dark and unreadable. "I've not seen you in these rooms before."

Ildikó's brain worked to concoct a suitable story, something plausible but that would still conceal her true identity. "My name is . . . Marika," she said. "I've been summoned to assist the countess with her wardrobe in her chambers."

The other guard was close to her now, *too* close, and Ildikó stepped back a little, wanting to feel the comforting presence of the stone wall behind her. The second man was taller than the first and thin, with deep-set eyes and hair that hadn't seen wash water in at least a season. There was a smell about both of them that Ildikó didn't like, different from the one that permeated the castle's rooms, but it was hard to place it beneath the stench of their unwashed clothes and skin.

"Marika?" the first soldier repeated. He met the gaze of his fellow guard over Ildikó's head. "What do you think the chances are that this"—he gave Ildikó an unpleasant-looking leer—"this skinny half-girl would have the same name as the busty young thing who services the countess as we speak?"

Ildikó flinched inwardly as the dual impact of the man's words sank in. Yes, they'd already guessed she wasn't who she claimed; worse, the real Marika was suffering under the countess's less-than-desirable ministrations right now. *I have to get in there and see if I can save that girl.*

"So," said the smaller of the two men, "the wench is *lying.*"

"True," agreed the other. His gaze raked her. "Besides, I really don't think she's the countess's type, do you?"

"Let's see." His oversized hand snagged one of her arms, fingers digging tightly into the skin. Ildikó tried to pull away from the uncomfortably cold and painful grip, but he only held on more tightly, then he shook his head and gave a nasty laugh. "With that short, dark hair and flat chest? Not likely."

His companion nodded. "You know, if we take her to the captain of the guard, he'll likely throw her in chains in the dungeon, leave her there until she starves and dies."

"It would be a terrible waste," the other agreed. "Of a good *meal.*"

The empty eyes, that too-cool touch . . . Ildikó jerked out of the guard's grasp just as his gaze flickered yellow and his facial features melted into a portrait of evil. She didn't have to look to know the other soldier was a vampire, too—were there others just like them where the hallway turned right at the far end? Here, God help her, was a prime example of the consequences of her inability to sense a vampire's presence—this creature had actually placed its filthy hand upon her and she *still* hadn't realized it was a bloodsucker.

She felt the larger vampire's spittle on her neck as he hissed in anticipation; it was cold and smelled of things pulled from a wet grave. Ildikó twisted away and brought her elbow up hard into the creature's nose as her right hand dug into her skirt and found the bag Rendor had given her, felt the comforting grip of the wood through the fabric. With his nose smashed, the guard's cry of pain was thankfully muffled, and she let instinct guide her—in less than a second, the stake, still encased within the fabric satchel, found its mark in the center of the first soldier's chest. Vampire dust exploded in front of her, and had she possessed the time, Ildikó would have been thankful for the absence of battle armor; as it was, she could only gasp as the other guard lunged at her and got a choke hold around her neck.

Her head immediately began to pound and black and gold sparkles flitted across her vision as her air was cut off. Growling, the beast crowded against her, forcing her back against the wall and giving her no room to get the stake up and into position. It took everything she had to snake one arm up on each side of his and clasp her hands, then angle them sideways until his grasp on her neck broke. She had one blessed moment of full air, but instead of backing away, he pushed her even harder, throwing his full weight against her slighter frame. Her precious breath went out of her lungs as she was slammed against the stonework and her arms flailed outward.

Fast as a snake, the vampire tried to bite her; just as quickly, Ildikó squirmed in one direction, then another. "No," she said through ground teeth. "I will *not* be your evening meal, you vile thing!" The beast pressed against her again and this time she let it; for a second, he hesitated, then she felt his entire body stiffen. The last thing he saw before he erupted into dust from the stake she'd driven into him from the back was her bright, victorious smile.

But Ildikó was anything but clear of danger. Caught up in the battle, she'd overlooked the noise they'd made—her furious statement, the grunts and growls of her two attackers. New excited voices drifted toward her, coming from just around that turn in the hallway—at least a half dozen men, probably more of the countess's guards come to check on their brethren. Her battle here was lost, and she had no choice this night but to retreat.

God would have to help Marika. Ildikó had lost her chance.

The screams of the night before weighed on Ildikó's mind, more so because she knew the young woman who had suffered so. Death was never good, but had her memory held the cries of a faceless stranger she would not have been as down in the heart, as . . . *connected* to the atrocities being committed somewhere within this heavily guarded stone fortress. She had saved many people from the village in her short time as a Slayer, but always the darkness had kept their faces from her, and hers from them. She had left her own family behind of choice, and while she respected Rendor and followed his guidance—more so of late—this was the first time Ildikó had seen or heard evil visited upon someone she knew personally, a girl with whom she'd shared conversation. It mattered not that their words had been far from cordial; the impact was far deeper because it had struck down a face she knew, a voice she had heard, a name Ildikó had uttered from her lips.

The morning dragged, with Ildikó's chores seeming meaningless and her mind spinning in all directions but unable to come up with any plan but to try the same entry tonight. The notion was fraught with potential trouble. The least of these was that the captain of the guard had doubtlessly noticed his missing men and his suspicions would be raised, resulting in an increased guard. Worse, what if the captain is himself a vampire, his men more of the same? If that were true, how convenient that such an army guarded Countess Elizabeth Bathory!

But there seemed to be no other option for Ildikó. If anything, even more servants wandered the area than in the previous days, even more soldiers and merchants. Each able-bodied man and woman who joined the castle's population this day decreased her chances of getting to the countess's chambers this eventide, and Ildikó became more frustrated as the hour wore late. If she did not figure out something soon—

"You there, girl. Come forward."

Ildikó almost missed the command, so absorbed was she in her own speculations. The old crone of a housekeeper, however, had no intention of letting it slip by; she reached out an aged hand and pinched Ildikó hard on the soft flesh on the inside of her upper arm. It stung enough so that the Slayer's head whipped around, and she nearly dropped into a fighting stance, then at the last second she remembered where she was and her need to keep her identity a secret. The housekeeper gestured angrily at her to heed someone behind Ildikó's shoulder and hissed something at her, the words too heavy with ale to be intelligible.

Ildikó turned and found herself face-to-face with the lesser of the countess's ladies-in-waiting, Kateline. The woman's face was, as always, drawn and tired, her dark eyes rimmed with shadows that testified to many sleepless nights. "You look of sound mind and health," she said. "We have need of your assistance with matters elsewhere."

Ildikó curtseyed, snatched up her cape and satchel from their spot by the fireplace, and obediently fell into step behind

Kateline. The older woman led her through the main hall and into the courtyard. Outside the shadows were lengthening and the cold was increasing, quickly bleeding away what scant heat the ground had managed to pull from the winter sun. The little village down the mountain always had a pall over it during the harsh winter months, but the houses this close to the castle, literally within its gloomy shadow, bore an atmosphere that was oppressive and unabashedly fearful in the evening. People rushed about as if their very lives depended on it, and if what she had encountered last night was any indication, finding shelter and safety before darkness fully descended really *did* mark the boundary between life and death . . . or undeath.

Ildikó's senses sharpened as Kateline guided her to a doorway that led out of the courtyard proper. Their footsteps crunched in the snow, and voices filtered through the sparse trees; not too much farther waited three more people—Jó Ilona and two more serving girls, their faces pale and terrified as they awaited the bidding of their mistresses. On the ground at their feet lay their task: the burial of two elongated shapes bundled in heavy fabric, clearly the bodies of two who had been considerably less fortunate. Ildikó barely hid her anger as she grasped the shovel handed her. *Is Marika one of these poor dead souls?*

Angry she might be, but common sense still ruled. Yes, she wanted to avenge these two and the others who had fallen victim to the countess. To do so, her objective was to find her way to the cause of their death, the bigger target back inside the castle. Out here she would hold her comments and tongue, and trust in her instincts to guide her actions.

Thanks to Ildikó's superior strength, the onerous chore went quickly, enough so that Kateline and Jó Ilona took note. Their work completed, the girls were herded inside and sent back to their normal duties, but Jó Ilona gestured for Ildikó to hang back as the others left. Standing before the crone, Ildikó felt . . . *soiled* beneath her gaze. Odd that Jó Ilona's eyes now seemed more than old, rheumy but far too knowing, tainted by the darkness of what had passed before them. When the old woman folded cool, dry fingers around her wrist, Ildikó had to search for a new strength within herself to keep from yanking away.

"You are assigned to help with cooking duties, yes?"

"Yes, mistress," Ildikó answered.

Jó Ilona nodded, the movement more a confirmation to herself than anything the young Slayer needed to interpret. The woman's eyes shifted left and right, as though she were making sure no one else was within hearing range. "A girl, strong such as you, and with aspirations to a better station in the household, could go far in the castle," she told Ildikó in a raspy whisper. "If she could hold her tongue about certain matters."

There was no mistaking that here, finally, was an avenue that might take her within striking distance of the countess herself. But caution was still called for; wary of appearing overeager, Ildikó made a show of giving Jó Ilona's words careful consideration. "You mean I am not to repeat to others what is seen or heard during the performance of my duties?"

"Exactly." The countess's lady peered at her and her fingers dug into the Slayer's flesh more firmly. "Are you capable of silence, girl? Be wise in your answer, for there will be no chance for turnabout."

Ildikó nodded solemnly. "I am most trustworthy."

Jó Ilona released her. "Very well, then. I will show you to your new post at Castle Csejthe."

And Ildikó followed the old crone down the steps into the farthest recesses of the castle, and into the very pits of hell.

* * *

There had been times in Ildikó's short span as the Vampire Slayer during which she had been cold and hungry, weary to the bone and injured. Yet even during the worst of those—her battle to destroy the nest of *vampyr* at Skole—never would she have imagined such a place existed as the dungeons maintained by the monstrous Elizabeth Bathory.

The rooms were unexpectedly well lit, but for once Ildikó would have preferred darkness and shadow—anything to help cushion the impact of her surroundings. After leading her down here yesterday morning, Jó Ilona had given Ildikó the barest idea of her assigned duties, then left. The last that Ildikó had heard of the woman was the sound of the heavy wooden bar being dropped into its iron brackets on the other side of the dungeon's main door.

She was trapped down here.

But she wasn't alone.

Ildikó hadn't found them until the crone had left, but at the farther end of the room, chained in place against cold walls weeping with moisture, were four girls. Shivering and moaning, they were delirious with fear and thirst, and while Ildikó murmured words of empty comfort and brought each fresh water, she could neither free them from the stout iron manacles, nor find anything to cover their nearly naked bodies. Sorely mistreated, each girl's flesh was a landscape of wounds, from bruises to cuts to bite marks that bore no resemblance at all to the familiar puncture of a vampire's teeth. A different sort of monster had preyed on these young women, and it was one that sorely needed destroying.

And so Ildikó waited, patiently tending to the girls and biding her time, replenishing the myriad of torches and keeping the single huge fireplace stoked lest the flames go out and they all freeze down here. Her stomach growled with emptiness, and she could only imagine what these pathetic prisoners felt, two of whom had shared the carriage with her only last week. Ildikó hadn't the tendency to hold a grudge, and it pained her greatly to see them imprisoned and in such pain, but while she checked their manacles dozens of times, her Slayer's strength was no match for the iron that encased their wrists and ankles.

There were other things down here, too. Alive and otherwise.

In the realm of the living there were the rats, squeezing in through the cracks and small drains in the stone floors and walls, safely using passageways too narrow for even the castle cats. Insects, too—huge waterbugs and other scuttling things for which Ildikó had no name. Those things, she could deal with—a well-placed stomp of her foot marked the finale for many of the pesky creatures—but it was the—*other* things, items made of wood and leather and iron, that horrified her almost more than anything she had previously encountered.

The rumors had not done this place true justice.

There were tables with stained leather straps, others with thumbscrews, pinchers, rope whips, and chain flails, all dark and nauseatingly heavy with the scent of blood. Had these things been used on the girls chained to the wall? If so, it was little wonder that the imprisoned girls seemed only a hair's length from death. But even though such implements were horrifying, they were dwarfed by the thing in the center of the room, a huge, metal monstrosity that gave Ildikó chills just to gaze upon it. Yet she couldn't *not* study the thing, try to figure out what it did to its victims, what purpose it ultimately served. It seemed to be some kind of . . . *cage,* and God help those caught in its grasp, because if she was understanding what she saw—

"I see you are fascinated by the Iron Maiden."

Ildikó spun, but the honey-coated voice belonged to no one in sight. Her gaze darted from the pools of shadow between each torch on the wall, but still she saw no one. *What manner of beast could hide so?*

Movement then, a blacker silhouette in a valley of darkness by the door—she'd been so focused upon the torture devices that she hadn't heard the stealthy removal of the locking bar, and someone had taken down several of the torches as she'd turned. Before she could speak, more figures moved into the room from the doorway, the heavier, taller figures of the countess's soldiers no doubt accompanying her for safety. As Ildikó waited, Kateline and Jó Ilona stepped forward, the first to cut off her view and access to the figure who could only be Countess Bathory herself. More soldiers hastened to accompany them—how odd that the woman felt the need for such protection from one scrawny serving maid.

But if the countess felt fear, she wasn't the only one. Her mouth dry, Ildikó swallowed and forced her voice to stay calm. She had miscalculated terribly, and Rendor's warnings about how isolated she would be came back in a nasty flood. The Slayer would find no help in this fiendish place, and it was clear that her Watcher, although highly regarded in the village, had been unable to send assistance or even gain entrance to the castle.

Still, there was no time for recriminations. She was where she was—alone—but she would not betray her fear to this monster in a woman's clothing. "I have never seen such a thing."

"It's quite beautiful, isn't it?" came Elizabeth Bathory's answer. The voice floated on the drafts in the dungeon like the ethereal version of a poisonous snake. "I had it made by a clockmaker at Dolna Krupa." If such a thing were possible, Ildikó thought she could actually *hear* the woman smiling. "Such a fine and . . . *efficient* piece of art."

Ildikó grimaced, not sure whether her expression could be seen in the darkness, not really caring. "Art? It seems more a work of cruelty to me."

The countess chuckled but still kept her distance. "Quite over-spoken, aren't you? A perilous thing in my service, you know."

The Slayer tensed, but no one moved forward. "My apologies, Your Highness."

The countess waved away her words. "No matter. You are different from the other maidens," she commented. "More robust, I think. Stronger. My sorceress tells me of your great stamina and health, that you are . . . special." A finger of unease stroked the base of Ildikó's spine. Even for one of Elizabeth Bathory's stature, it was bold indeed to admit to employing a person of the dark arts—of what other things regarding Ildikó did this so-called sorceress have knowledge?

The Slayer tensed again as one of the soldiers moved into the room, but he only set a serving tray on one of the heavy wooden tables, then returned to the shadows; on the tray was a waterskin, bowls of cold goulash, and a few hunks of bread. Even unheated, the smell of the food was enough to rouse the poor girls chained against the wall—no doubt it had been days since they'd had a meal. Still, their senses were too clouded by pain and hunger for them to recognize Ildikó.

"You will tend to these girls," the countess said. "And yourself, also—the cook tends to forget to bring meals to those in the dungeon. I fear this part of the castle makes her uncomfortable." The countess paused, and Ildikó again had that eerie sense of *hearing* the woman's happiness. "I rather enjoy its accommodations. Besides, my Maiden graces this room, and that, of course, makes it my first choice for . . . guests."

Ildikó strained at the darkness, but her heightened eyesight still couldn't make out the number of soldiers on guard with the countess. Nonetheless, she would have to chance it—her opportunities to be in the countess's presence were few and far between. With no idea whether she faced beast or human, her right hand slipped into the folds of her skirt and folded around the stake, then Ildikó risked a small step forward.

There was a flurry of motion in the darkness, of bodies suddenly moving and shifting. When Countess Bathory spoke again, her voice was farther away and muffled by the knot of people between her and Ildikó. "Don't worry, my pet. A serving girl as different as you should be treated as such, and we'll return to visit later. You shan't be down here alone too long."

A rush of footsteps and murmuring, and before Ildikó could cross the distance of the room, the countess and her passel of servants and soldiers had hastened through the doorway and barred it behind them.

Ildikó balled her fists in frustration, but there was nothing to be done about it—she was still trapped. Knowing it was useless to dwell on it, instead the Slayer retrieved the tray of food and carried it over to the four pathetic prisoners. At first eager, she was ultimately disappointed in the amount of food she could coax each to eat; beaten, sickly, and exhausted, one by one they drank a bit of water and fell asleep after only a few bites of the goulash. Her own stomach was rumbling with emptiness, so Ildikó ate a few bites of the bread and the rest of one bowl of goulash herself, finding it nearly tasteless and greasy, with a bitter edge to each swallow.

Setting the tray aside, she tried to think about what to do next, devise some sort of battle plan for when the Countess returned. But she was tired and it was hard to concentrate—the castle drafts made the torchlight flicker and wave almost hypnotically and she felt sleepy, pleasantly numb—

Suddenly alarmed, Ildikó stood.

And promptly fell face forward onto the filthy floor.

Gasping, with her cheek pressed against the stones, she realized that something had been added to the goulash—no wonder the prisoners, in their weakened states, had fallen asleep so quickly. This was far worse than anything she might have imagined, and suddenly her own mortality and inexperience sank in, her true powerlessness and *frailty* against this woman, the huge royal family, and seemingly endless army of soldiers and servants. She could not succumb to whatever potion or herb had been mixed into the goulash by the countess's sorceress, she *had* to stay awake—

Blackness.

Ildikó felt like she was swimming. In her childhood, her father and the tribe had once camped in a valley along the eastern border of Romania, where there had been a small lake. The water had been cold and not particularly pleasant even in late summer; it had washed over her skin and left chill bumps in its wake, making her want only to get out of its wet grasp in much the same way as she felt now. Oddly enough, she thought suddenly of Rendor, and the way he had rescued her from certain death three years ago, the warmth that had come when as a stranger he had thrown a heavy woven blanket around her shoulders and offered her shelter. If such a thing were possible, she believed to her soul that he would do the same for her now, that he had *been* trying; doubtless his efforts to provide assistance to her over the past week had come to naught. Had not her Watcher warned her countless times that her stubbornness might someday cost her dearly?

"Your skin is such an odd golden color," she heard someone murmur. *"It's as if you've somehow soaked up a measure of the sun—so different from the others."* Something touched her cheek, and Ildikó tried to pull away, then found she couldn't. Her head wouldn't move, her arms and legs were bound and completely immobile. *"It makes you quite beautiful, you know. Very appealing . . . desirable despite your leanness."*

The Slayer dragged her eyes open, then wished she hadn't. The headachy remnants of the sleep potion were nothing compared to the realization of where she was and her upcoming fate.

The countess stood on a raised platform in front of her, excruciatingly beautiful in a fine gown of green silk, her ivory skin and dark eyes accented by the burning torches around the room. Ildikó waited, expecting to see those fine features melt into the twisted visage of a vampire, but the noblewoman only stared at her.

"It is such a struggle to stay young," the countess said dreamily. She held out one hand, and immediately a soldier rushed to help her off the platform. "The very efforts of doing so are in themselves taxing, requiring a never-ending search. I have always known that the best blood comes from pure young girls, but you. . . ." Standing below the Slayer now, she reached up and ran a jewelry-covered hand down Ildikó's leg, and the Slayer started as she realized they had completely stripped away her garments. "I'm told you are not as other normal girls, that you possess special abilities. What benefits might I reap from one such as you, so strong and healthy, so *different*? What longevity?"

Ildikó tried to reply and found she couldn't—something cold and painfully hard had been pushed into her mouth and was being held in place by a strap. More bindings were around her head, neck, chest and arms, all the way down her body. She could feel a smooth surface against her spine, rear end, and the backs of her legs—metal?—but she couldn't turn her head to see what was holding her. Such a subtle mistake, the smallest of missed details, but devastating nonetheless . . . while she had thought her uniqueness would help her save the other girls and stop the evil, she had never realized it had served only as her undoing. Those same differences that had served her so well in the fight against the dark side—her strength and stamina, her lean and unfeminine skills—had pulled the countess's attention like a hungry wolf to fresh meat.

"Normally I have serving girls readied for me in numerous ways," the countess said matter-of-factly. Ildikó's eyes widened at her next words. "Heated pinchers or branding generally gets the blood flowing quite richly. But you . . ." Her voice trailed away thoughtfully. "I think it would be best not to blister such lovely skin, don't you?" The woman paced back and forth in front of her, going in and out of Ildikó's line of sight like a puppet in a street show.

"You showed such interest in my precious Iron Maiden earlier that I decided you should experience it firsthand, without all the bothersome distractions that preparation would entail."

The Iron Maiden? Ildikó tried to say something around the metal in her mouth, but it only came out as an unintelligible gargle. Now she wished she hadn't examined the torture device so closely, hadn't seen the hideous metal face on its front and the blood-encrusted spikes that sprouted from the insides of the two doors on the thing's front.

Spikes that would penetrate her body when those very same doors were pushed closed.

Ildikó tried to struggle then, staring down at the countess's dark smile as unseen servants on either side of the Iron Maiden began to slowly close it up. It was a useless effort—she was held fast within the unbreakable iron-spiked grip of the Bloody Countess's beloved torture device. There was no flash retelling in her mind of her own life as the first spikes pierced her skin and sank deep, no sudden divine inspiration about the things she could or should have done to make the world a better place or to banish evil.

There was only the building and excruciating pain, the silent screams of her own agony, and the fading sight of Countess

Bathory raising a goblet of collected blood—Ildikó's blood—and toasting her before lifting it to dark red lips.

And even as death enveloped her in its mercifully permanent embrace, Ildikó still wasn't sure if the beautiful, Bloody Countess was truly a vampire . . .

Or if, as a Slayer, she had died for naught.

Unholy Madness

Nancy Holder

FRANCE, 1789

Despite the fact that it was only autumn, the night was cold enough to freeze blood. Moonlight gilded the vast grounds of the Palace of Versailles, silver shafts that appeared sharp enough to pierce the hide of the fiercest werewolf. Garden statues that, by day, frolicked and gamboled—nymphs and fat cherubs and majestic sea gods—took on visages of demons and hell spawns. Their shadowed fingers contorted into monstrous claws. The water from the fountains in which they lurked curdled bloodred.

This is the world of evil, thought Marie-Christine, the Vampire Slayer, as she watched through the windows for the approach of her enemy. *By day, life is a parade of beauty. But at night, the truce with Death is lifted, and he sends his servants to collect his debts.*

She understood that debt all too well. Her own family was dead; she was the last of the noble line of Du Lac. She remembered nothing of her parents, not one sweet word from her mother, not even the scent of her hair. She had been told she had her father's quick-wittedness, but other than that, her life of wealth and privilege was their only legacy to their sole heir. Aunts, uncles, cousins, grandparents—she had none. All had perished in accidents or from illnesses before she could walk. It was as if the Du Lacs had never existed.

Her Watcher, Edmund de Voison, had also served as her guardian, and she had been raised in a manner befitting her station, in rank as well as in destiny. Once she had been Chosen, she was moved to the luxurious Palace of Versailles, the home of the king of France, Louis XVI, and his wife, the beautiful and regal Marie-Antoinette.

The young countess was now aware that someone was creeping up cautiously behind her. Aware, too, that whoever it was, was harmless. She closed the tapestry draperies and turned around with an air of expectation.

It was one of the army of palace servants. She did not know his name, and had no cause to learn it. There were so many servants, and after all, it was enough that he knew who she was, was it not? Not in the sense of her secret identity, but that she was a young aristocrat of the court, and therefore, someone he must serve and obey.

"*Oui?*" she asked imperiously.

"*Excusez,* Mademoiselle la Comptesse. Monsieur le Marquis has arrived," he said, his head bent low. He was dressed in black velvet knickers and a black velvet and silk jacket. His voice trembled, and she felt a moment's pity for him. The servants were terrified of the Marquis de Rochembourg, and they had great cause to be. Rochembourg was a sadist and a bully.

He is also a vampire, Marie-Christine thought. However, she sincerely doubted that this man knew that.

Marie-Christine put a hand to her elaborate white wig. Atop it, she wore a tiara of diamonds that sparkled as hard and white as the moonlight. The tiara was a gift from Amelie, a distant but much beloved member of the royal family, as thanks for fending off a vampiric attack on Her Royal Person during an evening stroll. Marie-Christine had killed off several of the vampire's minions, but the vampire itself had escaped.

The same vampire who lived in the world as the Marquis de Rochembourg, the "man" Marie-Christine was to dine with momentarily.

That time, he escaped. Marie-Christine smiled grimly. *Tonight is the night I acquit my honor. I shall turn* monsieur le vampire *to dust.*

She had carefully selected her *costume* for the occasion. She was dressed to kill—as the English liked to say—in an exquisite ruby-colored silk gown and volumes of white lace. Beneath her billowing skirts, she carried stakes; and her entire corset was made of wood, so that she could use the stays for weapons as well. The wood had been taken from the bell tower of the Cathedral of Notre Dame. It had been blessed by the Holy Father himself, and it was destined for the unbeating heart of the marquis . . . and any of his kindred haughty and foolish enough to accompany him this night.

"Very well," she said to the servant, smoothing her skirts. "I shall receive him in the Hall of Mirrors, where we are to dine."

"Oui, mademoiselle." He bowed again. His hands shook. She wanted to tell him that after tonight, the marquis would terrorize him and his fellows no longer.

But one can never be certain of that, can one? It may be I who die tonight, she thought, trying to temper her lust for the battle with cold common sense. *I am the Slayer because the girl who preceded me is dead. And so it has been for centuries.*

She lifted the sides of her dress, her skirts swaying gracefully as she walked across the parquet floor. Down the hallway she glided; then, as she approached the Hall, a waiting servant bowed and opened the doors for her. She crossed the threshold.

Before her, the glittering table was laid for fourteen—one place for her, and the other thirteen for her guests. The marquis brought with him a Judas—the vampire didn't realize that one of his minion-courtiers, Jean-Pierre Du Plessis, was a spy in Marie-Christine's employ. Jean-Pierre had revealed to the Slayer that the marquis knew her identity. Monsieur le Marquis also assumed that Marie-Christine was unaware that he was the vampire she had thwarted on Amelie's evening stroll.

Marie-Christine did not know what he planned—how he could possibly hope to kill her without alerting the palace household—but Jean-Pierre was certain that tonight he would attempt it.

The Council was very eager for her to make this kill. They had promised the French royal family that the French Slayer's first loyalty was to them, and then to the rest of the French aristocracy. After that, the royals and nobles of the other houses of Europe were afforded the Slayer's protection—including their colonies, if she could provide it. It was all very official; signed treaties and proclamations had been exchanged. Marie-Christine herself approved—for if the ruling heads fell, what hope was there for the natural order of things?

On all sides of the rectangular room, the exquisite mirrors for which the Hall of Mirrors had been named sparkled with gold and silver-backed glass. After consulting with Edmund, her Watcher, she had designed a number of elaborate bouquets of crimson roses, which covered nearly two-thirds of the length of the mirrors. Thus, the marquis would feel that his lack of reflection would go undetected. Marie-Christine had made sure to allow his servant, who had come to the palace with his acceptance of her invitation, to take note of her preparations for their dinner. He could then report to his master that, so far as could be learned, it was safe for him to attend.

It was a risk for the vampire, of course; but it would be riskier still to decline an invitation issued by one of the fashionable young aristocrats who lived in the palace. Even in the enlightened year of 1789, flouting the conventions of society meant the equivalent of death to the man or woman foolish enough to do so. Though the nobility reigned supreme over the bourgeoisie and the peasants, they needed the goodwill of one another to survive. Anyone who was cut out of the social order was generally obliged to move to another country, or to commit suicide.

Neither option would be attractive to a noble vampire, Marie-Christine reflected. *If he left France, he would be discovered and slain in an instant if he tried to curry favor with another royal family.*

She heard the tap-tap-tap of high heels on wood, fixed a dazzling smile on her mouth, and faced the entryway to the Hall of Mirrors.

"Monsieur le Marquis de Rochembourg," the servant announced, then bowed low as the man himself posed on the threshold.

His face was hard, craggy, and his features were sharp. He had a long, hook nose and very high cheekbones. His eyes were so deep-set she couldn't tell what color they were, but she knew that they were blue.

In his purple evening clothes, he was imposing and regal, every inch a high-born gentleman. Heavily wigged in long, silver-gray curls, he cast a quick glance around, noted the dense bouquets of roses with a look of satisfaction, and entered.

Careful not to bump her concealed weaponry, Marie-Christine swept a deep curtsey. *It would be so simple,* she thought, barely able to restrain herself from staking him right then.

"Monsieur le Marquis," she said breathily, "I'm honored that you accepted my invitation."

"But of course, Mademoiselle la Comptesse," he replied, coming forward. He took her hands in his, urging her to rise. His fingers were as cold as winter. *So simple, to bear down the tiniest bit, and crack them all like sticks. . . .*

The marquis's smile revealed perhaps more than he realized— it was more a grotesque imitation than an actual smile, his lips pulled back as if he intended upon ripping out her throat. He bowed again and took a step backward, made a sweeping gesture with his hand, and said, "I brought some members of my house."

"Of course. How delightful," she responded.

As the others filed in, she caught sight of Jean-Pierre, strolling in among the marquis's people, admiring the room as if for the first time with the marquis's other bewigged and bejeweled courtiers. It was quite a coup in their circle to be invited to dine in the palace. King Louis himself understood the magic of the place and had a standing policy that the peasantry be allowed in to watch him and his family dine in this very room. Marie-Antoinette hated the practice and only pretended to eat. Indeed, she bore such contempt for the peasantry that she never even bothered to remove her gloves, assuming they would not know the difference—they were nothing more than ill-mannered, poorly bred beasts.

"What an exquisite room, Mademoiselle la Comptesse," the marquis said. "What extraordinary taste, to reflect the beauty of so many roses in the walls of mirrors." He looked at her closely, as if anticipating a reaction.

Perhaps he suspects that I know what he's planning, she thought. *I'll have to stand doubly on my guard.*

"I can claim no credit," she replied. "The queen herself suggested the decorations. She received all these roses from the mayor of Paris, as a token of his fidelity to the Crown."

"The people love the king and queen," he proclaimed, as if it mattered one way or the other to such as he and she. She had never met a peasant, and had no interest in ever doing so. To what purpose?

"*Oui,*" she replied. "How nice. Shall we dine?"

Servants, of course, shadowed their every move. Servants led the marquis's entourage into the room. A string quartet of servants played while Marie-Christine's guests were seated—by more servants—at table.

Servants brought the elaborate meal—platter upon tureen upon bowl of fabulous delicacies. Servants served the high-born guests. Marie-Christine kept track of the actions of the dandies and coquettes, who were beautifully dressed, powdered, and wigged, trying to decide which of them were vampires.

The supper seemed interminable. Marie-Christine supposed she understood Queen Marie-Antoinette's dislike of playing at dining, when her mind was quite elsewhere. The delectable dishes of peacocks, oysters, succulent swans, and other exotic fare were quite lost on her.

A dessert of fruits, all re-created in sugar, was finally offered. Then came the cheese, and then the wines. So many wines. Marie-Christine did not invite the ladies to withdraw into another room, and as this was Versailles, and not London, that was not particularly remarkable. Instead, they grouped themselves on a collection of gold brocade chaises and settees, listening to the lilting minuet played by the quartet. The gentlemen assembled at the other end of the hall, smoking and discussing whatever it was they supposed women to be incapable of understanding.

Marie-Christine pulled out her silk fan and half-covered her face. At that instant, Marie-Christine's Watcher, Edmund de Voison, strolled in. It was their prearranged signal to prepare for battle. One by one, the servants withdrew, as they had been instructed to do, earlier in the day.

"De Voison," the marquis said appreciatively. Edmund had played cards with him recently, taking care to lose hundreds of sous to him. That, if not the supper invitation, would eventually draw the vampire closely enough to the Watcher and the Slayer for combat. The marquis always collected on his debts.

"*Bon soir, monsieur,*" Edmund said, bowing over his leg.

"A shame that you were not at supper. Have you been off conjuring the gold you owe me?" asked the marquis, and everyone chuckled. Edmund was famed as an alchemist. He spent most of his time in his laboratory, working with the arts of *l'occultisme.*

"Indeed not, but hoping to win it back from you, *monsieur,*" Edmund replied. "Would now be a good time?"

The vampire waved a hand. "As good a time as any, if la Comptesse does not object."

The ladies brightened beneath their pale complexions of white creams and heavily rouged cheeks. Cards and gambling were favorite pastimes of all high-born people.

"Games it is, then," Marie-Christine said in a loud voice.

The quartet stopped playing immediately and walked swiftly from the room. Then Marie-Christine and Edmund each moved to one of the long walls. Each pulled a golden cord, which had been secured behind the banks of roses, and swept to the center of the room. A hail of roses streamed to the floor, revealing the concealed portions of the mirrors.

The only reflections in the room were those of herself and her Watcher.

"Jean-Pierre!" she blurted, and her spy transformed his face into the hated mask of a vampire. His eyes glowed gold.

"It happened earlier this evening," he said, drawing his sword. "And I'm glad of it."

Their plan was ruined. Jean-Pierre was to have left the room to summon additional aid, in the form of palace guardsmen who understood the nature of these enemies.

"You stupid girl," the marquis hissed, transforming to his vampire form as well. The other guests did likewise. Marie-Christine and Edmund faced the vampiric mob alone. "Did you truly think I would not arm myself against you with everything in my power?"

Before she had a chance to answer, the vampires flew at her and Edmund in a rush of growls, fangs gleaming in the candlelight. They divided into two clumps; one of nine that came at the Slayer while the others rushed Edmund.

She reached under her skirts, grabbed a stake that had been attached to her corset, and took aim at the closest one. It was a female, hideous and brutish despite its fine clothes. Marie-Christine's weapon found its target. The vampire shrieked as it turned to dust.

Her hand was already wrapped around another stake, but her timing was off. Several of the vampires hurled themselves at her and knocked her down. Her skirts flew upward, obstructing her view—and theirs—as she grabbed another stake, this one in her left hand.

She plunged one into a male vampire that came tumbling over her skirts. Its heart was penetrated; it was sent screaming to the devil. Then she heard a muffled shriek and realized Edmund had dispatched one of his attackers as well.

Down to ten, she thought as her arms were grabbed and she was dragged along the floor. She didn't look up, but she smelled the fetid breath of half a dozen vampires as they tugged and pulled at her. Her wig came off and her brilliant red hair tumbled free.

"But this is too easy!" the marquis cried. The master vampire roared with triumphant laughter.

Then all at once, the room erupted with screams of agony. Marie-Christine felt small droplets of water on her face, and twisted her head so that she could see the hands of her captors. Blisters puffed up on their fingers, and as more water splashed on them, the vampires began to lose their grip on their prize.

Holy water, she thought. *Mon Dieu, we are saved!*

"Die, ungodly scum!" someone shouted. Marie-Christine was astonished. It was the queen herself, Marie-Antoinette.

Suddenly confusion reigned. The death screams of vampires collided with the warlike shouts of trained soldiers. The queen had brought the guards, and they were gutting the vampires with practiced hands.

"Aim for their hearts!" Marie-Christine reminded them. She got to her feet and finally yanked off her skirts, freeing herself for combat.

She went directly for the marquis, and he laughed again as he pulled his dress sword from his scabbard. It had a wicked tip, and it sliced the air as he executed a practice stroke.

"You are dead, wench," he sneered.

"If I die tonight, I'll send you to the devil first." She took aim, but he lunged directly at her with his blade extended. She was forced backward and sensed the presence of another body close behind her. She thrust back her leg, snap-kicking in the ancient style of the Chinese, and sent a male vampire skidding along the floor.

She left the creature there and focused on the marquis. One step, two, three . . . and he moved so quickly she couldn't follow his trajectory. Allowing her reflexes to take precedence over her reason, she moved slightly to the right, and threw her stake at him like a knife.

The marquis was struck in the chest.

With a roar of fury, he exploded into dust.

A momentary lull of shock ricocheted through the room. Then the surviving members of the marquis's entourage reengaged the enemy.

But their unbeating hearts were no longer in the fray; working with the queen's bodyguard, and Edmund as well, the Slayer made short work of the lot, deliberately saving Jean-Pierre for the last.

He knew she had him. He threw down his sword and thumbed his nose at her.

"There will be more," he promised. "One of us will kill you, and soon."

"That may be, but it won't be you."

She threw the stake into his chest, and he was gone.

Then the queen approached, flushed and excited, and Marie-Christine dropped to her knees.

"Majesty," she said, "I am sorry."

"You were caught unawares," the queen said stonily. "How could such a thing happen? De Voison?"

Edmund's face was torn and scratched, and his finery was coated with blood. He lowered his head and murmured, "My queen, I failed. I offer no excuses."

She regarded them both, Slayer and Watcher. Marie-Christine's face flushed with shame.

"The Council shall hear of this," Her Majesty declared. "They will decide what is to be done." She regarded Marie-Christine with contempt. "Go to your room and pray to God for His forgiveness. I cannot give you mine."

The Slayer could not help her flare of anger. She had saved the royal family from certain death more times than she could count. In return, the queen and king had showered her with rewards and deep affection.

Keeping her face a blank and hiding her balled fists behind her back, the Slayer walked backward like a scullery maid, bowing low.

The queen muttered, "For the love of God, girl, don't go out like *that*."

With as much dignity as she could muster, Marie-Christine hoisted her skirts around herself, twisting them into the semblance of a gown, and bowed again.

"We shall summon you at our leisure," Marie-Antoinette added.

As she left the Hall of Mirrors, she heard the queen say, "De Voison, we should request a new Slayer at once. She is no longer up to the task."

"Your Majesty," Edmund said, "that cannot be done. She is the Slayer until she dies."

The queen remained silent.

Marie-Christine was stunned. Marie-Antoinette couldn't mean such a thing. They were friends, the queen and the Slayer. She had even joined the queen's special circle of "milkmaids," who accompanied her to the lovely little hamlet she had had constructed on the palace grounds. There, the noblewomen had shed their fine clothes and dressed as simple milkmaids, sleeping in sweet little cottages and savoring midnight buffets along the stream the queen had so charmingly thought to include.

She's angry, that's all, Marie-Christine assured herself. But she wondered—would the Council actually execute a Slayer? If one of the crowned heads of Europe demanded her death, would the Council obey?

Impossible, she thought fiercely.

But after her maid finished preparing her for bed, she lay in the dark, alert to assassins and to the thundering of her own heart.

Three days passed, and Marie-Christine kept to her rooms. Her Watcher did not come to see her, and she wondered if he had been sent to London to account for himself and his Slayer.

Then, at last, Edmund came to visit. He was startled at her wan appearance and chastised her for not eating.

"For all I knew, my food was poisoned," she bit off as she moved nearer the sword she had been polishing at her night table.

There was a silence. Then Edmund said, "We are both in disgrace. But we have a chance to redeem ourselves. An excellent chance."

He sat on her bed and clasped his hands around his right knee. "A vampire named L'Hero is inciting the rabble. He gathers them into bands and sends them on missions of destruction, under the guise of demanding bread for their starving children."

"How absurd." She frowned at him. "There is plenty of bread. No one starves in France."

Edmund moved his shoulders. "You know how the lower classes are. They think they are entitled to every pleasure and delicacy, while they spend their days drugged with wine. And at night, they make far more children than they can afford."

Despite herself, Marie-Christine giggled, mildly scandalized. As the One divinely chosen by God to protect His elect, she was promised to a life of virginity—and happily so. She was the Slayer, and she had a vocation as sacred as any holy nun or priest.

"This vampire is quite brilliant," he continued. "He sets the peasants against any aristocrat he owes money, or who angers him."

"Why not use vampires?" she queried. "Or why not turn his followers into vampires?"

"I suppose to keep suspicion at bay," he said. "Remember, this report is from the Council, not the civilian government. Humans can do things for him that vampires cannot. And of course, he does have some vampire followers."

She nodded. "Such was the case with de Chambord."

Edmund raised a finger. "We must be careful. He's much more dangerous than de Chambord. Reports from London indicate L'Hero's followers destroyed Georgiu Rodescu."

Marie-Christine was amazed. Rodescu was a powerful magician. Many had tried to kill him, and all had failed. The Watchers Council had expressly forbidden her from even attempting to cross him.

"At any rate, the king and queen are afraid of him, and we have been ordered to dispatch him with all speed."

Marie-Christine smiled thinly. "Redemption."

"Redemption," he echoed. "Restoration. It's as good as done."

She shrugged. "We'll track him down and stake him faster than hounds after foxes."

"Indeed." He smiled. "But we must take great care. If it's true that he has killed Rodescu, he is a very formidable foe."

Impatiently, Marie-Christine nodded. She was already seeing herself in her mind's eye, receiving accolades and rewards from the hands of the queen herself for conquering a dread enemy.

"Since he's styling himself as a hero of the people, we're to go to Paris and infiltrate the lower classes," Edmund added.

"In disguise," she said. "As I have done with the queen, when we play at milkmaids."

"We'll have to dress in truly rough clothing," he informed her. "Your milkmaid costumes are far too grand. And we must conceal our polished speech." He smiled, clearly warming to the idea. "It will be a grand adventure indeed."

The Slayer nodded and pulled the bell cord beside her bed. After a few seconds, her maid appeared, curtseying to them both.

"Suzanne, champagne," she ordered. "And something to eat."

By nightfall, Slayer and Watcher had acquired ragged peasant clothing. Marie-Christine wore a coarse blouse of dull, tea-colored brown, and a skirt the color of pâté. A green woolen shawl was draped over her hair, the ends crossing over her chest and tied behind her back. Their beautiful coach stopped at the outskirts of Paris, and as they descended, Edmund stepped in a foul-smelling puddle and swore. Marie-Christine chuckled but allowed him his dignity, gazing around at the city as dusk settled over Paris.

It was not the Paris she knew—the wide boulevards shaded with plane trees, the magnificent hotels. There were men grouped around barrels, warming their hands, and a stick-thin woman trudged past the two of them, a sallow-faced infant dangling from her grasp. She stared straight ahead, and there was no sign of life in her eyes. Nor in the eyes of the men huddled around the barrel.

"Edmund, these people are zombies," she whispered. She felt in her shawl for her hatchet. As Slayer, she was heavily, if discreetly, armed with all manner of weapons.

"No." He cocked his head. "I don't think so."

Slowly she and Edmund advanced. One of the men glanced at them and grumbled something in gutter French that Marie-Christine did not understand. Edmund stiffened and turned around, taking her arm.

"Come away."

"What did he say?" she asked, easily catching up with him as he marched away.

"Nothing that need concern you." He sound prim, and she grinned. He glared at her and snapped, "I don't like your being here. It's not right."

"But it's all right if I risk my life in silk and satin?"

He shrugged. Curiously, she found she agreed with him. That was more acceptable to her as well. There was something unseemly about this project, and already she was a bit dashed. At the queen's mock village, the little cottages were sparkling clean. There were no smelly puddles, no men insulting ladies with crude language.

A sharp wind bit her shoulders, and she drew the shawl more tightly around herself. September was colder in the city than at Versailles. She should have brought something warmer. But no one in the streets wore anything that could possibly keep out all the cold. She gaped with astonishment at a frail urchin who bounded past them barefoot.

"What can his mother be thinking?" she asked Edmund.

He sighed with disgust. "That she can stay drunk twice as long if she doesn't buy her child some shoes?"

Marie-Christine nodded thoughtfully. Through the soles of her thin shoes, she could feel each piece of gravel in the dirt, each round pebble, as she and Edmund walked on. Their plan was to find an inn, and ask the patrons for information about L'Hero, explaining that they wished to join his band. Edmund, who had some small skill with languages, would do all the talking. Marie-Christine could not make the odd sounds of lower-class speech, and so it had been decided she would pretend to be mute.

As they walked, a window above them opened and someone shouted. Edmund grabbed Marie-Christine and pulled her out of the way as a waterfall of offal streamed down. Marie-Christine's stomach clenched with disgust, and she gestured to Edmund at a bottle-windowed building to their left, with a sign that read CHANTICLEER. It looked to be an inn.

Edmund nodded at her, and they went to the door. He hesitated, cleared his throat, and pushed his way in.

The room was a hazy mist of smoke and beer. Groups of men sat around wooden tables, more at longer tables around the perimeter of the room, and they all stared dully at the newcomers. Marie-Christine glanced at one of them and he grinned at her, revealing two or three jagged teeth, and moved his eyebrows up and down. She shuddered and kept her attention focused on the back of Edmund's jacket.

Soon they were placed at a table with two men, it being the custom to sit where there was room. The men stank so badly that the Slayer was afraid she was going to vomit, but she managed with great effort to keep down her gorge. Edmund ordered something for them, and when it arrived, she guessed that it might be soup. It was a murky brown, and chunks of orange and darker brown floated in the gruel.

Edmund sighed and manfully picked up his spoon. Marie-Christine did the same.

But after a moment's hesitation, she put the spoon back down. She couldn't do it. She didn't have to, and she wouldn't.

Slurping his soup, Edmund began chatting with the men, and soon the three were engrossed in conversation about meaningless things—whether there was work to be found, and how much bread cost these days. It was then that Marie-Christine realized someone was watching them.

Her Slayer's acuities focused, she turned slowly to stare at a man who sat alone in the shadows. He was very tall, and his face was sharply chiseled and very white. Black eyes gazed at her; blue-black hair tumbled past his shoulders. He wore a black coat and a rough workman's cravat over a muslin shirt. He was smoking a pipe, and the smoke eddied around his head, and he stared boldly at her.

His were eyes that were alive. His, a smile that made her swallow as it creased his face.

It is he, she thought. *It is L'Hero.*

Slowly she rose and walked to him through the crowded, close room. His eyes glowed ruby; she blinked, suddenly dizzy, feeling awkwardly for the stake concealed in the crisscross of her shawl. Something overcame her; she stumbled to the right, bracing herself against the back of an empty chair. Her eyes closed, and her knees gave way.

When she came to, she was sitting in the same chair, and the innkeeper was wafting a glass of brandy beneath her nose. She touched her forehead, aware she should not say a word, as Edmund studied her face. She tapped her mouth where a vampire's fang would protrude, then slowly turned her head where the vampire had sat, smoking his pipe.

She was not at all surprised that he was no longer there.

Their original plan had been to rendezvous with their coach and return to the palace for the night, but Marie-Christine's fainting spell had made them the center of attention. Edmund negotiated for a room, and he led Marie-Christine into a low, dingy attic room in which slept three other people in two beds. There was one more bed, and it was for the two of them.

They took off none of their clothes, not even their shoes, and pulled a coverlet matted with mold over themselves. Marie-Christine shivered as a sharp wind whistled through holes in the thatch overhead. Mice rustled in the straw, and she reminded herself that the palace was home to plenty of mice.

Edmund rolled toward her, whispering into her ear, "What happened?"

"I saw him. He was in the room," she whispered back. A rotund man in the next bed over began to snore like a trumpet.

"The . . . one?"

"*Oui.* He put me into a trance, I think."

"In the morning, tell me. For now, you're mute," he cautioned.

They lay side by side; slowly, Edmund's body heat warmed her right side, but by morning she had an abominable headache from shivering the whole night long. The rotund man never did stop snoring.

Downstairs, they had porridge for breakfast, and there were small white things in it that Marie-Christine tried not to see. Edmund took a few meager bites, paid their bill, and they left.

Outside, he said, "I'm poisoned, Marie-Christine. First that soup last night, and then that abomination. . . ." He clutched his stomach. "How can they eat such swill?"

"Perhaps we should ask the queen to reconsider," she ventured, "and kill us instead."

They shared an ironic chuckle, then moved into the busy Parisian morning. The sun was dull and the people as lifeless as they had been the night before. There were scores of beggar children, whimpering for coins from people who obviously had none to spare. Marie-Christine thought of the well-scrubbed faces of the children of the palace servants. These little ones were like creatures from a nightmare. With their thin faces and enormous eyes, they were barely human.

"Now tell me about him," Edmund said, once they had put some distance between themselves and the inn.

"*Mon Dieu.*" She crossed herself. "Truly, he is a king of demons. We must be on our guard, Edmund."

Nodding thoughtfully, he steered her around a steaming mound of horse manure, through which a mangy dog trotted quite joyfully. A heap of rags staggered beneath thick cords of firewood loaded on its back. It was an old woman, who pointed at Marie-Christine and cackled, then spat in the muddy dirt.

"She says you're a witch, because of your red hair," Edmund told her.

"How absurd." The Slayer pulled her shawl over her head. She wiped her face, feeling grimy and unclean. "This place is appalling, Edmund. The rudeness, the ignorance." She lowered her hand. "These aren't people, they're animals."

They spent the day surveying the filthy alleys and cramped rooms that passed for public dining places. Marie-Christine recoiled in horror when what they thought had been a pile of garbage turned out to be the remains of an old man. No one had taken his body for burial; he had simply been left in the gutter to rot.

As the sun sank and the cold winds blew, mobs of children scattered down the causeways and over bridges. Edmund asked a passerby who they were, and learned they were newly come from the workhouse.

"They are employed, and still have no shoes?" Marie-Christine asked, making a face at their cracked, bleeding feet. "It's so cold. Their toes must be frozen."

Edmund moved his shoulders with disinterest and said, "Let's make for the rendezvous with the coach. I swear I shall not spend another night in this hellhole." He scratched absently at his chest, then gave a little cry of indignation. "I have fleas!"

Marie-Christine jumped away from him. "Then keep away from me."

Something sharp nipped her collarbone. She slapped it, and held it between her fingernails. It was a flea.

Marie-Christine the Vampire Slayer shuddered with revulsion.

Their coach arrived, and they bundled into it beneath fur wraps and raced for home. Later that night, bathed and scented, tucked into her soft, warm bed, Marie-Christine began to doze. Her mind wandered. Everywhere, there were children with no shoes; mothers with gaunt faces; the cadaver of the old man, a decomposing obscenity in full view of an uncaring mob. . . .

A dull, ashen-colored fog pervaded the dream, leeching each tableau of its color and life. The streets, the cracks in the buildings, the tumbledown shacks, were coated with a hue of vast, bottomless despair. Rain fell, heavy: Christ was weeping. The bells of Notre Dame tolled *Bring out your dead, bring out your dead.*

Alas, a voice whispered. *Alas.*

Marie-Christine shifted, drifting more deeply into slumber. Behind her mind's eye, the merest whisper of a ruby glow brought the only color to the vast landscape of hovels and degradation. Rosy dawn, the first petals of a rose—the color was shockingly beautiful in a world utterly devoid of any warmth or comfort.

When she awoke, she was more tired than the day before. Knowing they must return to the streets of Paris, she forced herself to breakfast on buttery croissants and hot chocolate.

If the people knew they could dine like this, instead of wasting their sous on drink and lechery, she thought, *they would not allow themselves to be so base.*

Edmund joined her in his peasant clothes. They were the same ones he had worn the day before, and they had not been cleaned. She realized that she would have to wear her own peasant costume again as well, instead of exchanging it for clean rags and tatters. They had been far too well-groomed yesterday to fully blend in.

That was why L'Hero found me, she decided.

The Watcher declared, "I am grim but determined." She nodded, and they dined together in dreary anticipation of the distasteful hours that lay ahead.

When the coach let them off at the same place as before, they maneuvered with more confidence into the sloth and filth that was this quarter of Paris. Fortified with a good sleep and breakfast, Marie-Christine managed to avoid the piles of dog and horse dung, curling her lip at the lack of sanitation. Really, it would only take a moment to clean up after one's animals.

It's so typical of these people that they can't expend the slightest amount of effort to improve their lot.

Then she heard an odd sound, something low and breathy, and nudged Edmund in the ribs. He nodded, indicating that he had heard it, too, and together they moved into a wretched, tiny alley littered with refuse. As before, the Slayer had not come unprepared for battle; she had several fine stakes, an assortment of knives, and other weaponry concealed in her clothing.

It was a small girl, perhaps four, although she was emaciated and her features looked very old. Dressed in tatters, she was weeping and staring down at a broken doll.

Marie-Christine had no idea what moved her to the child's plight, but she squatted beside the child and said, "Your dolly's broken."

The waif stared at her, not comprehending, and Edmund

spoke next, in gutter language. The girl replied, lifting the doll off her lap and dropping it in the mud.

"She says that she can't eat a doll. She has not eaten since yesterday morning," Edmund informed Marie-Christine.

"Where is her *maman?*"

Edmund spoke to the girl. When she answered, his eyes lit up.

"She is fighting for justice," he replied.

"Do you think . . . ?" the Slayer asked.

Edmund spoke to the girl, asking questions, receiving answers.

"She is with a band led by a tall man. They are in 'a dark place,' near the river. I think she means the sewers."

The girl added something, and Edmund said, "Ah. A series of round bridges. I know exactly where she's speaking of."

"Then let's go."

Marie-Christine rose and turned on her heel, then paused. She looked at the little girl, staring up at them so trustingly, then at Edmund and said, "We should give her some money. For the information."

He frowned slightly, then pulled a coin from his pocket. The little girl's eyes widened.

"Give her another," Marie-Christine said.

He did so. The girl stared down at the coins, holding one in each palm. With a little cry she flung herself at Edmund's legs and wrapped herself around them, sobbing.

"She is thanking me." His voice was stiff. "*Mon Dieu,* I shall have fleas again."

Marie-Christine's heart tugged strangely as she watched the girl. Astonished with herself, she reached out a hand. The child studied it, then peered up at Marie-Christine, and very tentatively placed her tiny fingers against Marie-Christine's, at the first knuckle, as if she didn't quite dare to make full contact.

"Marie-Christine," Edmund admonished, "you're sure to contract a terrible disease from this little rodent."

"We may need her," the Slayer said slowly. "She can be our guide to her mother."

"Indeed." Edmund looked thoughtful. "How convenient. Do you suppose *he* sent her to collect us?"

"*Oui,* I do suppose," Marie-Christine shot back. 'But that doesn't make her any less hungry."

Edmund spoke to the girl, who babbled back at him. She tilted her head and grinned shyly up at Marie-Christine, then murmured a few additional words.

Edmund translated. "She thinks you are an angel, or possibly, the queen."

"*Petite ange,*" said the Chosen One to the girl. "Little angel."

The girl appeared to understand, slipping her hand more firmly into Marie-Christine's grasp. The three began to walk out of the alley.

"First of all, we must feed her," Marie-Christine announced.

"Oh, very well." Edmund's tone was grudging but compliant. For no reason that she could tell, Marie-Christine felt a wash of giddy happiness.

"She must have hot chocolate. I would wager a thousand sous she has never had it," she added.

The Slayer was correct: the girl, whose name was Mathilde, had never had hot chocolate, or croissants, or tender pieces of chicken simmered in wine. She had never, in her entire life, been unable to clean every morsel of food off her plate. In the café, she started to choke on a piece of cheese, and Marie-Christine had to physically stop her from overeating.

When the girl wailed in protest, kicking her ankles against the edge of the seat of her wooden chair, the Slayer said to her Watcher, "Tell her we will buy her more food later."

"She won't understand," Edmund insisted. "These people are incapable of planning for the future. That's why they live as they do."

"Tell her," Marie-Christine said, still restraining the girl. "It might even be true."

Edmund grumbled but did as she asked, and the girl looked dubious. She pointed to the food, and then to Marie-Christine's folded shawl, and the Slayer realized the chit wanted to hoard the leftovers.

"Explain to her that that's not done," the Slayer said.

The child must have understood her; she burst into tears and threw her arms across the meager chunk of cheese and a half-eaten slab of thick, sour peasant bread.

"Well . . . ," Edmund said.

The child stared at the Slayer, whose sacred duty of course, was to protect. *But not to protect such as she,* she reminded herself. *I was put on earth to protect those who matter to the world.* Still, Marie-Christine's irritation was mollified by the creeping realization that the girl was truly terrified of starving.

She had been warned by the fashionable ladies of the court that frowning created wrinkles, but she couldn't help her scowl as she watched the panicked urchin protecting the scraps. "What an awful mother she has. This poor thing has been terribly neglected."

"Their women are like turtles. They hatch their eggs on the beach, and wander off," Edmund snipped as the Slayer picked up the cheese and handed it to the child. Her grubby fingers closed around it, grasping Marie-Christine's finger. He grimaced. "Now you shall surely contract a disease."

Marie-Christine surveyed the child's clothing for a pocket, saw none, and plucked up the piece of bread. She carefully tucked it into her shawl. Smiling at the girl, she gave the bulge a pat and held her hand out for the cheese. Tears slid down the little one's cheeks, but she bravely handed it over, and the Slayer added the cheese to the portable larder.

The girl stared longingly at the concealed treasure, then sighed with a depth of resignation one might hear from a condemned prisoner.

"*C'est bon, ma petite,*" the Slayer assured her. The girl appeared not to hear. Marie-Christine reached a hand toward her chin; the child flinched, and Marie-Christine put her hand in her lap. "Oh, Edmund, do you suppose they beat her?"

"They probably do," he grumbled. When the Chosen One glanced at him, he cleared his throat. "We must go. We're not Sisters of Charity, we're warriors, and we must engage the enemy."

"*Oui.*" With firm resolve, she pushed back her chair and rose. The girl scrambled off her own chair, her eyes enormous as she stared up at Marie-Christine.

The trio left the café, the child, Mathilde, trailing timidly behind. They walked at a brisk pace, past squalid old buildings of mildewed stone and eons of grime. The buildings were uniformly so broken-down and filthy that it was difficult, though not impossible, to distinguish one from another. Brick, mortar, wood, and rock had ground against one another for so long that the tumbledown structures appeared to melt into one another, as though they constituted an enormous loaf of bread half devoured by rats.

Patches of the street revealed worn cobblestones, overlaid with coatings of rutted dirt. Willful orange geraniums sprouted from the cracks, and the desiccated bloom of a crimson rose lay in the gutter.

She wondered if a previous Slayer had ever walked these same streets. That other Slayers had risen from the soil of France, she had no doubt. She herself believed that Joan of Arc had been a Slayer.

Slayers were God's anointed, as were the kings and queens of Europe. It made perfect sense to her that there should be a hereditary legacy in her lofty role, as there was in theirs. Otherwise, there would be an inevitable and unending jostling for power, preoccupying those who had more important matters to pursue.

The world serves the mighty for a reason, she thought. *How else could civilization progress?*

Mathilde blurted out something in her unintelligible French, darting ahead toward a beggar propped up against a wall. The chit stumbled and almost fell, but clambered on, calling to the bundle of rags.

"What's going on?" Marie-Christine asked Edmund.

"I think she knows him." The Watcher cocked his head. "I can't be sure. Her French is a disaster."

The beggar had one leg; the other had been cut off at the knee, and the stump was wrapped in filthy bandages. The creature's head hung against his chest; slowly, like the lifting of a portcullis at the entrance to a drawbridge, he raised it as Mathilde darted up to him.

The girl spoke to him hurriedly, gesturing at Edmund and Marie-Christine. The man's eyes were dull and rheumy. Marie-Christine suspected he was blind.

She said sharply, "Get away from him, child," but Mathilde paid her no heed. Then she bobbed upright, hurried to Marie-Christine, and gestured toward her chest. The Slayer stared at her without a trace of comprehension, glancing to Edmund for aid.

"She wants the food. To give to the man," Edmund explained.

"Certainly not. *Mais, non,*" Marie-Christine told the girl, touching her shawl. "If I'm to smell of Camembert all day, it will be for her, and her only."

Still gesturing, Mathilde looked at Edmund, speaking to him, and the beggar on the ground growled something in decent French about kings and lies.

"He is a veteran," Edmund explained. "His leg was shattered by a cannonball. The army discharged him and he has no pension."

Marie-Christine moved her shoulders. "What has that to do with us? Certainly he understood the risks of his profession. I'm no lawyer. Perhaps he wasn't deserving of a pension. *I* don't have one, and I shall certainly die in my line of work." She looked down at the thin little face, whose eyes were spilling with tears. "Mathilde, stop it."

The one-legged man spoke again, and Edmund snapped at him. "He says the king turned his back on his troops, and that he cannot find work. Who will hire a one-legged man when so many other men with two legs are starving? And so he relies on the charity of those who love France."

"He speaks treasonously of his monarch, yet has the gall to ask for coins stamped with His Majesty's likeness?" Marie-Christine looked at the man with acidic contempt. "The Church can see to him. That's what the Church is for."

She turned away, considering the matter resolved. Before she had walked three steps, Mathilde ran in front of her and dropped to her knees, holding up her small hands in a pleading gesture. Marie-Christine huffed at her, waving her hand to urge her out of the way. Doggedly the child held her ground, shaking her head and babbling, pointing to the man, then finally, clutching up the dirt-caked hem of Marie-Christine's peasant skirts.

"She begs you to give the man her bread and cheese," Edmund said.

"I need no translation." Marie-Christine pursed her lips. "Tell her that if I give it to him, there will be no more food for her today. That this is all there will be."

Edmund complied. The girl answered, her chin raised, her head thrown back so that she could see into Marie-Christine's eyes.

"She understands. She still wants him to have the food."

"This is precisely why they are poor," Marie-Christine muttered as she retrieved the piece of cheese and the bread and handed them to the girl. "All irrational feeling, no sense . . ."

She watched in mute fascination as Mathilde ran to the man, gabbling at him, curtseying as she stretched out her hands. His own raised in front of his face, searching for the treasure, and Mathilde carefully placed the food into his grasp.

He bobbed his head, sighing, "*Merci, beaucoup merci,*" then fell to eating with a slavish urgency, as if he were terrified the food might be taken from him before he could finish it.

Edmund chuckled. "*Mon Dieu,* I've never seen anyone eat so fast."

Despite her Watcher's amusement, Marie-Christine felt supremely irritated. She was aware of something tightening in her throat, had no idea what it might signify, and snapped her fingers at Mathilde, as she might a lapdog or a pet monkey.

"Come along. We've wasted enough time," she insisted.

Mathilde appeared to understand. She got to her feet and darted back to Marie-Christine, babbling away. By the lilt in her voice, the Slayer realized the child was asking her a question.

"Oh, good heavens," Edmund blurted, rolling his eyes. "No, Marie-Christine, I won't even repeat it."

"She wants more food for him?"

"I refuse to tell you." Edmund slipped his snuff box from a pocket in his jacket and helped himself to a quick pinch. As he put it back, he said to the old soldier, "Take care, old colonel."

"Thank you, sir," the man replied. His French was decent enough after all.

Without another word, the Slayer swept away.

It wasn't until she was at least a hundred feet from the scene that she realized a tear was trickling down her cheek. She dabbed it with her sleeve, convinced that she was getting ill. How else to explain her overemotional soft-heartedness today?

"What did she ask?"

Edmund chuckled again. "For us to take the man with us. For us to find him a home."

"*C'est absurde*," Marie-Christine said to the girl, who stared up adoringly at her and chattered in her little voice.

"She wants to know why it is absurd to ask this of an angel of mercy."

Marie-Christine rolled her eyes. "She has no idea who or what I am. If anything, I am an avenging angel."

"That I will not tell her," Edmund said sternly. He spoke to the child, who nodded and replied. "She says that the bridge is not far now. It occurs to me, Marie-Christine, that she may be leading us on a fool's errand. Perhaps she's part of a band of pickpockets, and not at all associated with . . . our friend. She might even be a Gypsy."

"No matter," Marie-Christine said darkly. "I am the Slayer."

They continued on, moving through a morass of misery and poverty far beyond anything Marie-Christine had ever seen. The stones of the buildings themselves stank with disease and death; rats ran in packs, and everywhere, children wailed in hopeless misery. Marie-Christine was revolted; she doubted she would ever eat again.

"How do they live this way?" she said to Edmund. "If I were born into these circumstances, I certainly would not endeavor to bring more of my kind into the world. And yet look at their women, gaunt-cheeked and big-bellied, leading a parade of starving children while they await another."

She gestured with bewilderment at a woman who was clearly with child, two tiny, sticklike boys clutching at the hem of her skirt. Their faces were pinched, and there was no twinkle in their eyes.

"They may as well be dead," she murmured.

Mathilde appeared to take no notice. She began to speak rapidly to Edmund, who told Marie-Christine, "She says we are almost there."

"Thank God," Marie-Christine bit off.

The little child began to slow her pace. It was clear she was tired, and probably hungry again. If they were still together later on this day, Marie-Christine planned to feed her. Her threat to withhold food if she fed the beggar man had been an idle one.

The docks were reeking with sewage and dead fish; Marie-Christine's eyes watered from the smell, and Edmund waved a pomander in front of his face. The child rushed ahead, nearing a set of arched bridges, and called out in her strange French.

Consternation resulted, with muttering and whispered curses. Then at last a young, thin woman appeared from the shadows beneath the bridge, and she called excitedly to the girl.

"Good Lord, that wretch is Mathilde's mother."

"Are you there?" the Slayer called out boldly, meaning not the mother, but another, more sinister person . . . if a vampire could ever be thought of as a person.

From beneath the bridge, more faces appeared. They were weather-beaten and scarred; a woman squinted with one milky eye and one empty socket. Another man had no nose.

"They're common criminals," Marie-Christine said indignantly.

"*Mais non*," came a reply. The voice was deep and sonorous; the French was impeccable. "Their only crimes are poverty and starvation."

Marie-Christine closed her eyes for a moment as the voice reverberated through her bones. Edmund glanced at her, and she nodded.

"L'Hero," Edmund said. "Come out."

"Into the sunlight? *Merci, non.*"

"I will come in and get you then," Marie-Christine warned him.

The milky-eyed old woman garbled something at her and spat on the gravel at her feet. The thin one—Mathilde's mother—squatted on one knee and urged her child to come to her.

"You will not harm these people, and they will protect me with their lives," L'Hero said. "They are committed to the cause. They are my family."

"They're not my concern. And you have no cause." Marie-Christine wished she had her crossbow. They were at a standoff, she and this vampire.

For now.

"I know who you are," L'Hero informed her. "You are the Slayer. I called you and you came."

"Don't be ridiculous," Marie-Christine flung at him. "I certainly don't follow the orders of one such as *you*."

"Nor those of any such as these. You fight for dukes and their mistresses. For bishops and their courtesans." His voice dripped with contempt. "I have done more to help more people than you, Slayer. It would make more sense for you to join us."

L'Hero's people nodded eagerly.

"You live in squalor under a bridge," she said haughtily. She turned to Edmund. "We should light fires on either side and burn him to death."

"It would cause an uproar. The Council would not countenance your killing human beings." Edmund frowned. "But we can wait for the darkness to fall, and then you can take him with greater discretion."

She nodded. "Then we'll wait." She looked down at Mathilde, who had stayed with her, rather than go to her mother. The girl looked up at her and wrapped her fists in the coarse fabric of Marie-Christine's skirts. She looked exhausted and frightened.

"We have your daughter," the Slayer said to her mother.

The mother looked concerned. "Mathilde," she called. She babbled in her wretched French, gesturing to the girl. Then she looked up with concern into the shadows, presumably at the vampire. He replied in the same gutter patois.

"I reassured her that you will not harm her child," L'Hero said. "You are not allowed to kill human beings."

Marie-Christine narrowed her eyes. "Tell her this. 'That man in there with you is no man. He's an evil demon.' "

To her surprise, L'Hero did as she had requested. She had no idea if he was repeating her exact words, but the woman, and many of the others, burst into gales of laughter.

After the laughter had subsided, L'Hero said, "What can I say? They love me, 'evil demon' as I am."

"They don't know what you are," Edmund said.

"Oh, they *do*." L'Hero's voice was filled with amusement. "They know very well that I am a vampire."

Marie-Christine shook her head.

"They know what I am, and that I protect and care for them," the vampire cut in. "They know that I and my kind have certain . . . limitations, such as moving freely by daylight, and they help us. In return, I treat them well. I give them bread, and a place to sleep. And if they truly merit the honor, I promise them eternal life . . . once we have overthrown the monarchy."

"Treason!" Edmund cried as, without a moment's hesitation, Marie-Christine withdrew a stake and prepared for attack.

L'Hero guffawed. "Slayer, in your journeys through the fair city of Paris, have you not come to realize that the king and queen are worse vampires than I? That they have sucked the lifeblood of their people, until they are driven mad with hunger and pestilence? The queen herself has said, 'Let them eat cake.' Well, I say, 'Let them drink blood.' "

A chorus of cheers rose up among the people crowded under

the bridge. Their voices shouted the slogans of anarchy: *"Vive le Republique! Le rois, la-bas!"*

"This is intolerable," Marie-Christine shouted at them. "You'll all be executed if you continue this folly!"

"We'll die like dogs if we do not," someone shouted back. "It is our lot, to slave and starve! Why is it wrong to demand something better?"

Marie-Christine's temper flared. Raising her skirts to keep them above the mire, she trotted toward the clump of people. They drew close in, obscuring her view of L'Hero. When a young man moved to block her, she knocked him aside without a second glance. More came at her, including a man with a pitchfork. He was in the filthy river before he knew what had hit him . . . literally.

Of the tall vampire, there was no sign.

"Where is he?" Marie-Christine demanded as she pushed through the throng of peasants beneath the arched bridge. The mossy, rotting stonework reminded her of a dungeon. The stench was that of a charnel house.

But L'Hero was not among them. Somehow, he had disappeared. Again. Frustrated, Marie-Christine faced the mob and said, "Leave here! Get away from him. He is a demon! He is *evil.*"

A woman pushed through the crowd. She stood before Marie-Christine. "If he were the devil incarnate, I would do his bidding. He has saved us. All of us." She gestured to the woman with the rheumy eye. "Elizabeth would have lost her good eye, too, except for the medicine he gave her. And Arnaud"—she gestured to the noseless man—"they cut him for stealing one baguette."

"It is wrong to steal. . . ." Marie-Christine's voice was not as steady as she would have liked.

"It is wrong to *starve.* In the king's own city, it is wrong for babies to die because their mothers cannot feed them. It is evil to refuse medicine to people who are dying because they have no money. That is what is evil."

"The aristos dance and game," said a man, stepping forward. "And we die. We die every day, by the hundreds. But L'Hero . . . he has saved us. All of us."

The others nodded vigorously.

Edmund called out to her. "This is a battle for another day. Let us depart."

Mathilde's mother came toward her, speaking rapidly, pointing at her daughter.

"Of course she wants her back," Edmund said.

"Absolutely not." Marie-Christine wrapped her arms around the girl. "Tell her she is insane to expect good treatment from that diabolical monster."

The woman's lip curled in an ugly sneer as Marie-Christine spoke.

"She says that no matter where you take Mathilde, L'Hero will find her and bring her back to her. He has promised her that her child will have eternal life, and never starve or have to sell herself on the streets, as she has."

Marie-Christine shook her head. "Tell her that I will never hand this girl over to them. I—I will make her my ward and give her a decent, Christian upbringing."

"Marie-Christine," Edmund reproved.

The Slayer raised her chin. "It is what I will do," she insisted.

"*Maman*," Mathilde murmured softly, but she did not let go of Marie-Christine's hand. Silent tears streamed down her face, but not once did she allow a sob to escape her. Misery clearly warred with resolve in the little girl, and she kept hold of Marie-Christine.

"We'll have to feed her," the Slayer muttered.

"Indeed." Edmund moved his shoulders. "I can't wait to get back to the palace. I need a bath and a good night's sleep."

But there was something in his voice, a catch, a lack of conviction, and Marie-Christine glanced at him. To her surprise, he looked a little older than before. His forehead was creased and his mouth drooped.

He said no more until they were gone from the city. In the coach, Mathilde dozed against Marie-Christine's shoulder, and Edmund tapped his fingers against the thick woolen blanket spread across his lap. Marie-Christine's own mind wandered, replaying again and again the scene beneath the bridge. Mathilde sighed in her sleep, crumbs from a croissant charmingly dotting the corner of her mouth, like a trio of beauty spots.

"I will need to make a report," Edmund said at last. "The Council emissary will want to know how we're progressing."

"We discovered the lair," Marie-Christine filled in. "He got away."

Edmund snorted. "He lured us there. You and I both know it. He's a powerful creature. Charismatic in the extreme."

"Lucifer was the most beautiful angel in heaven," Marie-Christine observed.

There was a long silence. Then Edmund said, "In some of the other Watcher Diaries, it is said that the Slayer worked for the common people."

"To what purpose?" Marie-Christine queried.

Edmund took more snuff. He tapped his nostrils with appreciation and leaned his head back against the pillows. "The common good."

"What nonsense. There is no such thing."

"Agreed." Edmund exhaled. Then he began to snore.

Fast asleep, Mathilde was carried by a footman to Marie-Christine's maid's room. Marie-Christine thought with a flurry of nervous excitement that the peasant child's arrival would create a mild *scandale.* But the Slayer was resolute: she would never surrender the waif to her awful mother and L'Hero.

She and Edmund entered the palace, to discover that the Duc de Chambord was waiting for them in the small pink salon off the Hall of Mirrors. He was pacing, and frantic, as she curtseyed deeply to the duke, apologized for her disheveled state, and listened to his tale of woe.

"As you know, my family has an ongoing problem with certain . . . unsavory personages," he said, "and now those . . . creatures demand full payment on our, ah, obligations or they intend to marry their oldest son to my daughter. *Imagine* the *scandale.*" He whipped a handkerchief from the lacy sleeve of his shirt and patted his forehead. "A de Chambord, married into a family of demons!"

"Wealthy demons, however," Edmund pointed out. "And very barely demons. It is a well-kept secret in the circles of nobility. It's only by accident that you know of it yourself."

"That is not my fault," de Chambord said. "The rogue was losing at cards and, in his distress, revealed his demonic nature."

"Worse has befallen daughters," Edmund said, continuing on. "Recall Anne Bordeaux, who was married off to that epileptic idiot son of that Prussian prince?"

De Chambord blinked. "But—"

Edmund pressed on. "She has several fine children—no doubt from her lovers—and she has time and resources to serve as patroness to a very fine university. Her life is full and blessed."

The duke took pause. Finally he said, "I had not thought of it that way. And Clarisse . . . she's a flexible child." He shook his head. "No. I demand that you do what you must to keep my family's reputation from harm."

"The payment of your debt . . . ?" Edmund inquired discreetly.

"Is not possible at the present moment." He smoothed his coat sleeves with impeccable grace. "Besides, I suspect that they cheat at cards." The duke turned to Marie-Christine. "You are the Slayer. You must help me."

Marie-Christine thought of Mathilde's mother, who had been willing to sell her soul to the devil in return for bread. Then she looked at this man before her, extravagantly dressed, well fed, and her stomach turned with revulsion.

"I am engaged in another enterprise at the moment," she said crisply. "But as soon as I am finished, I—"

The man's lips parted. "I am boggled! I require, *non,* I *demand,* your immediate attention!" He scowled at Edmund. "Such insolence!"

"Mademoiselle is very tired," Edmund soothed. "She's not thinking clearly. Of course she will do whatever she must to satisfy your honor. It is her duty, and she knows that. Do you not?" He stared hard at Marie-Christine.

The Slayer swept another deep curtsey. "Forgive me, monsieur," she said to de Chambord. "I am fatigued beyond my ability to reason. Of course, I shall do as I am commanded. I must rest, and tomorrow, I will come to you for instructions."

"That is much, much better," de Chambord said, smoothing his wig. "Then I shall take my leave, and await you tomorrow." He gave Edmund a curt bow; he gave Marie-Christine an even curter one.

After he swept out, Marie-Christine said, "I won't do it."

"He has the right, and it is your duty," Edmund replied. He raised his hand. "That's all for now, *mademoiselle.* Sleep well."

Her face burned as she walked out of the room. He had dismissed her like a servant.

But what else am I? A terrier, sent to harry foxes and moles over gambling debts?

Before she retired, she checked on Mathilde, who was asleep in the maid's room on a makeshift bed of old blankets and pil-

0

lows. Suzanne smiled at Marie-Christine and put her finger to her lips, and Marie-Christine withdrew.

The days and nights dragged by, and the streets of Paris were rivers of talk of revolution. The Royal Court opined that the poor were bored with being poor. They coveted the vast estates and fat purses of the rich without a moment's understanding of the obligations that came with them. They vandalized the homes and businesses of finely dressed bourgeoisie, then moved on to the nobility.

The Watchers Council was alarmed.

They were right to be, for the vampire L'Hero took advantage of the political turmoil to wreak havoc on his betters. The demon led his people to the *Hotel* of Aristide De Nouville, a wealthy aristocrat who lived in town, and denounced him as an enemy of the people. De Nouville owed him money, but he didn't mention that. Instead, he reminded the beggars and cutthroats—and vampires—assembled around him that the rotund man had once voted to keep the poor out of the cathedral when the aristos attended Mass. No mention was made of the fact that he himself, as a vampire, could not face the cross.

Enraged, giddy with power they did not deserve, the rabble grabbed up torches and set the magnificent home on fire, laughing as De Nouville and his family and servants escaped in their nightclothes, in open carriages.

Next, L'Hero informed his followers that the three de Loury brothers had conspired with their tenant farmers to sell diseased wheat to the bakers who made the bread for the poor—neglecting to mention that the de Lourys also made the hosts for the priests, and for that reason, had incurred his wrath.

Incited to violence, his people stampeded the fields and demolished the homes of three local bakers, dragging out the mothers and daughters, forgetting who they were, and that they were human beings.

Like a fiery priest of the Inquisition, L'Hero urged them to drive out the goats and sheep of Martin Doree, whose land he coveted; and they not only drove the animals out of their pens, but also slaughtered them in a frenzy. His face dripped with steaming animal blood as he laughed at their hysteria and showed his fangs in the firelight; and his people danced around burning pens and haystacks, tearing off their clothes, drinking, cavorting, shouting, *"Vive la Republique! Vive L'Hero!"*

Some of these things, Marie-Christine heard about through palace gossip. Others, she dreamed; the dreams of Slayers are often said to be prophecies.

The gutters of Paris ran red with blood; the cobblestones were lumps in a gout of blood; everywhere that Marie-Christine walked, she slipped and fell in the puddles of blood.

Her hands were wet with death; she was a walking testament to her inability to exact justice, or revenge.

And then, in her dreams, he was whispering against her throat, gloating, "Stop me, if you dare. Or if you can find the time."

Marie-Christine satisfied the Duc de Chambord by threatening the semidemonic nobleman who owed him money. The creature agreed that it was in his best interest to keep the fact of his mixed parentage a private matter, and thus the forced marriage of the de Chambord heiress was averted.

Mathilde slowly won a few hearts, though the gossip surrounding Marie-Christine's decision to adopt her did not abate. Edmund declared that he was "flummoxed" by her actions and could only lay it down to her "illogical and emotional" feminine nature.

Meanwhile, more and more people died in Paris—not naturally, but from the kiss of the vampire. L'Hero had instituted a reign of terror such as Paris had never seen, turning his people, as he had promised them, and adding more to his army.

"And so, I beg you, let me go to the city," Marie-Christine said to Sir Stephen, an emissary from the Watchers Council in London. "So many people are dying."

The short, pock-marked Sir Stephen was perhaps twenty, if that; he had a high opinion of himself, and he expected Marie-Christine and Edmund to agree with that opinion.

"There is revolution in the air," he said as they sat in the pink salon. "The king and queen need you to stay close by. They must have your protection."

"But he's baiting us," Marie-Christine said. "He's killing people by the dozens."

"Paris has dozen and hundreds of dozens of people. You have one king. You have one queen." Sir Stephen spread open his arms. "Do I make myself clear?"

Edmund shot Marie-Christine a look. Seething, she lowered her gaze to the floor and swept a deep curtsey. *"Oui, monsieur."*

"The Council is most pleased to hear that," he snipped. "Upon pain of severe repercussions, do not stray from the palace grounds."

He droned on, and she nodded at appropriate intervals. But once the interview was concluded, she whirled on Edmund and said, "I'm going to the city. I'm going to run L'Hero to ground and stake him."

Edmund looked troubled. After a time, he said, "It's not our affair."

"He is a *vampire.*"

"We have our instructions." He balled his hands at his sides. "I know he's killing a lot of people, but they're royal subjects, the same as we are. And the king must come first."

"This is madness. Unholy madness!" she yelled at him.

"It's madness to assume you can do anything about it!" he yelled back.

Then she made two fists, and his eyes widened.

"Would you attack your own Watcher? Have you completely lost your mind?"

Without another word, Marie-Christine left the room.

That night, under cover, she made her way to the city. She didn't wear peasant clothes, but she kept her *costume* simple. Her jewels, she left at the palace. Likewise, her white, curled wig. Yet even as plain as she looked, she knew she stood out on the streets. That was good. It would make it easier for L'Hero to find her.

She told the coachman to return at dawn and paid him handsomely to keep his silence.

Walls dripped with moisture; fog rolled and coagulated at her feet, muffling the sound of her satin shoes. She walked proudly, boldly, hunting her prey.

At the end of an alley, she found an old woman, stiff and half-frozen from the cold. She was dead. Beside her lay a small bouquet of geraniums, as if perhaps someone had mourned her.

Moving on, she heard a child whimpering but could not find it. She saw everywhere the degradation of poverty, and the fine meal she had eaten earlier that evening was a heavy weight.

Perhaps half an hour later, she nearly stumbled over a dead youth, his skin marble white, his neck savaged. He had clearly been the victim of a vampire. A few feet beyond him, she found a second youth. He was lying atop a violin, which had been crushed by his dead weight.

After perhaps two hours, footsteps echoed behind her, and she whirled around with a delighted smile on her face.

"*Bon soir*, my Watcher," she said.

He stamped his feet. "Good evening? Are you insane? There is nothing good about it. It's freezing out here," he snapped. "You must come back at once. There is talk of a riot. Her Majesty is terrified, and they want you."

Her face fell. She had thought that Edmund had come to join her in her search for L'Hero.

"Riot?" She gestured around them. "What utter nonsense. There's no one on the streets."

"The spies report that the people are massing for a march on the palace."

"Spies who wish to sound important," she snorted. "So they can keep demanding to be paid." She gestured. "It's too cold to be out, shaking one's fist at the palace gates." Then she frowned and said slowly, "Except for those who feel no cold. The dead . . . and the undead."

He cocked his head. "They're about?"

"I found a number of corpses."

They regarded each other. He said, "I know you want to destroy him, but the queen needs you."

She huffed, inwardly torn. "She has a thousand men to guard her."

"She has the right to your company."

"He is *killing* people," she argued. "Now. *Tonight.*"

"But not important people," he countered. "Come now, you know that I'm right in this, Marie-Christine." He folded his arms across his chest and gave her a hard look. "It's that little girl, isn't it? Taking her in. You've become . . . motherly or some such thing."

"Edmund . . ." And she realized then that Mathilde, being at the palace, was in danger. Her heart caught in her throat.

"If not for Marie-Antoinette, then for me," Edmund said. "She'll have my head if you don't dance attendance on her. If we leave straightaway, we can be back before dawn. I've told her you are indisposed, but her patience will only last so long."

"*Oui, oui,*" she said quickly. "Let's go now. Quickly."

He was obviously relieved that she'd agreed to go back to Versailles. But they had walked only a few feet back when Edmund stopped, raised his hand, and asked, "What is that noise?"

The Slayer listened. In the far distance, there was a rhythmic stamp, stamp, stamp. She frowned, deciphering the odd noise, and looked at Edmund with horror.

"Cannon?" he asked.

"Footfalls, Edmund." Her spine stiffened, and she took a deep breath, preparing for battle. As usual, she was well armed. "The palace informants were right."

"We must go at once," Edmund said.

Then the world ignited.

There was no other way to describe it, as the wet streets suddenly burst with hundreds of figures carrying torches. Men, women, boys and girls, their faces unreal in the flickering light: a chaotic nightscape of grim, set masks; round, spectral holes of fury; undisguised terror and tears. Those unsure of what they were doing there were swept along by those who were certain. Drums beat and bugles blew, and the throngs surged forward.

"Holy Mother of God," Edmund murmured, crossing himself as they raced ahead of the crowd.

At that moment, Marie-Christine felt a gaze colder than the grave pressing down on her shoulders. She turned her head and looked up.

There he was, approximately one hundred meters away, standing atop a one-storey building, his black cap billowing in the smoky wind. He wore the true face of the vampire, and his fangs were dripping with fresh blood.

He did this. He started a riot, whipped his followers into a frenzy, and then the rest of the people caught the fever.

Then he flung back his cape, revealing Mathilde. She struggled in his grasp, her hands clutching at L'Hero's forearm as he pressed it over her neck.

No!

L'Hero smiled evilly at the Slayer, revealing his vampire fangs. He closed his cape over Mathilde's writhing form, hiding her from view.

"Edmund," she said, "he is here."

"Where?" Edmund swiveled his head left, right, and shook it. He scowled and crossed himself. "Ah, so he is. It doesn't matter. Let's go!"

"Warn Their Majesties," she said as L'Hero elaborately dipped his head in her direction. "Help them escape. I have to stay here."

"No! Marie-Christine!"

"He has Mathilde!"

"What does it matter? She's only a peasant. I order you to come with me," he shouted, but she left him there, racing toward the figure on the building. As she anticipated, L'Hero glided away, disappearing into the shadows of the chimneys and tall, sloped rooftops.

She kept running, slamming her way through the sea of bodies, dodging the torch fires, ignoring the shouts of protest.

Thousands of people swarmed around her. It was as if every inhabitant of Paris had risen from bed or grave or nightmare to exact revenge on two royal heads, for the crime of being chosen by God Himself to lead them. And yet . . . and yet, she had seen hungry children, and frustrated mothers unable to feed them. She was a witness to untold misery.

And didn't Christ say, "The poor shall be with you always"?

A wizened, ancient man rammed into her and shouted invectives, which she didn't understand; an old woman carrying a pitchfork yelled at him, and the two began to quarrel like little children. The woman aimed the pitchfork at the man, who balled his fists and snarled at her like an animal. Marie-Christine wondered if they were likely to kill each other.

She forgot them as soon as she moved on through the crowd, glancing up to the rooftops.

More people marched past her, and more; the streets were choked with them. Frustrated, Marie-Christine stopped in a doorway to catch her breath, shocked at the sheer number of rioters.

Do they hate the king and queen so much?

A brick sailed past her ear and crashed through a window. Another followed; throughout Paris, windows shattered and fires erupted. Smoke roiled above the rooftops. Still the people came, a thundering, mad army. It was Satan's feast day; it was an evil night.

All night, the Slayer searched for Mathilde and her captor. She had no luck. She saw no further trace of either of them.

Around dawn, she was accosted by a well-dressed man with blood running down his face. He fell to his knees, grabbing up the hem of her dress and burying his face in it.

"Thank God, a person of quality," he wailed. "I thought they'd killed us all. We must hide. They've taken Their Majesties prisoner."

"Surely not," she said slowly, gaping at him.

"They are threatening to guillotine them. Have you seen the guillotine? It cuts off your head." He wiped his forehead with shaking hands. "Cuts it off, and you live for three or four seconds after that. The pain . . . I've heard it is the most horrible way to die."

"This is insane. No one would dare to kill a king." She shook him. "You're lying!"

"I'm not." He threw back his head and wailed like a madman. "I wish to God I were, but I'm not!"

He was not. After Marie-Christine found an abandoned warehouse to use as her headquarters, she left the man there and combed the streets, gleaning news. By then, her clothes were filthy rags, and no one suspected her for an aristocrat.

The royal family was in custody. They had been stripped of their privileges and were being referred to as the Capet family. The talk was of regicide—the killing of a monarch.

As she made her way through the exhausted crowds, numbed by their victory and terrified of what was to come, she came upon a crowd pressed into a dark alley, all gathered around something on the ground. Two grime-covered soldiers kept order while a woman fell to her knees, shrieking, "Vampire! Vampire!"

Marie-Christine approached, expecting to see more of L'Hero's handiwork. But what she saw, by a thin stream of shady light . . .

Ah, mon Dieu . . . mon Dieu . . .

The Slayer staggered backward, and swayed.

What she saw . . .

Non . . .

. . . was the body of Mathilde's mother, her blue lips covered with caked blood. If she were not attended to, she would rise.

One of the soldiers said kindly, "Is she family?"

I will not rest until he's dead.

"You have to stake her," she said grimly.

"That one's nobility," someone hissed at the Slayer. "Listen to her accent."

"You'd better go," the soldier murmured. "Quickly."

She did, gathering her skirts and returning to the abandoned warehouse, where the half-mad man still cowered.

Her jaw set, her gaze unflinching, she spent the day sharpening stakes, although she had come back into Paris heavily armed.

At night she walked the streets, searching. She went to the palace but found it occupied by the human forces of the revolution, with not a vampire in sight. There was no sign of Mathilde, nor of anyone she recognized, not even among the servants.

She returned to the city. The streets were empty of vampires, although each morning, more bodies were discovered, astonishing numbers of them, their throats mutilated. The people decided it was the doing of Marie-Antoinette, who was cursing them with black magic from the depths of her prison.

Marie-Christine said nothing, only slept by day, half-listening to the ravings of the crazed nobleman, and hunting by night.

L'Hero eluded her at every turn. His victims were legion. He was building his vampire army, of that she had no doubt. The city was overwrought with tension and fear.

The next night, near dawn, Sir Stephen, the Council representative, beckoned to her from a darkened doorway in the most dissolute quarter of Paris. He was with a group of men she did not recognize, but their faces told her that they knew who she was.

"Where have you been?" Sir Stephen demanded. "My God, girl, look at you. You're a filthy, disheveled mess. At least most of us have kept enough dignity to maintain standards."

"Here," she replied, seeing as if for the first time that her once-beautiful gown was a sheaf of rags. "I—"

He silenced her with a wave of his hand. "Your Watcher reported your mutiny," he said angrily. "My orders from London were to kill you on sight. But the new Slayer. . . ." He waved a hand. "The Council members aren't thinking properly. Sooner or later, order will be restored here . . . by human beings . . . who will not look kindly upon a Council who did nothing to help."

"I saw L'Hero," she said simply. "I went after him because I believed he posed the greater threat."

"That's a lie," Sir Stephen flung at her. "It was that little girl. He had her. Edmund de Voison figured out the reason for your disobedience." He shook his head and regarded her with undisguised disgust. "Blood will out after all."

She frowned at him. "What are you talking about?"

"Come. Surely you know. About your parentage." When she remained silent, he sneered at her in utter contempt. "You're one of them, girl. A peasant. Born in the gutter."

"No," she whispered.

He smiled cruelly. "But of course you are. Your mother was a flower vendor. And your father, a common laborer. Didn't it strike you as uncommonly odd that you had no other family? The Du Lacs died out in medieval times. We used their name so that no one could come forward to claim you. And your fortune belongs to the king."

She shook her head. "But—"

"Enough. Tomorrow night, the Royals will attempt to escape in a closed coach. See that you're there to assist them. A coach will wait for you tonight in the usual spot arranged by you and de Voison. See that you rendezvous with it."

That was all he said. She blinked at him. He added, "Your Watcher will be with Their Majesties. He will share whatever fate lies in store for them, if you don't help them."

Sir Stephen melted into the shadows, rather like a vampire himself.

Within the hour she was on her way, but her heart shrank with misery. She could think of nothing but Mathilde and the fact that in a way, they were like sisters—children of the city of Paris and heirs to its misery and injustice.

Perhaps that explains my protectiveness, she thought. *I abandoned my post and betrayed my sovereign lady and lord because she is in many ways much closer in station to me.*

The thought gave her some modicum of comfort as well as pain.

The coach stood before her. The horses stamped their hooves to keep warm, their breath like hot fog. The coachman gave her a quick nod and she hurried toward the conveyance.

Suddenly the horses bolted. The coachman tried to catch up the reins and was unseated. He tumbled off the seat and landed hard on the ground. The coach took off. The man did not move. As Marie-Christine ran to help him, she saw that he was still breathing.

"Can you stand?" she asked, helping him to a standing position.

In answer, he shrieked in fear and began scrabbling after the coach as it thundered away.

The vampire was behind Marie-Christine. She felt him long before she turned and saw him.

L'Hero wore the hideous mask of the vampire. He was repulsive, and yet, there was something in his face that made her stare at him, almost as if he were beautiful. He was dressed in simple but very elegant black clothes, with a long cape, and around his throat he wore a red ribbon, which had of late become the symbol that someone in one's family had died on the guillotine.

In his grasp, as before with his arm across her throat, her little Mathilde struggled and whimpered. The child wore plain but elegant black velvet as well, and around her throat was a similar red ribbon. Her eyes were huge and pleading. Her lips trembled, but she didn't speak.

"*Bâtard*," Marie-Christine said, in a deadly low voice. "Let her go."

"She is hostage to your conscience," L'Hero retorted. "She is the only thing that compels you to do your duty."

She didn't understand, and so she said nothing.

"Which is to help the people," he filled in.

"That is not my duty," Marie-Christine reminded him. But her voice was not as steady as it once might have been. *I am one of them,* she thought miserably. *Unless Sir Stephen lied to me, I am a simple peasant girl, not a countess.*

The vampire's face curved into a cynical expression, if not exactly of contempt, then of weary amusement. "You are not my first Slayer," he told her. "The other one I killed lived on the Russian steppes. And do you know, when she died, she had never seen the czar. She wasn't even sure that he actually existed."

"That is nothing to me," she said uncertainly. "I'm certain she fulfilled her duty as it was presented to her."

"Her Watcher was a feeble old woman who could offer her nothing. The Council had lost track of them both years before. That little Slayer killed perhaps two vampires before I killed her. She also killed a rooster someone told her was possessed." He chuckled. "My point is, she did what she knew to be right. She died a good death. I'm certain she sleeps with the angels. But what of you, *mademoiselle?*"

She had good, sharp stakes hidden in her rags, easy to grab. She took a breath, composing herself for battle. "Let Mathilde go."

He laughed and squeezed Mathilde's neck. The child made a retching sound, staring in terror at her angel of mercy.

"Go save the Royals," he said dismissively. "It won't stop this revolution. These people are sick to death of suffering."

"Suffering you are helping to inflict." She narrowed her eyes at him. "Don't pretend to be some kind of patriot."

"I have done more good for the people of Paris than you," he sneered, "even if you include the many I killed. But you are the lapdog of an elite few. You shame your office."

"How dare you." Her voice was deadly calm.

"This is how I dare. My friends?"

Previously obscured by the darkness, figures seemed to separate themselves from the buildings and gathered behind L'Hero and Mathilde. She recognized many from her encounter with L'Hero under the bridge. Their arms were thin, their faces drawn, but as she watched, all became vampires. They were undead, all of them, and yet for the first time, they seemed *alive* in a sense she could not properly define.

"I know that you've been told to save the Royals. You may leave. I give you safe passage."

"Mathilde comes with me," she said, and he shook his head.

"She is my price." He gave his head a regal toss. "Go. None of us will attempt to stop you. You have my word."

Marie-Christine shook her head. "Let her go. *Now.*"

"She belongs with us," said a voice, in very bad French.

Mathilde's mother stepped from behind the vampire. She looked dazzling in a simple gray gown, her hair swept up in a becoming style. She put a hand on L'Hero's shoulder. Then she let her face change, and she was hideous.

The soldier didn't stake her, the Slayer thought. *He must have had her buried, and then she rose.*

Mathilde's mother's hand trailed past L'Hero's shoulder to his neck, which she caressed with a lover's touch.

"I challenge you, Slayer," the vampire said. "You may go. But if you stay, you will die tonight."

Marie-Christine glared at him. "And you will turn the people of Paris into ravening monsters."

"It has been done for me, already."

"By the king and queen?" Marie-Christine could not hide the sarcasm in her voice.

"She begins to learn," L'Hero said to his band. Some of them made a show of giving her silent applause.

Then a cry startled them all. L'Hero looked past the Slayer, his eyes widening. Marie-Christine did not turn. She kept her gaze fixed on him.

"It has happened! They have been caught!"

It was a boy of about thirteen. He danced a jig as he ran up to the others. "They've been thrown back into prison, and there is talk of beheading the lot tonight!"

L'Hero's people chorused cheers. L'Hero patted the boy on the back, and the boy transformed into vampire form.

"What of the Watcher?" L'Hero asked.

Marie-Christine's stomach tightened with fear for her guardian. *He lied to me,* she reminded herself. *He told me I am noble. But perhaps it is true. Perhaps Sir Stephen is the liar, trying to manipulate me in some way.*

The boy looked pleased. "To be beheaded, for certain. They are taking him to the guillotine even now!"

"Non," Marie-Christine whispered.

In her distress, she launched herself at L'Hero, her stake in her hand. His reflexes were on point; he dodged her lunge as one might a sword-wielding opponent, then slid out his leg to trip her. Despite her heavy skirts, she leaped over his leg, switching her stake to her other hand, and tried again.

She failed again.

He thrust open his hand and called, "Sword!" One was thrown to him from the center of the crowd. He parried the stake as she lunged again, and the tip of his blade sliced her skirt from waist to midcalf, revealing the intricate corsetry beneath.

He grinned viciously at Marie-Christine, then clasped Mathilde's mother around the waist. She tipped her head to the side and he bit into her neck, sucking blood lustily, as another man might pause for an invigorating taste of wine.

Then he was on her—advance, lunge, parry—swinging his sword like a saber. Marie-Christine gave ground, aware that she was in an extremely defensive position, and that if this continued, she would lose the duel.

Edmund, she thought, *forgive me.*

"You're free to go," L'Hero reminded her. "I do not compel you to stay. You only have one Watcher. But you will have enemies like me until the day you die."

She pressed her lips together, as her right heel hit a barrier. She had not kept good track of her surroundings. All she could manage to keep within her sights was his sword as it flashed in the moonlight.

"He will train you, make you a better fighter," L'Hero continued. "He will help you prolong your life. And if you wish it, you may begin saving the lives of the people, and not just their masters. Now that your eyes have been opened."

With that, he jabbed at her face. She jerked her head; his sword point nicked the corner of her eye and blood streamed down her cheek. She whipped back her head, aware of the spray of crimson. Reaching her hand behind herself, she found the corner of a post and flung herself around it, in a semicircle, standing behind it for the meager protection it offered.

From a distance away, drums sounded a slow cadence.

A death march.

Edmund, she thought desperately. *Not Edmund!*

"They're driving him to the scaffold," L'Hero taunted her. "In an open cart. The people stand on either side, pelting him with rotten fruit and excrement. He is looking for you, wondering why you have not come to save him."

That's true, she thought frantically. *If he knew what I was doing, if he could see this duel, he would never forgive me.*

I'm not sure I shall forgive myself.

The thought propelled her forward. Her sword moved as if of its own accord. Mind connected directly to body; she was unaware of her movements as she made them. It was as if she had stepped away and the Archangel Michael himself took over her fight.

She could only see L'Hero's face in a blur of white flesh and fangs; the dark holes that were his eyes darted across her field of vision like black fireflies. But she knew he was afraid. The tide had turned, and she was winning.

"Give me Mathilde!" she shouted. "I'll leave you alive!"

"My people will kill you, if I do not," he told her. "The people *you* should have protected."

Somehow, by the intervention of the Divine, she rushed the tall vampire and thrust her stake into his chest. It was as if all Paris screamed as he exploded into dust.

"Mathilde, come!" she cried, reaching out a hand to the child.

Then they were after Marie-Christine, chasing her as she burst down the streets, screaming, "Edmund!"

Over bridges, along the filthy sewers; past trees and gardens and shops. Following the sound of drums, the moon above giving her sight, she flew as fast as she could to the killing place, and saw the scaffold, and Edmund climbing the stairs to the platform. The guillotine towered into the night, its blade shining in the light from a hundred torches as the crowds pressed against the scaffolding that supported the dais.

She waved her arms above her head, screaming, "Edmund, I am here!"

The noisy crowd hushed, intrigued by this apparition: a beautiful, half-naked woman, her face gushing with blood. She ran toward the dais, but a soldier stepped in her way. She pushed him aside, to murmurs of astonishment. Another took his place and aimed a weapon at her.

"Marie-Christine," Edmund said, half-turning from his progress toward the machinery of death, "stop."

Her Watcher's fine clothing had been ripped to shreds. His face was bruised and bleeding.

Her chest heaving, she looked at the grimy men grouped around the guillotine, understanding them to be simple, common folk, and clasped her hands together in supplication.

"That man was forced to go with them," she said slowly, in case they didn't speak proper French. "He didn't want to. He was forced to."

"Marie-Christine, stop," he repeated. "This is a lost battle. Do not lose the war as well."

"What is he to you?" asked one of the men, in a workman's accent. Poorly clothed and rough featured, with grizzled gray-and-white hair on his cheeks and chin, he looked at her with interest, as if gauging the thickness of her neck.

"He is . . . he is my only friend," she told him.

"Then I pity you, because soon, you will be friendless." As the crowd chuckled at his wit, he gestured to the others to place Edmund's head between the twin boards of the guillotine, one hanging down above Edmund's head, one sticking upward from the base of the contraption. A half-circle had been cut into each board, to enclose the neck of the condemned.

His head was secured, much as one would be locked in a stocks for thievery in a simple countryside village. Then a hush descended while a list of Edmund's crimes were read. They were described with what had become commonplace revolutionary statements: *Crimes against the people, disloyalty to the State, which is the people. . . .*

Moving to the front of the crowd, she looked up at Edmund as he faced downward and said, "I . . . I took care of *him*. You know. *Him*."

For a moment he paused. Then he said, "Oh, I feel ever so much better." The sarcasm in his voice cut her more deeply than any other injury she had ever endured.

She whispered, "Edmund, I am the Slayer. I had to protect . . . to protect the innocent."

He looked straight at her. "Once a peasant . . . ," he said contemptuously, and her heart broke. It was true. She was a child of the lowest classes.

"But . . . but I am the Slayer," she said.

But he didn't seem to hear her. She realized that if she spoke the words more loudly, he still would not be able to hear her. They would make no sense to him.

He didn't know what a Slayer was.

"They have taken over all Paris," she said desperately. "But I killed . . . that one. It will stop now."

He laughed bitterly. "It will not stop. These, these . . ."

"*Revolutionaries,*" said one of the men gathered around Edmund. His voice rang with pride and conviction. "He is quite correct, *mademoiselle.* We shall not stop until every aristocrat is dead! We shall become the liberators of all France!"

The people went wild with cheers. Trumpets trilled. Drumbeats rippled.

"You see?" Edmund shouted at her above the tumult, his face paling as the blade was raised. She could see it moving upward, preparing for its descent. "Do you see how miserably you have failed in your duty?"

Shortly before the blade fell, someone called out, "Death to all tyrants!"

The blade fell, and Edmund's head tumbled toward her. Not even a basket had been put in place to receive it. It slammed to the ground, and the crowd roared with victory.

As the Chosen One fell to her knees in mute shock, the child, Mathilde, slipped her hand into the Slayer's, and squeezed it.

Her flesh was as cold as the grave.

Mornglom
Dreaming

Doranna Durgin

Two entities in need.
  They find each other.
  The primary is demonic in nature, carnal of flesh; it hungers.
  The secondary is spectral in nature, ephemeral of flesh; it craves.
  Together, they haunt the mountain hollers.

The resounding noise of offended piglets filled the barnyard. Within the barn, Mollie Prater picked out the shouts of her equally outraged younger brother as he struggled to herd the creatures inside without letting the big mean-as-spit sow through the low door.

From the loft above her, Lonnie gave a low laugh, forking down another bunch of last fall's hay for the evening cow feed. "Ferd never gets any better at that."

"Easy for you to say, seein' as you're free of the job now." Mollie scooped a handful of charcoal from one bucket and a handful of hardwood ashes from another, dumping them both in the pig slops and stirring vigorously with the flat wooden paddle she plucked from its spot on the barn partition.

"Count yourself lucky," Lonnie grunted, sending down another forkful of hay. "You bein' a girl and all—you missed that particular chore."

Mollie said nothing as she stirred the pig slops and worm tonic. No point in it. Girl children had one set of chores, boys another; such was life even if she *had* always been plenty strong enough to handle either. Soon enough she'd have a whole 'nother set of chores—wifely ones. At fifteen, she was well ready to be wed, and after two patient years of courting, Harly Meade was ready to have her. Her daddy reckoned him as a good provider and a faithful man in all ways, and that suited her; a man had to be steady to make his way in these mountains.

She liked, too, that he was tall and straight limbed and had a sweet smile—and that he so often turned it on her, making her feel entirely uncertain of her feet against the ground. In a few more weeks she'd be Mrs. Harly Meade and she'd find out just what there was to being woman of her own homestead, a modest starter cabin in a small scoop on the side of the steep hill.

It was the impending wedding that had her feeling strange these days, she figured. She blamed her excitement for that day she'd woken up with the odd sensation of her own blood tingling through her body, lending her strength a woman didn't expect to have—and for the times since then that she'd tripped over her own movements simply because things came easier than she expected, easier even than her own normal vigorous efforts. She blamed the wedding for her dreams, too—although they didn't seem to be wedding sorts of dreams at all, but mornglom dreams full of darkness and roaring and startling smells.

She'd always had a knack for dreams, but . . . she couldn't recall dreaming in smells before.

Real-life pig stye stink rose to fill her nostrils, dispelling thoughts of early morning dreams. "Pee-yew," she said in disgust, and decided she'd stirred the charcoal and ashes worm tonic quite well enough. She flipped the latch to the narrow gate blocking the small aisle between the dirt-floored pigpen and re-peated, "Pee-*yew*."

"Can't be no worse than it ever is," Lonnie said with all the airy assurance of someone who hadn't done the pig-worming chore since Mollie had grown tall enough to carry the buckets. He jabbed at the hay, peering down at her through the square entry door in the floor. "You want to worry on something, think about the hay. I hope we've enough to last through the spring cutting."

Mollie might have answered him—if outside, Ferd's triumphant whooping hadn't turned into a shout of protest, a warning that the furious sow had slipped by. If at that same instant right above her, Lonnie hadn't made a surprised and alarmed noise of his own, shouting her name in warning as he fumbled the pitchfork.

She couldn't say if time had slowed, or if it had sped up so fast that events slicked right past her, with her own part in them a thing of startling instinct and speed. She saw clear enough as Lonnie dropped the pitchfork through the loft door right above her, sending it stabbing down at her head just as the old sow charged in with the piglets, and by God didn't that pig have blood in her eye. Slaver flew as she jabbed the air with her sharp tushes, rampaging right through her own squalling babies to squeeze into the aisle with Mollie as her target.

Shouting—pitchfork—squealing—charging—

Mollie snatched the pitchfork out of the air a hair's breadth from her own head and whipped it at the enraged sow.

"Mollie Prater!" Lonnie gasped as the tines jabbed the ground directly before the infuriated pig; the reverberating handle whacked the sow hard on the nose, blocking her path. Stunned, the sow stopped short as Ferd ducked through the pig and boy-size door cut into the side of the barn, clambering barefoot over the pen slats to the main barn; she gave the world a sullen look and backed up until she reached open space again. Ferd took in the scene with a puzzled look on his rounded boy's face, and Lonnie, crouched over the loft door, seemed to have lost most of his words, for all he could do was say, "Mollie Prater!" once more.

Mollie looked at her hands—her impossibly fast, incredibly coordinated, startlingly strong hands—and said the only thing she could. " 'Tain't like I could throw it *at* her. She's still got those babies to suck."

Ethan Bentley stood in the open air of the train caboose platform, watching the twisting rails recede behind the train to be swallowed up by equally twisty hills. He considered it a wonder that the crews had even carved out a place to lay track, with so little room between these unending ridges for anything but deep, narrow gorges and watercourses. No wonder they chose to follow the curve of the hill itself, somewhere between top and bottom—until it reached those places where the hills crammed together and there was nowhere to go but over.

The hills themselves were thickly covered with spring-green trees, poplars and oak and evergreen hemlock—except where the bones of the mountains jutted out, rough granite with mica chips that sparkled in the bright sunshine. A view so different from the streets of New York City, it was a wonder Ethan's eyes could take it in at all.

You have an assignment, the Council had told him—good news and bad. Good, because it meant he would finally fulfil his destiny, taking up the job for which he'd been trained instead of hanging around the dockyards of the city to keep track of the murky creatures who congregated there. Bad, because it meant leaving the city haunts he knew so well and plunging into this deep mountain world of which he knew nothing, and into which he could hardly hope to blend. And *bad,* because it meant a Slayer had died.

Assignment didn't always mean the death of a Slayer; sometimes it meant the death of a Watcher—which was far more preferable. Watchers could be replaced. A Slayer with experience could not. As often as not the new Slayer hadn't been identified or trained before the calling. In this case she lived in an area so remote that Ethan would be hard put to find her at all in the crumpled, winding hollers of Pike County, Kentucky; he'd certainly have no opportunity to study the situation, to introduce himself to the new Slayer, or to ease into an explanation of her calling. There would be no crowds into which he could blend, not Ethan Bentley from New York City. Already he was used to the wary glances, the quick assessment, the challenge of the slightly edged question, "You're not from around here, are you?"

No, these people weren't used to outsiders. The rails and ties unwinding behind him made fresh track, a train route less than a year old and laid in place to haul the precious bituminous coal of southeastern Kentucky. It was 1886, and the world had come to Pike County.

The world, and Ethan Bentley.

Mollie churned milk to butter, sitting on the steps of the cabin and listening to Lonnie talk of coal towns, and how joining up with one seemed the certain sure way for a fellow to put a mark on the world. Why putting a mark on the world had to be important, she didn't know; she'd never wanted or expected anything more from her life than seemed likely to come her way—a good husband in Harly, a family to raise, the chance to look down the holler and take in the beauty of it, green and ripe and full of life. Or in winter, with the frost sparking hard off the trees and the day's sun come to melt it away, bringing enough warmth that most days were just as easy outdoors as in and with only a handful of snows each year.

"I could work my way up to a boss spot," Lonnie was saying, though her daddy just grunted a response, and not any kind of happy-sounding grunt, either. Lonnie must have taken a good hint to change the subject, but she wished, listening, that he hadn't thought to tell about the barn that morning. Or that he hadn't stretched the tale so tall, for surely what she heard wasn't really the way it had happened. She'd been lucky, that's all—not so fast as he described it, nor so calm-headed and deliberate. *Not so oddly—*

Cra-ack!

Mollie looked at the broken butter churn handle in dismay. It had been new-made.

But the jagged ends of the ash wood handle were good and broke. Some hidden flaw in the grain, no doubt. She sighed, set it aside, and examined the gash it had made on her palm, blotting the blood on her apron corner so she could hunt for splinters, ignoring the funny feeling that crept along her spine, the one that said the handle had been perfectly fine, inside and out.

Her mommy came onto the porch, wiping her hands on her own apron after she set down a basket of laundry. "Take these out for hangin'," she told Mollie, and then tsked loudly over the broken churn handle. "What's happened here?"

"Must've been crooket inside," Mollie said, picking out a last splinter and scowling at her hand.

"Pour you a little turpentine over that," Lila Prater said, tilting over Mollie's shoulder to have a good look. "Wouldn't want it to come up bad, not with the wedding so close."

Mollie nodded. "Maybe Lonnie'll bind that handle back together long enough to finish this batch."

"I suspect so," Lila said, looking up the long lane leading from the cart road by the creek that ran down the center of the holler. "Here's Adalee, Mollie. She'll keep you company."

Mollie raised her head to discover her best girlfriend coming up the road, heavy with the burden of a sack and the baby within her besides. Mollie waved a hand in greeting and gathered up the laundry basket to meet Adalee by the clothesline. "Aren't you looking fine," she said, admiring Adalee's plumping belly.

"Won't be *me* everyone's looking at come next Saturday," Adalee said, grinning a sly grin. She held the sack out. "I brung you something. For your wedding chest."

Mollie took the sack, untying it to discover a set of pretty white bedsheets, the linen fine woven and the top edge finished with Adalee's lacy tatting. She gasped with delight, and barely stopped herself from pulling the top sheet free so she could see it all at once. "No," she said, "I'll keep it specially clean until the night of the wedding."

"Won't Harly like you on these sheets," Adalee said, conspiracy in her tone. "Him and his fine long legs and good broad shoulders."

"Adalee!" Mollie said, trying for a scandalized tone and hitting only a giggle. "You've been looking at my Harly!"

"I look where I please," Adalee said airily, taking the sack from Mollie to close it up tight again. "There's herbs in there, too, so those sheets'll be pretty-scented when you first use them."

Mollie gave herself a rare moment of anticipation, of herself and Harly in their own little cabin. Harly who loved her, who held her hand as though it were a thing made of china instead of work-calloused toughness. Harly with his shy grin, and who made up for the lack of a certain intuitive spark with his persistent determination. Harly, who knew what he wanted—and that want was Mollie.

Then she turned to the laundry, heaving the first of her father's water-heavy shirts over the fraying line. "Wisht I thought laundry would feel less of a chore in my own household—but I'm looking forward to it anyway."

Adelee grinned; Mollie heard it in her voice as she settled onto an old stump, awkward with the new shape of her body. "It'll get just as old," she said, but then she swapped subjects altogether, becoming more somber. "Mollie, you hear of the christening at the head of Dry Creek Holler?"

Mollie glanced over her shoulder to see the worried wrinkle that drew Adalee's fine brows together. They were much alike, she and Adelee—honey brown hair with summer sunshine streaks and amber brown eyes, both petite of figure and feature. Mollie had better teeth; Adalee had a straighter nose, and they'd both spent much time facing opposite corners in church Bible teachings when they were younger—though the somber Preacher Peavey hadn't ever convinced them that giggling was a sin.

He'd have liked the look on Adalee's face now. "It was for one of the west edge Meades," Adalee said. "You know, that woman what keeps losing her babies before they're born? This time she had herself a live one, a real pretty little girl. Way I heard it, you never saw a man so proud as hers."

"Must've been a right nice christening, then," Mollie observed, twitching the wrinkle out of one of Lila's aprons and moving on to hang Lonnie's britches and frowning her puzzlement at Adalee's somber expression.

"That's what makes it so sad," Adalee said. "So purely awful." She took a deep breath. "This . . . *thing* done come down from the hill, squallin' something fierce, and it stirred them folks up like a pot full of trouble. And it kilt the Meade man, and a Peavey from down near Poor Bottom."

"It *killed* them?" Mollie's hands, full of clothespins and wet cloth, dropped to waist level, and she twisted to look at her friend. "What do you mean, *thing?* Some nasty spring bear, or a wolf?"

"I surely don't. I mean it was a man-beast, a *thing*. I hear its eyes were tore out and weeping vile slime and it still come at them folks like it could see every bit of 'em."

"I never! You're fibbing me!" Mollie turned back to the laundry line with an indignant jut of jaw.

"Cross my heart, I ain't," Adalee said, and the earnest note of her voice made Mollie hesitate as she jammed a second pin down on a kitchen rag. "I'm telling it just like I heard it. It ought to have been the biggest, happiest day of those folks' lives, and it done turned into the worst. They're laying out the bodies even now, and you can go see for yourself if you don't believe me."

"Seein' dead people don't prove a thing," Mollie said, having regained some of her composure.

"It'll prove something when you see what's left of 'em," Adalee said promptly. "It surely will."

Mollie pulled another shirt from the basket and snapped it briskly to straighten the sleeves, pretending to be unaffected by Adalee's words . . . but somewhere along the way, Mollie's head and her heart had turned back to the fading edges of dawn dreams that had been all screams and roaring and fear.

The scent of sorrow on the wind is as sweet as the blood that will follow. Trailing the scent down from the ridge to the crinkle of a holler, the spectral entity soaks up communal grief such as only a funeral brings. He feels the demon's hunger as well, melded as they are—but the demon has learned quickly. From sorrow or joy, from whatever intensity of emotion the humans have emitted to betray themselves, the specter wants more. The demon might feed on his tidbits of flesh, but the specter feeds on that which he failed to allow himself in life.

So the blind demon chases the gathering, knocking over the corpse in its coffin with barely a notice. The demon harries young and old, guided by the specter until that which was once a man has supped his fill on the torment of others.

At that the demon kills swiftly and skillfully, two instead of one after his unusually long pursuit. He unfolds his gruesomely long sixth finger to prepare his feast for eating.

Mollie didn't tell the tale to Harly, and she didn't tell of her uneasy nights. Just nerves, he'd say to that, and most likely be right. As for Adalee . . . "You got to make allowances for a woman with child," he'd said more than once, especially after learning how Adalee had sent her smitten husband walking down the holler after dark, hunting out a neighbor with a bit of sweet pawpaw butter left over from the previous fall.

"Just got to chink the logs," Harly said now, his voice full of pride and pulling Mollie back from her thoughts to the here of things on side of the hill and the new home perched there. *Her* new home. Logs all of the same size neatly dovetailed and debarked, a couple shuttered windows in front to take in the rising sun as it peeked over the top of the opposing ridge. Mollie could well imagine flowers lining the front of the house, some pansies and maybe some hollyhocks at the corners.

"It's beautiful," she said. "It's just purely beautiful. Can't hardly believe you done this all by yourself."

"Not all of it, you know that," Harly said, but he ducked his head at her pleasure and reached out to take her hand. They stood there that way a moment, long enough for Mollie to realize he'd taken the hand she'd cut only the day before, and she felt no pain of it. To remember her astonishment that morning when she'd opened her eyes and discovered not a gash, but healing pink skin. Pink, with a last splinter working its way out.

She'd always been quicker'n most anyone to heal up a cut. But this—

This went beyond *quick*. Way beyond.

Thinking of it, she almost missed the way Harly turned away from both her and the cabin, even while holding to her hand. "What is it?" she asked him.

"I been thinking," he said, and still wouldn't look at her. "So many men're headed toward Black Creek. Spend the week there, come back for the weekend . . . it's a new kind of living, Mollie. They got a company store with special prices for the men, and the kinda goods might elsewise take us years to collect. Things that could make life easier for you, like one of those special clothes washing tubs . . . glass for the windows . . . ."

Mollie stood stunned. "Why, Harly," she said, and lost her words. Finally she managed to blurt, "is that what you *want?* To leave this place? To spend your time in the dark underground of those mines?"

Harly's fingers fumbled on her smaller hand; he said nothing.

Mollie felt her throat grow tight. She hadn't thought of him as a man with strong intent, with a drive for other than what he had. She'd thought of him as easily content—maybe *too* easily content, but there were so many worse things a man could be . . . . "Harly, should we have our babies, you'll miss all their growing up. You'll miss *me*—"

His hand tightened hard enough to choke off her words; he turned and looked at her for the first time, his dark hazel eyes earnest. "It's you I'm thinking of, Mollie Prater. What with your own brother talking about heading for the mines an' all . . . I wasn't sure it would suit you to be up here in this small place of ours, watching him bring in fine things for his own."

"Nonsense," Mollie said. "He don't even *have* his own yet, and when he does they're welcome to what he can give him. *This* is what we talked about together. This kind of living, like what was good enough for my folks and yours. Are you changed on that?"

Harly's face was all relief. "No, ma'am, I ain't. I don't care for the idea of being down in those mines, and I don't care for the thought of leavin' you here alone of the week. But it seemed right to offer it to you."

She shook her head. "I reckon to make a marriage right, we ought to live it each in the same place."

He grinned, tugging her onward. "I'm for that," he said. "Just as everyday as it gets, you and me. Say, come around back, I'll show you what I got started of the garden."

Mollie looked at her hand, suddenly just as alarmed as she'd been moments ago. Pink, healing flesh; not even prodding it brought out pain. This sudden healing fit was as far from *everyday* as Harly would ever imagine.

She curled her fingers around her palm and followed Harly out to the garden.

Pikeville wanted Ethan no more than Ethan wanted Pikeville. "Don't swagger," his superiors had warned him. "You won't be on the docks now."

Ethan had never thought to miss the stink of fish and humanity. Or the occasional reek of demon, providing him with such ample training and research grounds—*A Complete Guidebook to the Dock and Pier Demons of Northeastern Harbors,* his pet project while waiting for assignment. "Don't swagger," they'd said all right. "And don't neglect your studies in favor of compiling a guidebook for which only you see the need."

They had never forgiven him for blending so quickly into the city streets upon arrival from London, and a decently upper-class upbringing, he was sure of it. Why else send him . . . *here.* Here, where he'd already had several days of delay simply because the locals didn't know or trust him, professing complete ignorance of the existence of any such person as Miss Mollie Prater.

Meanwhile, his day's explorations revealed that the Pike County courthouse opposite his hotel held the crude records of the births of not one, not two, but seven Mollie Praters of the right age group. Not to mention the *Molly* Prater, and one *Moly* Prater he rather suspected was as much a candidate as the others. Not one of them lived in town; each and every one of them lived in a different holler, as if he could distinguish one of these innumerable wretched hollers from another.

Ethan made a disgruntled noise and stepped into the muddied street, glad that the strong spring sun of the region had dried a walkable path even if he'd packed—and worn—clothes meant for the more severe New York weather. He'd see if the hotel manager could be of any help. The man had become more cordial after several days of prompt payment for the tiny room he'd assigned to Ethan.

Otis was the manager's name, and he greeted Ethan at the desk with something akin to true welcome, his wild old-man's eyebrows twitching in a way that gave Ethan the impulse to flick them off Otis's forehead and stomp them dead. "There's been another one, did you hear?"

As if anyone else in this town would tell him anything, even for the pleasure of spreading gossip. Ethan shook his head. "Another what?" he asked, assuming it would be another in the Hatfield-McCoy feud killings that currently rocked the area. Roseanna Hatfield, modern-day Juliet, lived only a block away from the hotel.

"Set of beast murders, that's what," Otis said with a sense of triumph, seizing on this pristine gossip ground.

Ethan didn't have to fake his surprise. "Murders? Here?"

Otis nodded, leaning over the high counter in a conspiratorial manner. "Worse than murders. Bodies all tore up in strange ways, and it ain't the first time it's happened these past weeks."

"How many times, then? And the bodies . . . may I ask—"

"Four," Otis said, holding up the requisite number of fingers. "First time, just one killin'. After that, it's always been two at a time. And always at a gatherin'—it's been a christening, a funeral, and two weddin's, and didn't that man-beast chase everyone into a palsy before doing the killin'. And them bodies . . . ain't nothing like no one's seen before. There's the marks of the killin', and then afterward. . . ." Otis leaned even farther over the counter, and Ethan automatically did the same, then recoiled as casually as possible at the man's breath. "Afterward, the man-beast makes cuts in the poor soul's back, and sucks out the innards!"

Ethan blinked. He remembered to put on a face of startled horror instead of intense thought, but his mind was already racing, filtering through hours of study and memorization. *Raksha demon?*

Except the Raksha was a fastidious diner who killed one victim at a time so as to be able to dine on the freshest possible tidbits. And those tidbits didn't consist of *innards* but of two small identical glands sitting atop the kidneys.

He wished he had all his books with him instead of just a few crucial volumes, so he could check his memory. And he wished, dammit, that he could find Mollie Prater.

He had the feeling his time had just run out.

That *her* time had just run out.

Mollie drew her thickly knitted shawl more tightly around her shoulders, not so much in cold as in sympathy. Below the gathering, thigh deep in cold spring river water, Lallie Beamis and Gerrald Mullins stood shivering, listening to Preacher Peavey and waiting the shock of a full dunking baptism. Mollie shifted toward Harly, who tipped his head down to hear her muttered words. "Believe I would have waited till warmer weather to get so faithful," she said.

Harly was quick about squelching his amusement with a stern whisper. "That ain't respectful, Mollie."

Her father turned around to eye them, so Mollie shut her lips on her reply. If Preacher Peavey caught wind of her disrespect, he'd feature her in a sermon quick enough. Then it would be *her* having to renew her faith with a dunking.

She heard a scuffling in the woods to the side of them where sycamores, willows, and raspberry canes lined the banks of the river in thick cover her gaze couldn't pierce. It came again, and she thought there was a faint grunt as well; she stared at the spot, frowning. Harly gave her a puzzled look, and she kept her voice as low as possible. "Didn't you hear—"

With a sudden bellow, something of gray mottled and flaky skin burst from the underbrush. Gasping, Mollie clutched at Harly; he gave her a little shove. "Run!" he shouted at her, but the creature was already loping manlike toward the small clutch of the Bolling spinster sisters, and Mollie couldn't help a horrified stare as the sisters broke apart and ran screaming for their lives—Myrtle, the oldest of them, darted right for the river and fell in the water at the bank.

Oddly, the beast veered away from her, snarling and hooting and slavering, knocking elderly Mr. Carter on his back but not stopping to hurt him further. Instead it lumbered up the bank at Mollie's own family, scattering them—and veered again, heading at the church where several families had taken shelter.

Mollie just stood there, so flummoxed by its massive man-form, by the odd twisty horns curling down the back of its mis-shapen head like hair, the odd, matted texture of its skin, the clumpy look of its hands . . . but somehow the thing that just plain turned her stomach was the weepy old scar tissue of its eye sockets above flat nostrils, looking like a man with his nose cut off. She gagged at the sight of it, and suddenly realized that Harly had all but scooped her up and run off with her. His fingers dug painfully into her arm as he tugged to no avail. "Mollie, you got to *run!*"

She crashed into the woods with no particular path to follow and someone's dying scream at their heels. "Harly!" she shouted at his back, knowing that scream could have been her mommy, could have been her little brother. "Harly, we can't leave them—"

He slowed. Stopped, and turned fiercely on her; it didn't escape her how he'd stayed by her side, her and her stupid gaping self rooted to the spot. Now he said, "Mollie Prater, you got a case of the crazies? That thing's worse'n a chicken-eating dog in a henhouse!"

"But—"

Nose to nose they were, all-out yelling at each other like they'd never done before, barely listening to each other anyway.

"But, nothin'! I go back there, it'll be with a gun in my hands!"

Mollie cocked her head, held up a hand. "Harly, wait—"

"A gun in *both* hands—!"

"*Listen!*" she shouted back at him, practically on her tiptoes to put herself on a closer level to his.

They glared at each other in silence, and eventually Harly realized just that. The silence. No screaming, no inhuman hooting and grunting. "It's gone," Mollie whispered.

Harly only shook his head. He let her take his hand and lead him back toward the church, angling through the woods.

They came upon the body without warning. It wore Gert Peavey's pretty flowered dress . . . its radically twisted head had no face to speak of. Two discreet blood trails ran down the exposed back. Mollie went silent and white, and looking at the thing that used to be the preacher's wife, said hoarsely, "I got to find my kin—"

"Mollie!" Harly shouted, yanking her back and throwing himself out in front of her—between her and the beast thing, which crouched silently at the edge of the church clearing, blending right into the trees as it dipped its uncurled sixth and seventh fingers into the back of another limp body, routing around with concentration until the long-clawed fingers came up with a bit of reddish brown organ on them, a tidbit it licked off like a fastidious cat.

It hesitated, sniffed the wind just once, and turned its blind face to them, for an instant—before it charged. Charged hard and true and shaking the ground with its steps, and to Mollie's horror, Harly stepped out to meet it.

It slapped him away like a fly and came for Mollie.

Mollie, feeling absurd and small and terrified, snatched up a dead limb and stepped aside from the charge to whack the creature a good one, a blow that rocked her arm—and stunned the creature long enough for her to dart past and grab Harly as he stumbled to his feet—and this time they found the church path and they ran good and hard and long until Harly couldn't run any longer.

He stopped, bent over with one hand on his knee and the other on his side where the awful inhuman man-beast had hit him, and he stared at her with a look in his eye that Mollie found just as alarming as the creature itself.

Then she followed his gaze, and discovered she still held the dead limb. Not any old dead limb, not of the size a bitty thing like herself ought to have been able to run with. A limb as thick around as her thigh, freshly broke from the tree; she suddenly felt the weight of it.

She'd torn it from the tree. She'd wielded it against the savage man-beast. She'd run with it, kept up with Harly, *surpassed* Harly. She stared at it.

He stared at her.

*   *   *

"—Mollie Prater," said the whisper on the streets. "Trickle Creek Holler." Loud enough for even Ethan to hear, to go to Otis and to hear the old man say it. "Mollie Prater. Whomped that creature with a stick and lived to tell the tale. Saved her man-to-be. An' to-morrow they'll be married."

Tomorrow. He had to get there before the demon. Before more people died. Before they lost a Slayer who didn't even know she'd been called.

Mollie wrapped a damp-palmed grip around her bouquet, only to have her mother gently remove it from her hands and set it aside. "You'll bruise 'em," Lila said, carefully tweaking a flower into place. It was too early in the season for much but tender early blooms, spring beauties with some phlox and bright yellow coltsfoot. "I swear, Mollie, when did you become such a fidget?"

Mollie turned to the wavy image in the speckled mirror, twitching at the blouse of her best dress, a blue-flowered print she'd only worn three times and which now bore slick satin ribbon bows at the cleavage and hem. Her hair was caught up in a ribbon of the same material, and her shoes were new for the occasion. She plucked at the bow by her cleavage and thought of Adalee's sheets fresh-laid on her wedding bed.

Lila slapped lightly at her fingers. "Leave it be. Lord have mercy! Let those menfolk get theirselves ready out there before you pluck yourself apart."

Lonnie and Ferd were out setting up sprays of bright yellow forsythia and pussy willow branches, and her daddy had gone to fetch the visiting preacher. But Mollie, rather than put herself to work outside or in the kitchen, was relegated to the back room where her parents slept, hidden away until the moment of the wedding itself.

"I'd ruther be hanging laundry," she said. "Or hoeing the garden. Or—"

"Harly will be here soon," Lila said, betraying her own emotion as she fussed with Mollie's hair—primping, touching, in the end not changing a thing.

Harly, and the cabin that would be theirs. Harly and the fresh-sheeted bed. Harly, with a baby at his knee . . . Mollie stopped fussing with her dress long enough to envision it, to play it out in her mind's eye like pretty pictures. After today, her whole life would change, and she was ready for it.

Someone gave a discreet knock on the door, and Lila let out her breath in a gust of relief. "About time!" She scooped up the bouquet, pressed it into Mollie's hands, and guided her daughter to the door with a firm hand betwixt Mollie's shoulders. On the porch, they hesitated, looking out at the gathering that filled the front yard and spilled over toward the chickens and the toolshed. Neighbors, friends, family—people she barely knew, besides. People who needed a joyful thing after a hard run of tragedies. Adalee was up near the preacher; she gave Mollie a wave as though only the two of them could see it.

At the edge of it all, a city-looking man sat on a cranky-eared mule, a cap pulled down over his forehead and determination on his face; it gave him a jut-jawed appearance.

She had no idea who he was.

Let him enjoy the wedding if he chose. She forgot his strange presence and found Harly standing up near the preacher with a foolish grin on his face; the grin grew bigger when he saw her looking.

"Go on," her mommy said in an understanding whisper, her nudge subtle against Mollie's back. "Go be growed up, Mollie mine."

Mollie stepped off the porch.

She couldn't say then if time had slowed, or if it had sped up so fast . . . .

With a warbled hooting, the matted-skin beast-man charged from the woods and straight into the middle of the assembly. The stranger's mule reared and dumped him; Harly shouted a command, and two of his cousins lifted rifles they must have had on hand against this very moment.

Mollie found herself over by the toolshed, having dodged easily through the panic of the yard, already eyeing the man-beast's likely course. "Adalee!" she shouted, trying to grab the attention of her awkwardly pregnant friend—but Adalee stood dazed in the middle of it all, one hand on her belly and the other stretched beseeching in midair, as if it were making up its mind which way she should run.

"This doesn't make sense," someone muttered, and she knew without turning that those clipped syllables belonged to the stranger from the mule. "It's *blind,* bloody *blind,* and it's herding these people like cattle—"

She turned to glare at him. "You know about this man-beast?"

His shoulder was muddied from his fall, but his cap remained in place, its angle more rakish than before. He met her gaze without defiance or apology, although he pretty much owed her one or the other just for being here. "Raksha demon, actually," he said, raising his voice above the sudden bout of screaming.

Mollie flinched against the toolshed, jerking around as Harly yelled, "Shoot it!" somehow knowing it was the wrong thing to do—and watched in horror as the man-beast bounded to Harly's cousins and laid them both out with a single blow of enormous strength. *Dead.* Only a broken neck sat anyone's shoulders at that angle—

"You're the one who can stop this," the man said, coming up closer behind her, his manner as familiar as if he'd known her all her life and then some. "You're the *only* one." His hand landed on her shoulder, a touch beyond familiar. "You're the Slayer, and you were born to—"

She whirled around, catching him up by the throat with one hand, shoving him hard against the toolshed. His cap hit the ground; his face turned dark red. His struggles were useless. His booted toe hit her shin, and Mollie looked down.

She'd taken him right off his feet.

Despite the differences in their sizes, in their man's and woman's strengths, she'd taken him right off his feet.

She dropped him, aghast, the world swirling around her in a series of screams and hideous hooting and two already dead. "Mornglom dreams," she whispered. Dark predawn dreaming of screams and roaring and startling smells. . . .

"It started a few weeks ago," he croaked, relentless, one hand rubbing her finger marks at his throat. "You're stronger, you're quicker, you heal like a bloody miracle—"

"Shut up!" she shouted at him. "You're tetched in the head, you don't belong here—"

"Ethan. And neither," said the crazy man, pointing to the yard, "does *that!*"

The man-beast. The *demon.* It slowed by the scattered chickens; it turned its blind face toward the center of the yard.

"Adalee!" Harly shouted, even as Mollie silently mouthed the same. "Adalee, look out!" He lunged into the yard from his safe spot behind a hemlock, throwing himself between the demon and Adalee. Mollie should have screamed, but it stuck in her throat, making her whole body quiver as the demon struck Harly down and turned back to make the kill. To kill *Harly.*

"*You're the Slayer,*" Ethan croaked beside her, but he needn't have said a word. Mollie had already snatched the scythe from beside the shed and fit it to her hands, quickly realizing that the curve of handle and blade made it an unwieldy weapon. She stepped on the end of the thin metal blade, snapping off the narrowest part of the hook so the remainder was short and wicked and jagged at the end, and then she charged up to the monster from behind and whipped that scythe at the back of his legs with hours of weed cutting behind her every move. Weed cutting and something else, the speed and strength she shouldn't have and yet did.

Stringy muscle parted with the creak of dry, tearing leather; the demon staggered. It left Harly and whirled on her, its curling-horn hair snapping to stand on end, its extra fingers straight and splayed and reaching for her.

She should have stumbled backward. She should have screamed or fainted or fallen back on her bottom, helpless in fear. She should have died.

She killed it.

Afterward came a complete and sudden silence, as if the whole world stopped itself to take note of her deed. Not a sob, not a cough, not a rustle. Mollie felt the stare of every single person there, people who had gathered for her wedding and found themselves at a slaughter. But she couldn't tear her eyes away from the dead thing at her feet, not for the many long moments of silence. Then, finally, she dropped the scythe on top of it and turned away.

The movement became a signal; someone let out a sob and then everyone started talking at once. Mollie looked down at her own hands, expecting to find gobs of blood and killing gore. They were clean and ready to clasp her bridegroom's. But as she finally raised her head and looked around, finding the members of her family—*safe*—finding Harly and Adalee—*safe*—and seeing that for all the fuss and screaming, no one after Harly's two cousins had died, she saw too the first glimmerings of something that scared her more than even the demon.

They were uncertain of her. They were wary of her. *Harly* was wary of her.

When little Betts Mullins shrieked and pointed her way in fear, Mollie's heart fell away. But from the direction of the toolshed came Ethan's still croaky voice. "What the bloody—" She whirled around, realizing the pointing wasn't for her at all and terrified at the thought of the demon climbing to its feet behind her.

No demon. Instead, a wraithlike hant, all wispy and wavering murk—until, even as Mollie gaped, the thing's facial features jumped into clear, hard definition.

As one, the gathering gasped. Ethan eased up behind Mollie and with leftover harshness whispered, "They know him. Who—?"

Someone else answered, not even knowing the question had been posed. "Asa Peavey! Mean as a skunk even from the grave!"

"Preacher Peavey's grandfather," Mollie added in a murmur, suddenly more trusting of the only body here—stranger or no— who hadn't eyed her so doubtfully. "He passed before I was born, but I hear tell his heart weren't nothing but mean."

Even now, the hant's visage was distorted with anger; it gave a wordless howl of rage that ended, to Molly's ears, in something like a sob. "You've kilt it!" the hant moaned, as much anguish as anger as it looked down upon the mottly heap of dead demon. "I wandered so long before I found it, and you've kilt it!" As it looked up, its features wavered. When they solidified again, its expression had changed—become crafty and determined. "I'll take one of you, then. I'll by-damn take what I need!"

A high, scared-to-thin woman's voice said, "*She* done it! Not us!" and though Molly whirled to see who had betrayed her, she found them *all* looking at her—and her family full of worry, keeping silence. Half convinced.

Ethan stepped up beside Molly—not like Harly, tall and broad shouldered and full of strength—but with a kind of confidence that made her desperately glad for the company. "What," he said with perfect calm, "is it that you need?"

"What I never had," the hant said, as if it were perfectly obvious. "Them things I never felt. All them high feelin's, good and bad. All I got on my own is mad and I'm *wicked* tired of mad."

"Ah," said Ethan, his matter-of-fact tone startling her into taking her gaze from the hant and latching it onto him. He'd resettled his cap, she saw, and he kept a thoughtful look about his fox-narrow features. "Classic situation, really," he said to Mollie, as if they were the only two there with the hant. "An angry ghost who felt little else in life, now doomed to go hunting for what he missed when he was alive. I suggest you all forgive him."

Dumbfounded, Mollie just said, "Do *what?*"

"If he was an angry man, he left a lot of people angry *at* him, feelings they passed down to their children. And if he wasn't still blocking those other emotions, he'd feel them for himself. Forgive him, and he can feel his own feelings instead of hunting down weddings and stealing joy."

"Well, ain't you the smart one," Mollie muttered, confounded by the man all over again.

Ethan gave her a rakish grin, one that vanished as he turned to the gathering. "Forgive him!"

As one, they stared back in stubborn resentment. The hant laughed. Anger-tinged, knowing laughter. "I'll take what I want, be it bodies to use or feelin's to have," he said. "I always had to."

"Ain't that the truth!" Granny Lil shouted at him. "You was a bastid!"

"No!" Mollie said. "When he uses me up, what do you think he'll do? Go away, nice and quiet?"

"He'll come for someone else," Ethan said, quite sensibly. "And another, and another. He'll haunt this community until there's no one left to haunt. But now—look at him now. What a pathetic excuse for a man he is. What a miserable man he must have been! Who among you would choose to live without love? Forgive him, and let him go." But then he made a wry bit of a face, scratching up under his hatband at the ear. Mollie's hand print still stained his throat. "Of course, it won't work unless you mean it."

"Miserable!" the hant said; Mollie would have said he'd sputtered, if he'd only had lips to do it with. "Miserable! I had a good farm!"

"You near starved every winter," Harly's daddy observed.

"I had a family!"

"They hated you," spat Granny Lil.

"I had a long life!"

"And you took it out on every one of us who was alive to bear it," said Uncle Erd, arguably the oldest man in Pike County. "You ain't worth hating, you was so miserable. I forgive you, and you're welcome to it."

The ghost's marbled features wavered into a stricken expression. "You can't do that! I helped this demon kill people!"

Granny Lil said, "Only 'cause you was too miserable to do it your own self." She scratched under her bosom in an unself-conscious gesture and said, "I reckon I don't want to bear the burden of hatin' you anymore."

Harly stepped up beside Mollie; she felt a little leap of hope come in to erase the despair she'd felt at his earlier wary expression. "I've heared tales of you all my life," he said to Asa Peavey's hant. "I guess they're something to marvel at, that a man so mean as you lived in this world. I thank you for those tales."

It was the final moment to free them all—Mollie's neighbors and kin alike. In a babble of overlapping shouts, they forgave the hant that had been Asa Peavey.

The hant gave a screeching wail and with a final pop! that Mollie felt inside her ears, he disappeared.

After a startlingly awkward silence full of people looking at Mollie, the assembled kin and neighbors quietly left, gathering the two dead young men and slipping away with muttered good-byes, as if some silent voice had told them there would be no wedding here today . . . or ever.

Mollie turned to Harly. Tall, broad shouldered, straightforward Harly. Harly who wanted a normal mountain life—and a normal wife. Harly with the wariness back in his face, and sadness in his eyes. He looked at her; he looked at the demon—that which had killed so many and now lay slain by her hand. He knew as well as she that her life had changed forever, and it showed on his face; Mollie felt it deep, in that same place that sent her dreams.

Only the dreams had never hurt so much, never felt so desperate.

Harly opened his mouth to say something; he shook his head instead. And then he turned and walked away.

Mollie turned her hands over, checking them again for some sign of the battle they'd won.

The old gash on her palm wasn't even pink anymore.

"Everything I ever wanted," she said, dazed. "Everything I planned for. My life . . . It's all changed." *Right in this moment.* Or maybe when she'd first felt the tingle of her own blood, or when Lonnie dropped the pitchfork . . . or when Harly walked away. "It won't never be the same."

Ethan took her strong hands in his, hesitated, and gave a firm shake of his head.

"No, it won't," he said. "You're the Slayer."

She didn't know what it meant. But she knew, somehow, that he was right. And she knew—somehow—he would be there with her through it all.

Silent Screams

Mel Odom

MUNICH, GERMANY, NOVEMBER 9, 1923

How does one sum up one's life if that one is convinced that life may end violently at the hands of a monster in only moments?

Does one talk about the noble things one has done, or is that too self-aggrandizing? Or should that one talk about the failings that one has experienced while trying to perform those

Damn! I can't even conduct myself properly while filling out this journal entry. Now I've gone and stained these pages with errant ink. Not that it would hardly matter.

This feather I've taken from a dead woman's hat hardly makes a precision writing instrument. I managed to cut a nib for it with the small Swiss-made folding knife I've learned to carry over the years. You won't find the fine penmanship I'd prided myself on for so many years on the final pages of this journal.

And they will be the final pages. Of that, I am very certain.

I look at the writing that covers these pages and am appalled. When I was teaching primary school in Berlin I would never have accepted such work from a student. My ink-stained fingerprints are all over these pages because I cannot sit still. Every small noise scares me because I keep imagining it to be the shifting inside one of the coffins of this mausoleum.

At present, there are nearly two dozen coffins around me. I don't know how many generations of Kesslers reside in this place. But I do know that I'm the only one that has been interred alive in this place. However, that shall be soon corrected when it wakes.

My tears cause some of the stains on these pages. It shames me to admit that, but it is true. I know there are men—and even young girls—who can meet their Maker with calm acceptance.

I am not one of them.

My name is Friedrich Lichtermann. I only now realized that whoever finds my body may not recognize me. My captors took pains to strip my regular journal from me. God, when I think of the things that they can learn about the Council from what I have written down over the years it makes me ill.

My trainer told me in the beginning that this might happen, that the journal I so dutifully kept might not end up in the hands for which it had been intended. Our enemies are great and powerful. I'd been told that ever since the Council had admitted me for training, but until I met them face-to-face, I never really knew the evil that they were capable of.

Oh God, how can I be so lax in the details you—who *have found these papers*—will need to know to ensure that they get into the right hands? And, trust me, you'll be better served to get these papers to the proper authorities posthaste. If you do not, some of the foul fiends that arranged my death will arrange yours as well.

I am a Watcher, put to task by the Watchers Council to oversee the training of a young girl who may one day become the Vampire Slayer. Though many girls may have the skills to become a Slayer, only a few are chosen. My job has been to train and educate the young girl in my charge so that she might be ready for the mantle of the Slayer.

That was my assignment here in Munich. The potential Slayer that I was given charge of was named Britta Kessler. After instructing her the last two years and having nothing happen, I had begun to lose hope that Britta would ever become the Slayer.

Of course, some of my contemporaries would say that such hopes on my part would be very ghoulish. You see, the only way a young girl becomes the Slayer is when her predecessor is slain by one of the foul creatures she was born and trained to hunt.

Slayers never get to live out the years allotted to normal woman.

God, that damned scratching of the rats is near enough to drive me insane. I can see them in the shadows watching me. Even in the dim light of the candles I'm working by on top of this stone tomb, I can see their fears and hungry eyes glowing red and orange. Perhaps they can smell my fear, or perhaps they can smell the blood that still stains my clothing and my hands.

Let me begin at the beginning, where I now see I should have begun in the first place. There are so many things to tell about what has happened, so many things the Watchers Council will want to know.

And if you're not a believer in the foul fiends that have done for me, then I know you can only take this last note as the final diatribe of a stark-raving madman. I promise you that it would be better for you and your families if I were a lunatic who howls at the moon.

The members of the Kessler household began this day—or, more correctly, *yesterday*—with a large breakfast in the dining room, as they normally did. As usual I, too, was in attendance.

Herr Kessler sat at the head of the table and was in rare good humor. Perhaps you know of Herr Kessler. He is one of the most influential among the German industrialists that rose from the bloodbath that had been the Great War.

I, myself, served as a motorcycle messenger during the war. Occasionally Herr Kessler and I would share a stout drink in his den and talk of the things we had seen during that terrible conflict. I was only in my early twenties during that time.

I served my country as best I could, but I never really understood, or cared to learn, the full ramifications of the politics behind the war. One thing I've learned about wars, they are generally fought by people trying to take something from other people who are trying just as desperately to hang on to whatever it is the first people want.

Herr Kessler was in his late thirties and a family man with much more at risk than I. Miraculously, he and I both made it through the war intact. But the instances of our survival were enough to warrant that occasional drink shared by two men who had learned to appreciate being alive.

I think that appreciation for life was what allowed Herr Kessler to be so close to his six children. He genuinely enjoyed them. Fräu Kessler ended up being the sterner disciplinarian between the two of them, but you would never doubt her love for those children either.

Britta was the oldest at seventeen. She inherited her father's red hair and freckles as well as his tall and slender build and flashing green eyes. She had striking features, and I've seen several boys her age turn their heads to watch her as she passed by. She was such an innocent that she barely even kept track of such notice, and if her mother were to point it out—as Fräu Kessler sometimes did because she considered her daughter to be of marrying age—Britta's face would turn scarlet.

I sat to Herr Kessler's right, as was the custom. The three older boys sat to my right, all of them giggling and whispering among themselves as they usually did unless their father was in one of his sour moods, which he seldom had. All of the boys had their mother's blond hair and blue eyes.

Britta sat across the table from me to her father's immediate left. Her younger sister and youngest brother sat on her side of the table as well. The youngest boy was only three and tried to entertain us with his obnoxious eating habits. The Kessler family always reacted in mock horror at his antics.

The telegram came while we were at breakfast. Klaus, the butler, brought it to me on a silver plate, saying a messenger had dropped it off only moments ago, insisting that I see it as soon as possible, for it was marked *Urgent*.

I thanked Klaus, then—curious—I opened the telegram. Only one short sentence greeted my eyes, but it changed my whole world.

From this moment on, Herr Lichtermann, always be at your best.

It was not signed. There was no need. I knew immediately that it had come from the Watchers Council, and I knew what it meant for Britta, though I had seen no sign of the changes in her. Does any Watcher ever know that he is suddenly watching the Slayer until that moment is announced to him? You would think that such a drastic change in his charge would be immediately noticeable. But I had seen nothing, and I felt very much discomfited by the idea.

"Is it bad news then, Herr Lichtermann?" Herr Kessler asked politely.

"No," I said, perhaps a little too quickly, for I saw the ashen look that suddenly manifested on Britta's features. "Just a polite reminder about some new business."

"Father," Britta gasped, still overcome by the truth she only suspected, "may I be excused from the table?"

"Britta," Herr Kessler asked in consternation, "what is the matter?"

"I think I'm going to be sick." Britta covered her mouth with a hand.

I grew immediately concerned myself. What if her father suddenly suspected that the telegram I had received was the reason for Britta's sudden sickness? As for myself, I didn't know what to think. Britta and I had discussed on occasion the probability that she would become the Slayer. It was remote at best, I told her. There were plenty of girls who were being trained. But she had the potential, and we couldn't allow that to be ignored.

From my studies as a Watcher, I knew that upon being notified that she was the new Slayer, a Slayer-in-waiting could experience a gamut of emotions. Some girls relished the mystical appointment, while others lamented the fact that their lives—and, indeed, also their deaths—would never be the same. Becoming the Slayer was a cruel reward at most. But it was a task that Britta had known she might someday have to undertake. Both our fates were sealed with that one telegram.

"Of course," Herr Kessler agreed, somewhat puzzled in his concern.

Britta threw her napkin onto the table and ran from the room.

The other children immediately started discussing among themselves exactly what kind of sickness might have assailed poor Britta. Fräu Kessler excused herself as well and went after her oldest daughter.

"It's these damned sicknesses," Herr Kessler said irritably. "They seem to hang on longer and longer after each winter."

"It's probably nothing," I said to reassure him, for he did worry so much about his children. I think it had to do with some of the things he saw in the war, some of the things he had still never discussed with me, although we had talked about the war in some detail. I, too, had my horrors that I never shared with him. However, I've seen the haunted looks men get on their faces when they remember the things they've seen in combat. The expression Herr Kessler had on his face was one such haunted look.

"Still, even if it is only a transitory thing, it could be a month before it passes completely through this household. Then what'll we have but a bunch of runny noses and coughing at all hours of the night. It's pure hell on earth for a man who has to work for a living."

Although his days as a common laborer had been gone for fifteen years and more, except for his service in the German military, Herr Kessler worked six days a week most weeks and put in long days to make his company grow. Since the war, there were a lot of new opportunities for a man with vision and a willingness to work. At the same time, the German economy was very unstable.

I turned my own attention to my breakfast. Plates heaped with breads, cheeses, jams that Fräu Kessler made herself from her grandmother's recipes, fresh fruits, and an egg casserole. Despite my own slender build I usually made a formidable attempt on Fräu Kessler's breakfasts. The house cook tended to all the actual work, but it was Fräu Kessler who constructed the menus.

Only a few minutes later, Fräu Kessler hurried back to the dining room and looked at me. "Herr Lichtermann, Britta is asking for you."

"She is?" Herr Kessler asked in surprise.

Fräu Kessler nodded vigorously. "Oh, I believe she is just fine, husband, but for some reason she wishes to see Herr Lichtermann."

Herr Kessler regarded me with no small surprise and perhaps a little suspicion. He had hired me as his daughter's tutor on the recommendation of a friend of someone on the Watchers Council. Herr Kessler only wanted the best for his daughter and did not know about the Watchers Council and the rampant beasts that hunted in the nights. He was convinced that his sons were getting a good primary education, but he was not so convinced Britta was getting a good secondary education from school. Part of that belief came from his friend, who had then influenced his decision to hire me.

It helped that I had impeccable credentials as a teacher. I passed Herr Kessler's interview, as well as the much harder interview presented by the Watchers Council.

I looked at Herr Kessler with a nervousness I desperately hoped did not show. "With your leave, Herr Kessler."

He nodded. "Of course, Herr Lichtermann. Please let me know if there is anything you need."

I assured him that I would, then took the telegram and my leave of his table. I went through the lavishly furnished house quickly. And Fräu Kessler kept pace with me, surprising me when her short legs managed to keep up with my much longer ones.

I went up the stairs to the second floor and knocked on Britta's door. My own room was in one of Herr Kessler's three guest houses. Staying inside the house would have been too unseemly for the family's modest morals.

"Who is it?" Britta asked through the door. Her voice sounded anxious and rushed, not at all the calm girl I had known from these past years.

"Herr Lichtermann," I answered. "Your mother is very worried about you, Britta. She's standing here with me now." Since her parents did not know that she was in training to be a Slayer, Britta and I had had to figure out how to communicate effectively and secretly. Subterfuges like that had always made me feel guilty.

Still, how could a Watcher talk to the parents of a prospective Slayer and convince them that helping their daughter risk her life on a nightly basis would be for the betterment of all? That was why, when a potential Slayer was identified that was part of a tightly knit family, her Watcher had to approach her with the stealth of a thief. It was much simpler when a girl who was identified by the Council was an orphan or otherwise alone in the world.

"I'm fine," Britta answered brightly. "In fact, I think maybe I'm feeling better than I ever have."

"Then you need to hurry back downstairs to the breakfast table," Fräu Kessler admonished. "You are worrying your poor father needlessly."

"I will, Mama," Britta apologized through the door. "Oh, and Herr Lichtermann, I should like very much to postpone this morning's lessons so that we may take a ride. I think the fresh air might better clear my head."

"Of course, Britta." Knowing that my young charge surely wanted privacy for us to speak of the matter of the telegram, I looked at Fräu Kessler. If anything were to be done inside a German family, it would always be done through the mother. "That is, if your mother has no objections."

Fräu Kessler studied me with pursed lips and a doubtful expression. "Has she been good at her studies, then, Herr Lichtermann, to warrant such release?"

"Yes, Fräu Kessler," I answered. "I've seldom seen a student who applies himself or herself with the diligence shown by your daughter." Thankfully, that was a very true statement, because Fräu Kessler was extremely sensitive to lies—as her children well knew.

Filled with excitement, I returned to the Kessler breakfast table and tried not to think anymore about the telegram in my pocket and Britta's advancement to the mantle of the Slayer.

I'd become acquainted with the legend and the reality of the Watchers Council and the Slayer during the Great War.

While traveling with a dispatch in Vauquois where our army

battled the French with great vigor, I came upon a German military field ambulance broken down at the side of the narrow dirt road. In those days, early 1916, the Butte de Vauquois was a bloody battlefield. Our army and that of the French strove their hardest to blow each other to pieces with mines they planted all over the hillside. Both armies had also cut long trenches through the terrain.

During my duties as a motorcycle dispatch rider, I had occasion to see dozens of men, German and French, pulled from the muck and the mud of those trenches. But never had I seen what I was to witness that night.

I had run out of fuel nearly five miles back and had been pushing the motorcycle since. The motorcycle was a Triumph Model H with the relatively new three-speed gearbox in use by the British and the Germans. It was lightweight but reliable. My only struggle was the mud that caked the road due to the rains that had flooded the area for the last three days.

I was dressed in a thick, woolen overcoat, gloves, cap, and goggles. Covered in mud and sleepless the last thirty-four hours, I wanted only to find someplace warm and dry where I could sleep for an hour or two.

When I saw the military field ambulance my spirits lifted. I thought perhaps I might be able to borrow some fuel and a little food. In my sleep-deprived state, I had failed to question why the ambulance had parked over to the side of the road.

I left the motorcycle beneath a tree, pulled my overcoat tighter, and walked to the back of the ambulance. Even the pain-filled moaning that came from within didn't raise alarm in my mind. I'd thought perhaps the ambulance attendants were working on some poor soul who might have fallen afoul of one of the many German and French mines that lay under the Vauquois countryside.

I knocked on the ambulance's back doors. The noise within quieted almost immediately, and only the eerie sounds of the night remained except for occasional distant cracks of rifle fire and basso thumps of Granatenwerfer grenade launchers.

In the next instant, the ambulance's back doors exploded open and a monster appeared before me. A weak flicker of lightning lit the garish features of the demon. The cold, cruel eyes regarded me in disdain. The monster's mouth opened in a savage snarl that revealed pointed fangs.

As a motorcycle dispatch rider, I was always armed with both an 1888 Commission Rifle and a DWM 1914 military artillery Luger. I pulled the rifle up from my side, letting it hang from its sling, slid my finger onto the trigger as I lifted it toward the monster before me, and fired. The rifle's heavy recoil caught me off balance and knocked me into the muddy road.

I knew that my bullet had taken the creature full in the chest, but the demon was only staggered for a moment. I'd never shot a man before, but I knew that the heavy round should have knocked him from his feet. No blood showed on his clothing. I frantically worked the bolt action and tried to feed the next shell home.

Lightning flickered across the dark sky again. When the creature leaped at me, I knew I was going to die. The demon knocked my rifle from my hands and seized me by the coat lapels, easily lifting me from the mud.

In the next moment, the vampire—as I was later told the demon was—turned to dust. I fell back to the ground. Still yelling in terror, I gazed up at the man before me who held a simple wooden stake in his hand.

I later learned the man was Alfred Gantry, a Watcher. He too had been in the ambulance. At that point, he believed himself perched on the edge of death, and perhaps he was, but he made it through the next morning and regained his strength. What he told me in those few moments, though, changed my life forever.

He also entrusted me with his journal, kept meticulously, and asked that I take it to the Watchers Council for him. He gave me instructions on how to find them before he passed out. At the time I'd been certain that he'd died.

All through the night, as I sat in what I was certain was a deathwatch over Alfred Gantry, I read his journal. The rain drummed the ambulance, but I have scant recollection of it because I was so immersed in Gantry's entries. The idea that so many demons walked through our world killing whoever they chose was appalling, and I became sworn to the Watchers Council's cause, though I'd never before known of them.

Gantry had been on the vampire's trail for months and had finally managed to track the foul beast to the French countryside. The foul creature had slain his charge, the Slayer that he had trained for years, all those months ago, and the Watcher hadn't been able to give up the hunt till some kind of justice was served.

Gantry wore no uniform and thereby risked being shot by either the French or the Germans as a spy. He had been wounded in an earlier fight with the vampire and stood before me on what very nearly turned out to be his last legs.

The other man in the ambulance who had been moaning died within hours, and I listened to his fevered and wretched moaning for hours, feeling nauseated the whole time. There was nothing I could do to patch his torn neck.

I took care of Gantry throughout the night with the supplies available to me in the hospital field ambulance. No one else came along that deserted road the whole night or the next morning.

When by the next morning Gantry had recovered enough to care for himself, I extracted a promise from him to introduce me to the Council he served. Their war against the demons that inhabited our world made more sense to me than the Great War where I now currently served. The Great War, historians say, was the war to end all wars, but it never addressed the war we fought against the demons that walked among us.

After the war, I received four years of training as a Watcher, then was put into the field because the Great War had disrupted many Watchers that had already been in place, and the Council's need there was strong. Watchers had been killed throughout Germany because they monitored the activity of the monsters drawn to the bloodiest battles.

Britta Kessler was my first assignment. My education background before the Great War proved to be a perfect cover for becoming a Watcher for a young lady who might one day become the Slayer.

"Look!" Britta exclaimed. "It's as we talked about, Friedrich! I am stronger and faster than I've ever been!"

And indeed she was that. I watched her race through the forested lands north of Herr Kessler's estates where we normally rode. She was like the wind, barely touching the ground before she was gone.

As usual when we took our rides, I'd brought along the lacquered wooden chest of weapons I'd been using to train her. All my life, my own interests had ranged far and wide. Aside from being a secondary education teacher, I was also a fencer and a pugilist. I'd even trained for a while in different Chinese fighting styles. The Watchers Council always tries to be very thorough.

But even they, with all the vast research and experience at their fingertips, can't plan for everything. I don't fault the Watchers Council for the horror that later occurred to young

Britta and myself. If anyone is to blame, then the blame must lie with me.

We practiced with the weapons that day, from the simple stakes to the saber to the crossbow, and discovered to Britta's delight that her already more than ordinary skills with those weapons had increased even more.

I'd never had occasion to meet an actual Slayer before. There simply is no time. A Slayer's life is unfortunately very short, and the young women are spread throughout the world. Part of their defense and part of their effectiveness relies on them being discreet.

Observing Britta glorying in her newfound abilities as she was now, I realized how hard it must be for the girls who become the Slayer to keep their amazing abilities secret. To suddenly wake up one morning—or be seated at the breakfast table, or wherever else these young women may be when they inherit the Slayer's abilities—has to be a heady experience.

That morning, much to my chagrin and my own delight, Britta bested me in every practice. Two days ago, that had not been so. That allowed me to pinpoint the passing of the last Slayer, though I didn't mention that to Britta.

The young woman I faced in our mock combats handled me as easily as if I'd been a child just learning to do the things we had done for the last year. In fact, no matter that I was in the best shape of my life at thirty-four, I was soon left winded and panting while Britta acted as though she could go on for hours.

Finally, I ruefully called a truce.

"What's wrong?" Britta asked.

I continued putting the weapons back in the chest and didn't much feel like looking at her. I know I should have been proud of the way she conducted herself, of the amazing abilities she suddenly exhibited, but my own pride stung. "We've done enough this morning," I declared. "If we stay here any longer Fräu Kessler will start to become worried. I'd rather not endanger the relationship I enjoy with her."

"Now that I am the Slayer, you mean?"

I looked at Britta then to let her know she should be more properly contrite. But, you see, the Slayer is always a young woman inexperienced in so many things. She is hardly ever more than a child. "Yes," I told her bluntly.

Britta helped me tie the chest to my horse again. "If it helps," she said in a more properly chastened voice, "I was getting tired there at the end."

"Were you?" I didn't properly understand the physical changes the Slayer went through, and no one I'd ever talked to on the Watchers Council knew either, but I thought perhaps she should have been stronger.

Britta started to answer, but I saw the hesitation in her face that marked the beginning of a lie. Over the last two years I'd gotten almost as skilled as Fräu Kessler at picking out Britta's attempts at lying. Thankfully, the lies Britta told were only small ones concerning her own well-being. Her lies were usually over such things as whether or not her feelings were hurt. Above all things, Britta was a very private person.

"Well, not really," she admitted. "But I thought it might make you feel better if I told you that."

I smiled a little at her. Over the past two years, I had developed a fondness for Britta. Watchers aren't supposed to become personally involved with their charges. Although I knew from reading the records of past Watchers that even that edict had been broken over the years. However, the close proximity forced on to me by acting as her tutor as well as her Watcher had taken away much of the distance that such a relationship might usually entertain.

"No," I told her, attempting to keep the rancor from my voice, "once I get past my own hurt pride, I realize that you should be quite well prepared for any of the monsters that you may now meet. I choose to take pride in my part in that."

"You've met a vampire."

"Yes."

She was quiet for a moment. "What was it like?"

"It was," I assured her, "quite possibly the most frightening thing I've ever done. And as I have told you, I would have died that night had it not been for Alfred Gantry." I took my glasses from my jacket pocket, cleaned them, and put them on. "That experience quite literally changed my life."

Britta took the small bag of treats that she had packed that morning from her saddlebags and sat on a fallen tree at the clearing's edge where we normally sat to catch our breaths after a workout. Some days we worked on lessons there or I tried to answer some of the seemingly interminable questions my young charge had. Thankfully, Britta was a bright student and interested in most things I taught her about, even the subjects that had nothing to do with vampires and demons. She remained curious about the wanderlust inside me that had driven me from my home at an early age and through two different universities before the Great War. I'd lived the kind of life that she only dreamed of.

Looking back on events now, I feel certain Herr Kessler knew his oldest daughter very well. I think he knew that I would bring more to Britta than simply a book education. We talked of the places I'd been, the people I'd met, and the things that I'd seen.

We sat on a fallen tree and ate apples and strong cheeses, then washed that down with a bottle of cool spring water. I could tell Britta was thinking deeply but I knew better than to ask. She would only talk whenever she was ready, and I respected that.

"Do you think, that when the time comes to face a monster, that I will be brave?" she whispered.

Her question took me by surprise. After two years of working with someone, you'd think you knew him or her. Then again, after a lifetime of living with yourself you would think you would know yourself also.

"Yes," I said. "I think you'll be very brave." After all, how could she not be brave? I'd trained her.

But I knew how she felt. We'd been in training together for two years and had not seen any of the demons that she would now be responsible to hunt. To be truthful, it was somewhat disconcerting to know that she was now the Slayer, yet there were no enemies about.

Those of you who are Watchers who have had Slayers in the past probably know what I'm talking about. The moment a Slayer comes into her own, the demons begin to seek her out. Not to say that they intentionally hunt for her—although I've heard that some have spent time hunting Slayers—but a Slayer and those she hunts always seem to find each other.

"I wish I knew for sure," Britta said.

"You'll know soon enough," I told her. I didn't know how prophetic that statement was or how close the demons were.

"Did you know her?"

"Who?" I asked even though I knew precisely whom she was talking about.

"The girl who was the Slayer before me."

I shook my head. "I didn't know who she was." I believed that, because it was two years since I had last known of a Slayer. Given the longevity, or lack thereof, of a Slayer I really doubted it was the same young woman.

"I wonder if she had family." Britta bit into the cheese.

"I don't know." Suddenly there seemed so much I didn't know.

"At least she had her Watcher."

I didn't say anything regarding that. I knew from my studies that not every Slayer was identified in time to provide her with a Watcher.

"I am so ashamed."

"Why?"

"Because only moments ago I was celebrating these new powers that I had been given, glorying in the fact that I had become the Slayer. I didn't even stop to think that someone had to die to give me these powers."

"I think you'll be forgiven that."

She looked at me then, and there were tears in her eyes. "It all sounds so good, doesn't it? I get to be the Slayer, one girl in the entire world, a Chosen one. Like a fairy tale from one of the Brothers Grimm that Poppa used to read me when I was a little girl." She paused. "But this isn't a fairy tale, is it, Friedrich?"

When we were alone like that she often called me by my first name. When I had objected mildly, she had told me that we had a partnership and she had learned from her father's business that partners were equals. Only some partners were more equal that others, judging from the amount of risk each took on a venture. We both knew who the more equal partner was between us. A Watcher may train the Slayer, but a Watcher will never *be* a Slayer.

"No," I told her gently as I could. "Being the Slayer is not a fairy tale." I took no more of the fresh strawberries and blueberries she'd brought for our midmorning snack because they were suddenly ashes to the taste.

A moment passed, and then Britta asked the question I knew that she would ask and that I dreaded most. "How do you think she died?"

I recalled all the accounts I had read from past Watchers that had lost Slayers. All of those accounts suddenly seemed to take on new weight and meaning. I looked into her green eyes and knew I could not lie to her.

"Horribly, I'm sure," I replied in a voice that was whisper thin.

The breeze rattled through the branches and rustled the leaves. The clearing felt hollow of a sudden, and we seemed a million miles away from anything we knew.

"I can't help wondering," Britta said, "if she died alone. Surely, that must be the most horrible thing of all."

I didn't say anything for I didn't want to make mention of any of the terrors that past Slayers had faced. Those young women led solitary lives apart from their friends and families till the day they died.

"Don't think of dying, Britta," I told her. "Think instead of living. I have trained you well, and you have been an exemplary student. You will succeed where others have failed. I believe that." At the time, I didn't feel like I was lying. I desperately wanted to believe what I was telling her.

Britta placed her hand on top of mine. "Promise me one thing, Friedrich."

I hesitated and tried to cover that. "If I can."

"Promise me that no matter what happens I won't die alone." Then she realized how that sounded. "I didn't mean that you should die with me, only that you would be there should the time come that I would be killed."

I looked at her. What else could I do? "I promise you," I told her, "that you won't ever die alone."

After we had returned to the Kessler family home, Britta found that her father had left a surprise for her. A coach and team stood waiting out in front of the main house. Her mother quickly explained that Herr Kessler had left a list of shopping that he wanted Britta to attend to.

This lifted Britta's spirits immediately, as I knew it would when I heard her father's request. Fräu Kessler had no real desire to take a long ride into Munich or to deal with all the people that lived there now. Fräu Kessler was from old peasant stock and very proud of her roots.

I excused myself and retired to the guest house where I had lived these past two years and dressed in a suitable attire to accompany Britta. I believe that my accompanying Britta made it easier for Herr Kessler to send Britta into the city. Fräu Kessler made a point to always ask Britta about the promising young men she might have seen in the city. Subtlety was never Fräu Kessler's strong suit. And should Fräu Kessler ever learn of my opinions in this regard, please offer her also my strongest apologies—for everything.

I dressed slowly, for I knew I would be waiting on Britta. However, on this day I was much surprised to find the young woman talking to the driver and waiting for me. She chided me for being so slow and I apologized profusely.

In short order, we departed the Kessler estate and made our way toward the city. The road was in good shape and well traveled. I noticed that Britta's conversation was more with Herr Kauptmann, the driver, and with Fräu Kinkle, her chaperone, than with myself.

I maintained my silence and spoke only when spoken to, following the lead set by my *more equal* partner.

Still, riding with Britta was always an enjoyable event. Those who knew her in any regard knew her to be a stimulating conversationalist. Britta had the knack of hearing any story and being able to repeat it word for word, gesture for gesture, and in the same manner in which it was first heard, if even years later.

Other instructors she'd had when she was much smaller told her she had the mind of a writer, the soul of a poet, and the elegance of an actor. I believed them. If Britta hadn't been slated to become a Slayer, she could have been any of those things. I think

Herr Kessler had in mind to make her part of his company when the time was right, but now I will never know.

Two motorcars passed us as the horses pulled the coach. One of them was going into Munich and the other was on the way out.

Britta acted like a child again as she watched the motorcars. "Oh look, Herr Kauptmann!"

"I see them," the gray-haired old man in livery stated, nodding his head.

"Wouldn't you one day like to drive one of those big motor-cars?" Britta waved excitedly to the motorcar's driver, who waved back to her enthusiastically.

"Oh no, Fräuline Kessler. A coach and a team of horses suits me just fine," the old man said. "Me and those fine horses of your father's, why we understand one another."

Britta had been striving to convince her father to buy one of the motorcars for the family, but Herr Kessler refused, insisting that there was no place a motorcar could go that a good team of horses couldn't go as well. I think Herr Kessler equated the mo-torcars with the Great War. Those battles were the first fought with men and mechanization. I truly believe that it was the most horrifying war ever fought.

The second motorcar, trailing a cloud of dust, was soon out of sight, and Britta's conversation with Herr Kauptmann returned to the stores she needed to go to and the order that she wished to go to them.

The winding, tree-lined road widened and appeared more trav-eled as it neared Munich. Even from some distance away I could see the three-hundred-foot twin towers of Frauenkirche Cathedral, which was built in the fifteenth century, in the old section of the city that sat along the western bank of the Isar River.

Most of the buildings along the Marienplatz, the best-known square in the city, had been built with baroque and rococo architecture. The bold centerpiece next to the Church of Our Lady Cathedral was Neues Rathaus, the city hall.

When I had occasion to spend time in Munich, I loved walking the streets and drinking while reading a book or making entries in my journal in the beautiful beer gardens. While Britta was shopping, I usually spent many happy hours in the shadows of the Sendlinger Gate or the Isar Gate, and now and again strolling through the Hellabrun Zoo or the Haus der Kunst, an art museum that I favored among many others I'd had opportunities to visit before the Great War and my new calling.

Herr Kessler owned a printing shop that provided stationery and printed books, a factory that made optical and precision instruments, another factory that made railroad parts, and the brewery he'd inherited from his grandfather on his mother's side. By current standards, Herr Kessler was a wealthy man even before considering his estates and farmlands. He had escaped the bankruptcy that seemed to stalk the middle-class German after being made responsible for reparations after the Great War.

We left Herr Kauptmann at the public stables and began making our rounds. By this time, I knew most of Britta's routine, though I seldom stayed with her these days. However, after receiving the telegram, I felt the need to stay close to her. She wasn't overjoyed at the prospect, but I think we both managed as elegantly as we could while serving our own agendas. Fräu Kinkle remained a discreet distance behind us.

Besides doing her parents' shopping, Britta also enjoyed looking at the latest fashion trends. The city housed a number of textiles factories and clothing manufacturers and brought in many new dealers to trade fairs and international exhibitions.

I don't know quite what I expected as we wandered the city. I'd read many accounts of the Slayer's purported abilities. Besides the incredible strength and speed that put her on a more equal footing with her savage prey, Britta was also supposed to be able to take more damage than a normal human and heal much more quickly.

And she was supposed to, by some arcane method that had never been quite explained, sense vampires and other demons.

I suppose, as we wandered around on her shopping errands, that it was this sensing of vampires that I awaited. I watched warily. As a mecca of industry and the arts as well as possessing an international flair, I felt certain that Munich was home to any number of foul fiends. How could it not be?

After two hours of shopping, though, the only things that Britta and I accumulated were packages and parcels. I trailed after her through the aisles as she purchased everything on the lists she'd been given. Herr and Fräu Kessler's lists tend to be extremely detailed and complete.

While Britta seemed to be indefatigable, I found myself soon exhausted.

"Herr Lichtermann," Britta said, addressing me formally as was her custom in public places, "you do look preoccupied. Perhaps you'd like to spend a little time at that bookstore you enjoy so much."

I straightened my spine resolutely. Standing in the dress shop with my arms filled with boxes I didn't look like the man of action I always viewed a Watcher as being. I had met no few such men while I was in training, and the ones I constantly looked up to were the ones who always appeared rough and ready, as Theodore Roosevelt had always been thought of.

"I shouldn't leave you here," I replied, though in truth, I longed to get out of the shop. Britta had the extraordinary gift of being able to look at the same merchandise again and again, seemingly with the same interest she'd had the first time.

"I'll be fine," Britta told me, smiling.

"Are you sure you haven't . . . *sensed* something?"

"You would be the first to know. Go on and enjoy yourself, Herr Lichtermann. If something should come up, I would find you and let you know immediately."

Knowing neither of us would enjoy ourselves if I didn't heed her suggestion, I took myself down to the book dealer's.

I bought a new leather-bound journal I had been eyeing in the shop for some time, thinking now that I was the official Watcher for the Slayer, it was time that I made a better presentation of my work.

The book dealer's is a small yet roomy place, filled with bookshelves and small, round tables that guarantee privacy for those who want it, as well as a gathering place for those who wished to meet and exchange ideas on whatever subjects caught their fancy.

I sat at one of the back tables against the western wall so that the sunlight fell on me. Perhaps I was more sensitive to the sun now that I thought vampires might be pursuing my young charge as well as myself. The foul creatures can't walk into full daylight lest they burst into flames and be consumed.

I tried writing for a while, but looking at the pristine, white paper before me only intimidated me. What could I write about? That my young student could now run faster and was stronger than she'd ever been? How helpful would that be for the next Watcher who had to care for the Slayer assigned to him?

That, I realized after only a moment's reflection, was a particularly morbid thought. I sighed in disgusted defeat and closed the new journal. Was there ever an instance of a Watcher and a Slayer who hadn't encountered vampires and their ilk throughout their career? I wondered. How would I ever write the treatises and articles and monographs on the Slayer and her work if we never encountered the foul denizens we existed to stand against?

Now, of course, as I sit here in this mausoleum and listen to the skittering claws of rats crawling through the tombs, I realize how foolish I was in that moment.

Thankfully, I spied a used copy of William Blake's *Songs of Innocence,* which I had not read in a few years. Of late, all my reading time had been consumed with manuals and treatises on demonology and other related topics. I purchased the Blake book as well and spent a little time reacquainting myself with the great poet's works.

After what seemed to be only a short time, but which I judged by the descending sun and the third beer stein I had emptied while I read was a few hours, Britta swept into the book dealer's shop.

Her beautiful angel's face looked radiant, and I knew something exciting had happened.

I stood so abruptly I almost knocked over the table. "Britta," I said, looking her over carefully to see if she'd suffered any damage. It was the first time outside of a practice session that I'd ever done anything of the like and I realized later that an onlooker could have misconstrued the whole event.

"Have you enjoyed yourself, then, Herr Lichtermann?" she asked.

"Yes, thank you," I replied. "And how has your day been?"

"Most productive. Mother and Poppa will be very pleased by the progress I have made."

"Progress? Then you are not finished?" I'm afraid I must have had a sour and disappointed look on my face at this point.

"It won't be much longer," Britta promised. "The rest of the shopping is only a matter of picking up regular orders. In the meantime, I've discovered something."

I looked at her hopefully, my heart hammering in my chest. A vampire? I wondered. A demon? What might it be?

"I was talking to Marta—you know Marta?"

I did know Marta Bruesehaber. Herr Bruesehaber owned an estate nearly the size of Herr Kessler's only a few miles away. Herrs Bruesehaber and Kessler had competing breweries but managed several stationery stores together in other cities.

I nodded.

"She just told me that there is a movie company in Munich this very day," Britta went on excitedly. "She said they're here to make a new picture called *Silent Screams*. It's one of those morbid horror pictures like *Nosferatu*."

Of course, I was very familiar with *Nosferatu*. And I was vaguely familiar with the picture-making industry that had found a home in Munich.

"Why is this picture so interesting to you?" I asked.

"Because it's a picture," Britta said in mild exasperation. "I've never seen a picture being made before."

I shook my head. Pictures were a novelty for me. I rather disliked the idea of sitting in a crowded theater with strangers watching the flickering black-and-white images parade across a screen. I found someone else's imagination too stultifying to entertain me. I much preferred a good book, such as the Blake I had so recently purchased.

"And Marta told you that you could watch this new picture being made?"

"Yes," Britta said. Her green eyes flashed. "She met a young man named Gunter who is one of the film studio's key people. They've become friends. The motion picture agency rented one of the mansions in the old part of the city. Marta's father has invested some money in the picture, so Gunter invited her to the open house the picture company is putting on this evening."

"And she in turn invited you?" I asked.

"Yes. Oh Friedrich, please say that you will go with me. I know that Poppa won't go to something like this, and if you don't go I know he won't let me."

I heard the desperation in her voice and wanted to ignore it. But I knew how much Britta enjoyed new experiences.

"Please, Friedrich," she said. "After all that talk of death this morning something like this would be so much fun."

I looked at her and tried to remind myself to be stern. I was the Watcher of the Slayer now. Didn't that put frivolity behind me? And behind her as well?

My head said no, but my heart said yes, and before I could believe it I heard myself telling her I would go with her. If I had known then what the consequences of such a weakness on my part would have been, I would have been able to change so many things.

But it's just as probable that even more people would have died had we not gone. I shall seek some solace in that meager belief.

In the end, Herr Kessler agreed that Britta and I could attend the motion picture party at the rented mansion. Herr Kessler, I might add, didn't give in to his daughter's wishes as quickly as I had, but I defend my own weakness with the fact that I knew how drastically her life had changed that day and he still had no inkling.

At seven o'clock that evening, Marta and her driver picked us up at the main house in the spanking new motorcar her father had purchased only that day. Herr Bruesehaber had chosen to move on into the twentieth century, and I knew that decision would be a source of great debate with Herr Kessler the next time they went birding.

Riding in a motorcar wasn't a new experience for me, but Britta was positively thrilled. She and Marta chatted on like two magpies while I shared the front seat with the driver. The man went very slowly, and I could tell he hadn't much experience with any kind of vehicle.

Since we rode in an open touring car, only the diamond-studded night and the leafy canopy of the trees that lined the road were over us. For the first time ever, I felt strangely vulnerable.

"Ah Fräuline Marta, I'm so glad you chose to join us on this evening's grand outing."

"Thank you, Gunter," Marta said politely, waving a hand toward Britta and myself. "I'd like to present my friend Britta and her escort for this evening, Herr Friedrich Lichtermann."

Gunter extended a hand toward me, taking my own hand in a strong grip that was cool and dry. He was very Aryan, with blond hair and blue eyes and a blocky build. He wore a perfectly tailored black suit that made me very aware that my own suit needed replacing or expert attention.

"Please make yourself at home, Herr Lichtermann," Gunter said, waving us into the old mansion.

The mansion had a magnificent ballroom that was properly festive for the occasion. Long tables laden with cheeses, fruits, and breads as well as punch bowls covered the floor around the outer perimeter of the room. Serving men and women catered to every desire of the audience. A chandelier that looked properly celestial hung over the ballroom. Double spiral stairs against the opposite wall wound up to the spacious second floor.

"Quite the place, isn't it?" I whispered to Britta. Then I noticed she seemed preoccupied.

"The chandelier," Marta whispered back across Britta, "is rented from Herr Andriessen. I have that on good authority."

I nodded, as if I found the information intriguing, then took Britta by the elbow and steered her toward one of the tables. "Would you like some punch?" I suggested.

"Yes," she said, as if only then distracted from a daydream. "Thank you."

She let me lead her across the Italian marble tiled floor. A sizeable orchestra played on a spacious balcony on the second floor. It was one of George Handel's operas that he'd written for his London audience. I do recall that.

"What's wrong?" I whispered as we crossed the ballroom.

"Gunter is wrong," Britta replied.

"What do you mean?" I guided us into a line for one of the punch bowls.

"I don't think he's . . . *normal*," Britta answered.

"In what way?"

"I don't know." Britta glanced over her shoulder at the man as he continued to greet people and invite them into the rented mansion. "I don't very much care for him."

"He's a motion picture person," I replied. "I've heard from a few friends that they're often not very likeable people." Those friends were other Watchers that I sometimes exchanged letters with. You see, Watchers write about all kinds of subjects.

"It's not a matter of likeability," Britta replied. "It's something more basic than that."

"What?"

"The way he moves."

I watched Gunter at the door. I saw nothing wrong with the way he moved and told Britta that.

"He's too fluid when he moves," Britta insisted. "Everything is too perfect. Normal people don't move like that."

"I'll take your word for that," I told her. Suddenly, I was very glad that I had put stakes into my jacket pockets.

"Stay with me tonight, Friedrich," Britta said, holding more tightly to my arm.

"I will," I told her.

"Good evening, ladies and gentlemen," a booming voice declared overhead as the final strains of Handel's opera faded and the orchestra became silent.

Conversations around the room stopped and everyone's attention turned upward.

"Welcome to my house," a dark-haired man with a goatee and mustache said from the second-floor balcony in front of the orchestra. "Please, don't let my little announcement disturb you while you eat me out of house and home and drink all my finest wines." He laughed and the audience laughed with him. "I'm Erich Sahr, director and star of the special motion picture you're going to see tonight."

A brief murmur rose from the crowd.

I'd not heard of Erich Sahr as either a director or an actor, but the motion picture business was still very young, and as I have said, I hadn't very much interest in it, though I had occasionally exchanged those letters about it with other Watchers. I assure you, I read more about it than I wrote about it. As a medium of entertainment, I preferred a good book that would totally unleash my own imagination.

"Perhaps many of you don't know what an impact German filmmakers are having on the American motion picture industry," Herr Sahr continued. "However, should you get the chance to travel to Hollywood one day and look up some of the talented people now working in that business, I guarantee that you would be very surprised. Now I come to you tonight to show you my opus, *Silent Screams*. It is a horror film, and, like *Nosferatu* before it, will hopefully disturb audiences that see it." He chuckled. "In a good way, of course, which would be very profitable for me and the investors who trusted me in this venture."

The murmurings from the crowd grew more excited.

I, myself, was more than a little concerned about the men we'd come to see after Britta's reactions to Gunter. Vampires, I'd been told, tend to congregate rather than stay alone. I was beginning to feel very much like the fly in the spider's parlor.

I watched Herr Sahr with acute interest. Did he move differently from other men? Was there something he did that set him apart? If he did and there was, I couldn't tell it.

"Please avail yourself of the refreshments for a few more brief moments," Herr Sahr said. "At the end of such time, there will be a showing of the picture in the next room." He stepped back from the balcony.

True to Herr Sahr's word, ten minutes later we were indeed watching the movie. The plot and the pacing were very intense.

I don't know if Hollywood will ever show something as nightmarish and bloodthirsty as *Silent Screams*. I pray to God that they don't. I don't know how an audience could stand it. And if the true nature behind *Silent Screams* is ever discovered, I can't see how it could ever be shown.

The violence and the killing in that picture, you see, are real.

But the audience last night

—*my God, can it only have been last night?*—

didn't know that the deaths they saw in the picture were real murders executed by foul demons who knew no mercy.

The story in the picture centers around a flesh-eating Bavarian baron played by Herr Sahr that was bitten by a seductress while on a voyage to South Africa after the Great War. The picture also took a note from the National Socialist German Workers'

Party—the Nazis—by making comments on the vanishing middle class in Germany and what had to be done about that.

The picture followed the baron's first hunts as he gained cunning and skill, through his confrontations with the various men and women who'd wronged him. All of those confrontations were bloody and vicious, and the audience drew back and farther back till they couldn't go any farther back in their chairs.

The picture ended abruptly. Baron Strasser's final scene showed him talking over the body of his latest victim with his aide, a deranged murderer played by Gunter, about gathering all his enemies together in the city on the pretext of a party, then killing them all.

The last was relayed to us through dialogue that we read in between the scenes.

The film ended, and harsh, white light splashed on the small screen, making me wince in pain. I blinked again as Herr Sahr gave the order to relight the room's lanterns.

"What did you think about the film?" Herr Sahr asked as he stepped in front of the screen.

A few comments came from the audience, but I felt they were too stunned by the cruel viciousness they'd seen to properly react. Most of the comments Herr Sahr got were positive, complimenting him on his masterful acting and director's skills.

I didn't have a compliment. I just wanted to get out of the room, out of the house.

But it was already far too late for many of us. You see, a vampire can't enter your home except by invitation. But he can invite you to his own house any time he wishes. And if you accept there is nothing to stand between you and the vampire.

"I'm so glad all of you could come out," Herr Sahr said. "This really wouldn't have worked had there not been a good-size turnout. The final scene of the picture needs to be shot."

I think some of the less drunken and more suspicious among the crowd then began to get the gist of what was going on.

Several of the men got up and started pulling their wives into motion. But it was already far too late.

Herr Sahr snapped his fingers imperiously. Instantly, liveried doorman stepped in front of the room's two exits and locked them with ornate brass keys.

The audience screamed in fear. A few of the audience members remained uncertain whether the situation was a joke. Some of them even tried to laugh it off.

Britta rose from her seat, as did I. I reached into my jacket and brought out one of the wooden stakes I had hidden there.

"Run and hide or fight if you wish," Herr Sahr taunted. "It will only make the picture much better for it." He stepped to the corner of the room and yanked a tarp from a camera while another man went to operate it.

As I looked at the man, his features changed, switching from human to something much more bestial. Gunter and a dozen other men also changed. Then they fell onto the audience with their great fangs flashing.

For a moment, I stood frozen beside my seat, remembering the creature I had faced back in the Great War. I trembled all over, no longer in control of my body. My chest seized up tightly, and I could no longer breathe. I recalled how the vampire had leaped at me and bore me to the ground, leaving me no option to defend myself. If Gantry had not been so close behind the demon that night, I knew I would have died.

Despite my calling and interest in being a Watcher, I was afraid. Most of the other Watchers I'd read about were afraid as well at one point of their careers or another. Fear was something you had to conquer before you even conquered the demons. That realization suddenly crystallized in my mind. I'd gone through the whole Great War without being killed or killing anyone.

Beside me, though, Britta acted immediately. I saw the clean set of her jaw and the intensity flashing in her green eyes. She took two stakes from her handbag, gripping one in each hand. Then, dressed in the black evening gown she'd chosen from her wardrobe to wear that night, she attacked the vampires.

One of the demons turned to face Britta confidently, his lower face a mask of blood as he held a dead or dying woman swooning in his burly arms. The Slayer gave him no chance at all to counter her attack. She shoved the stake in her left hand under the demon's rib cage and through his heart.

The vampire exploded into dust, and again I was reminded of how the creature had died at Gantry's capable hands. One of the vampire women turned toward Britta after seeing her fellow demon seemingly so easily dispatched. Britta attacked the vampire woman without mercy, something I'd never seen in her during our practices. My student had always been good in action, but she'd never had that hard edge to her that I'd read the Slayers must have and all seemed to share.

The vampire woman blocked Britta's attack, knocking her hand away in a move that reminded me of the Chinese fighting styles I'd studied and taught Britta. The Slayer, and I call her that because last night in that mansion Britta was that entity, failed to make contact with her thrust. Stepping to the right, the Slayer whirled and performed a spinning back kick that caught the demon in the face and knocked her backward, lifting her from the floor as if she'd been catapulted.

The demon struck the wall behind her and smashed through the plasterboard. Amazingly, the vampire pulled herself from the wreckage of the wall and stood once more. I know she would have returned to the fight, but the Slayer didn't give her a chance.

Britta kicked her opponent in the face again, then sunk one of her stakes into the demon's heart.

The vampire turned to dust and disappeared.

I don't know if I took pride in Britta's training at that moment because I was still locked in the fear of the past and what was going on then. Where was this great and fierce Watcher I was supposed to manifest into? Where was *my* change—the change I'd read about in the notes and journals of other Watchers?

It's true that many Watchers did not fight at the sides of their Slayers, but that was because the mantle of the Slayer is a lonely one. Whatever young woman currently fulfills that position is usually left to her own devices and spends much of her time alone.

Now I knew why. Most normal humans, even the ones who have knowledge of the foul beasts that prowl our world and stalk us, can't face the demons. There is something inherently frightening about the very inhumanness of them.

I offer no real defense for how I acted last night. These are only the things that I suddenly thought I understood.

But I know from my studies that a good number of Watchers did, in fact, battle at the sides of the young women that they trained.

However, I stood there unable to move, buffeted only by the frightened people around me who screamed and tried to flee for their lives, not knowing at all which way to turn. My breath was tight in my chest, and the back of my throat burned. I had a death grip on the stakes that I held.

Britta turned from her last vanquished foe. "Friedrich!" she yelled across the room. "I need you!"

I looked into her eyes and knew that she did need me. Even though she possessed the strength and skill that the power of the Slayer had brought to her, she was also still the young woman I knew who doted on her younger brothers and sister, the one who dreamed of seeing so much of this world.

Forgive me. I know this page is much more messy than the others before it, but the memory of Britta standing in that room, so beautiful and deadly, but yet somehow retaining that innocence about her, breaks my heart.

These young women—no, they are girls, surely I offer no disrespect by terming them so, and God knows that I mean no disrespect toward those unfortunate souls—have not even really begun to live their lives. I can't help but think of all the things they miss out on as I sit here in this mausoleum writing this by flickering candlelight.

Even the years that they have to them are fierce and savagely spent ones away from the comfort of family and friends.

And how many of them fall alone, surrounded by the monsters that they seek to defend the rest of us from? Do they go largely unmourned and unremembered?

I leave that question to you, the discoverer of this document—the last I shall ever pen in this life. The rats' claws scraping on the stone floor of the mausoleum echo around me again. The sound is maddening, but it isn't so maddening as the whir of the cameras that I know have been strategically placed throughout the mausoleum.

When I first discovered the cameras in here, I tried getting at them. However, my captors very cleverly put the infernal devices into places behind closed gates so that I cannot get at them. They also left bright candles burning throughout the rooms of the mausoleum, probably just enough so that the cameras can pick up the movements I make.

Perhaps they even think to steal my papers from me after the foul thing that they've locked in here with me kills me. But they either don't know about the use I have in mind for the small artesian well at the back of this grand building. The well was probably originally put in for the comfort of visitors or as a decorative feature that would provide the soothing voice of bubbling water.

Or perhaps my captors have forgotten about the well or have decided I am not very intelligent. But I have investigated that artesian well and discovered that I can get an arm down inside it. The empty wine bottle I found will also fit down inside the well.

I know that I don't have much time left to me. When I judge that I can no longer work on this journal entry, I will roll the papers up, shove them in the empty wine bottle, and put the bottle and these notes into that artesian well. Then I will pray that my work has not been in vain and that someone will discover the bottle and the papers inside. Surely the well leads out into the Isar River at some point. God, let that be so!

I digress. All of this you, the reader, will know when you find that bottle with this note. Perhaps you will think these pages only the ramblings of a madman, or perhaps you will read these pages some years later and laugh, thinking all of this is a sick joke. It could be that you will check the records in Munich to see if some bloodbath such as I describe actually did take place in that illustrious city and find no mention of it.

I will bet that you will find no entries relating the events I'm telling you about in these pages. Munich is a city of industry, of investments, and the future. The city fathers will decide they can ill afford such a debacle to be known about their municipality. As always happens in such a terrifying attack by these demons, the true event will be lost and only a small mention of several mysterious or accidental deaths will remain.

I beseech you that when you find these papers, you let the families of those poor, unfortunate souls know the truth of what happened last night. And let them know that they may all be in danger. Not every person that dies at the hands of a vampire will rise from *the grave the next night, but I believe that may well have been the intention of Erich Sahr—to unleash a pestilence of violent horror upon this city that will live in infamy.*

Probably all you will really hear about last night, November 8, 1923, is about the attempt Adolph Hitler and the National Socialist German Workers' Party is making to take over the Bavarian government. Only before I left Herr Kessler's house this evening I found out that Hitler and his cohorts were unsuccessful. People are calling this event the Beer Hall Putsch, and as near as it came to succeeding, I suspect they will remember Hitler and the Nazis much longer than they do the mass murders that took place last night in the old part of the city.

The infernal rat scratching is growing more prevalent. It must be after midnight now. God help me, the time will be soon now.

But let me return to the events of last night while I still yet have time. There is more, my amazed reader, that you will need to know.

"Friedrich! I need you!" Britta yelled at me.

Even frightened as I was and surrounded by screaming people equally as afraid as I was, I heard the steel in her voice. Somehow that timber in her voice gave me strength when I had none.

I went to her, pushing my way through the mad mob that tried equally to shove me away and to hang on to me, crying out for me to save them.

"We've got to get these people out of here," Britta told me.

I nodded, because I didn't trust my voice.

Her green eyes caught mine and held them as two vampires made their way toward us. "Remember your promise to me this morning," she told me.

"I do," I croaked, knowing full well that we were both about to die.

But I had not, even after reading so much of the exploits of the previous Slayers, taken into consideration the power that was Britta's to command. I cannot, in all honesty, claim responsibility for all that I saw Britta do that night. Part of the Slayer's skill lies in her training, but so much of it seems to come naturally once the power has manifested itself within her.

The Slayer ripped a hunting tapestry from the wall beside us and brought it down onto the two vampires coming directly for us. The tapestry was heavy and unexpected, and succeeded in knocking them down. Before they could regain their feet, Britta sheathed her stakes in them, unerringly finding their unbeating hearts and reducing them to dust.

A female demon approached me, her face a tight mask of bloody rage. Crimson stained her white evening gown, I remember that explicitly. It's an image that will die with me. Only one among many, I'm afraid.

Erich Sahr yelled orders at his fellow demons, bringing them all to bear on Britta. Evidently by that point he'd realized who she was. But no matter how complicated things got in that room, Herr Sahr made sure the cameras kept rolling. Somewhere, that film exists. The Watchers Council should know about it. I can't get the thought out of my head about all those horrified faces trapped forever in black and white, all those silent screams as they were killed.

Britta battled her way to the doorway that led to the grand ballroom. The vampire blocking the way there tried to stop her, but he had no chance. He threw a flurry of blows at Britta, but the Slayer stopped them all, then buried a stake in his heart. After the demon turned to dust, the Slayer kicked the locked doors open, freeing the surviving people inside the room.

Once a means of freedom was before them, the survivors of the movie showing had no qualms about using it. They fled en masse.

And to my shame, I fled with them. I tried desperately not to leave, but when the doors opened and the way to the street was seen to be clear, I ran, joining them with some herd instinct.

"Friedrich!"

Startled by the terror in Britta's voice, I turned as I ran through the mansion's main doors. Peering into the grand ballroom where we had dined by invitation only a short time ago, I saw a half dozen vampires holding Britta so that she couldn't escape.

I stopped.

"Friedrich!" she wailed. "Remember your promise to me! Remember that you told me you wouldn't allow me to die alone! You *swore* to me!"

God in heaven, I swear that I shall never forget that horrible cry. I've not slept since last night, and I know that I could not without hearing poor, poor Britta over and over in my nightmares.

In the next moment the vampires bore her to the floor and someone closed the mansion's doors.

"*Friedrich!*" Then they covered her and, mercifully and selfishly, I heard her no more.

Forgive me, but I only gave fleeting thought to trying to return for her. But how could I, who was only human, stand against the demons strong enough to slay the Slayer?

I stopped, as I said, but it was only for a moment. Then I kept running.

I hid out all that night, not daring to return to Herr Kessler's estate after I had let his beautiful daughter perish alone and untended. I watched from a rooftop as the bodies were recovered from the mansion the next morning. Evidently those in charge of the recovery of the victims had some small experience with vampires, because they didn't try to go into the mansion at all that night. Of course, being involved with Adolph Hitler and the Nazi party occupied a lot of their attention during the night as well.

I couldn't help thinking that Herr Sahr had planned well, and wondered if he had somehow known Hitler would make his move that night. Now I know that I shall never know. But Hitler's efforts were defeated, and I shall take some cold comfort in that. Things here in Germany are hard enough after the Great War without madmen running around fomenting unrest.

I spent the day scared and alone, thinking only of my desertion of Britta and how I'd broken my promise to her. But I was no Slayer. I was just a man, a very scared man up against monsters that could have snapped me like kindling. I did the only thing a sane man would do.

Later that evening, knowing what Herr Kessler would do, I made my way out of the city and down the long road to his estate. Poor Britta's body had been discovered with the others that had been taken from the mansion. As much as Herr Kessler loved his daughter, I knew that he would want to see her laid to rest as soon as possible.

I waited outside the mausoleum as the family, dressed all in black, conducted the funeral after Britta's body had been interred. Then, shortly before sundown, I gathered the stakes I'd carved with my Swiss-made knife and sneaked into the mausoleum like a thief.

I didn't know if Herr Sahr had attempted to Turn her when he killed her, but I didn't see how the demon could resist corrupting the person who was supposed to stand against him and his kind. I tried not to think of poor Britta as some soulless hellion, but the image of her features turned bestial and cold wouldn't leave me.

I also knew that Britta, at least the part of her that survived to welcome the demon into her body, would remember my betrayal of her. It was with great trepidation that I made my way into that ornate mausoleum.

I went immediately back to the wing that was slated to hold Herr Kessler and his family and spotted the casket I had seen carried to the estate earlier by a funeral coach trimmed all in black. My heart pounded in my chest as I stared at the sleek wood.

But I knew what I had to do.

Resolutely, I took up one of the stakes I'd shoved into my belt and approached the casket. All I had to do was pierce her heart with the stake, then there would be no coming back for her. My hand trembled and sweat poured from my body like I was a dish towel being wrung out in Cook's strong hands.

Moaning, not wanting to see Britta this way, I reached for the casket lid and lifted. The freshly oiled hinges opened without a sound to reveal the empty bed inside. My breath froze in my throat as I wondered if she'd already risen.

"No," a voice said behind me. "She's not there."

I whirled and found Herr Sahr standing inside the mausoleum. I trembled as I stood there, a disheveled and humbled man, I assure you, and one still very much afraid for his life.

"Where is she?" I croaked.

Herr Sahr grinned at me. After his night of bloodletting and filmmaking, he looked sartorially perfect.

I hated him for that. I hated him for what he'd done to Britta, and for making me feel so helpless and pathetic to prevent it or do anything about it now.

"Fräuline Britta is still here in this place." Herr Sahr took a cigarette from a silver case inside his jacket.

"Is she—is she—" I could not bring myself to say it.

"Dead?"

I made no reply. My throat would have only strangled anything I might have tried to say.

"Oh," the vampire said, "she's dead. Very much so." He blew a smoke ring into the still air in the mausoleum. "It is a very difficult thing to turn a Slayer, you know." He regarded me. "Or perhaps you don't. You look every bit as inexperienced as your young protégée."

I started toward him then, the stake clenched tightly in my fist. It wasn't that I was suddenly brave. It was that I was so frightened that I could no longer stand still.

Before I took my second step, Herr Sahr moved with incredible speed and slapped me down.

I fell to the stone floor, smelling the old death that reeked around me. I tried to get up, but I couldn't. My muscles wouldn't obey my mind, and I teetered on the brink of unconsciousness.

"Before young Britta died, Herr Lichtermann," the vampire taunted, "and she died screaming, let me assure you of that, I remembered how she'd screamed at you in the mansion. She reminded you that you had promised she would never die alone."

Guilt hammered me, smothered me in its cloying embrace.

"You promised her that she wouldn't die alone," Herr Sahr repeated. "She won't forgive you for that, you know." He glanced down at the stakes on the floor. "I'm leaving you your toys. It's only fair that you be armed. Still, I don't think it will be an even match. I think she will still kill you, but perhaps you will surprise me. At least the exercise should provide a modicum of amusement for your audience."

Abruptly, a chugging, hammering noise filled the mausoleum. I recognized the sound immediately.

Sahr smiled. "Generators," he said. "For the cameras, you see. Your final confrontation here in this place is going to be saved on film, my friend. However it turns out. I've taken the liberty of placing men behind the gates of the various passages in this mausoleum. They will film your final moments."

A small hope dawned within me then. Perhaps Herr Kessler's main house was not so very far away—

"The sound of the generators," Sahr assured me, "will never be heard by anyone in that home. And if it is, I will kill them as well." He leaned toward me, still smiling that mocking smile. "I'm going to make you a star, Herr Lichtermann."

Before I could move, he stepped forward and kicked me in the head. Everything went black.

I awoke in the mausoleum some hours ago only to find Herr Sahr had seen to it that I was locked in. No one at Herr Kessler's estate has heard my pleas for help, nor the incessant thumping and banging of the generators that provide power to the damned cameras that tape my movements. The mausoleum is too far away from any of the main houses, and the groundskeepers seldom come out this way. When I checked through one of the barred windows—too tight for a full-grown man to slip through—I'd seen sundown rapidly approaching.

After that, I'd searched frantically through the mausoleum for Britta's body. If I could have found her before she rose again in the middle of the night, I could have stopped the horror that I knew would be coming.

But although I searched everywhere I could think of, I couldn't find her. The Kessler mausoleum is an old one, filled with a number of passageways that were gated off. I didn't have the strength to open those gates, so I can't help but think Britta was hidden behind one of them. The rats that infest this place kept me company and still do.

So do the cameras that Herr Sahr had installed. Perhaps he has rewritten the end of his picture. I wonder about the audience for such a thing. Will it be made up of demons? Or—even more horrible to consider—will that audience be made up of men with the hearts of demons?

I don't know. Perhaps you will learn.

I must close now and try to get the papers in the wine bottle and the wine bottle down into the artesian well. I'm certain that the last scratching noise I heard wasn't the sound of rats' claws. It was more like the pampered nails of a young woman rasping along stone walls.

Now I hear her. She calls my name, and although I recognize the voice as Britta's, I don't recognize the mocking tone.

God, I am so scared. Nothing can be more horrible than this! But both our fates have already been sealed, haven't they? Only the final scene needs to be played out—the one Sahr orchestrated so carefully.

Even though I am afraid of her, I am more afraid of death. Perhaps tonight, though, she and death are the same.

I will fight.

I know that.

God forgive me, I have NO CHOICE. I cannot allow her to continue the wretched existence she has begun if it remains within my power to stop her.

She comes toward me coyly, like a shy lover. I know this because the sound of her nails along the stone walls approaches very slowly. I cannot hide from her; I know that she can smell my blood wherever I go. And I know that after wakening from her recent death she will be ravenous.

Please get this message to the Watchers Council. I've included one of the postal addresses they use in Berlin.

As for me, I shall take up the stakes I carved during Britta's funeral earlier and wait to meet her. One way or the other tonight, I shall keep my promise to her.

She will not die alone.

I pray only that my arm is swift and that I remember the girl I knew is dead, her place taken by the foul creature that will hunt me as surely as I hunt her.

God have mercy on us both.

Sincerely,
Herr Friedrich Lichtermann

And White Splits the Night

Yvonne Navarro

FLORIDA, 1956

She had always loved the swamp.

At seventeen, Asha Sayre was tall and well muscled for a girl, graceful as a snake as she walked along the mushy ground on the edge of Lake Okeechobee. The ebony tones of her skin were a natural camouflage, melding smoothly with the heavy, sunlight-mottled greenery. Still, she was mindful of the 'gators and cottonmouths that twisted silently through the underbrush and the swamp—they would not be so easily fooled. Any spot of standing water could be home to a territorial, hungry reptile, and their ranges spread far and wide. The hunting knife that hung off the belt of her denim jeans, serrated with a spiked guard along the knuckles, would split an alligator wide open with one swipe . . . but only if she saw it coming. Caught from behind, she'd be dragged into the water and drowned, then wedged under a rock or something beneath and saved to be a tasty later meal.

Such a damp, dangerous place, but Asha turned her face upward and smiled, enjoying the feel of the heat on her skin. There was so much *life* here—river otters and muskrats played in the water, as if daring the 'gators to chase them, swamp sparrows and marsh wrens sang while herons walked amid the grasses, their spiky legs keeping them above the low water level. Occasionally she'd catch a glimpse of a red-shouldered hawk dive-bombing toward earth, and Asha knew that some poor swamp mouse had met its end. Damselflies and skimmers skipped above the water lilies and pogonias, all beneath a sheltering umbrella of loblolly bay, willow, and bald cypress trees. Movement was everywhere, the dance of existence itself.

But there was death here, too.

Something dark and unnatural that didn't belong with the threat of the 'gators and poisonous snakes.

It took her awhile, but Asha finally found it. She'd been wandering, really, traveling southward along the lakefront and deeper into the swampier areas on nothing more than gut feeling. It was the smell that drew her the final yards, the sickening stench of decomposition, and now she stood and studied the corpse half buried beneath the dense Possumhaw and bayberry leaves. A wave of her arm sent a cloud of horseflies skyward, giving her a few seconds to glimpse bare flesh before they resettled. Mother Earth was quick to reclaim dead material here, and already beetles and rodents had joined the flies in their feast. But that two-second look had shown Asha what she most needed to see on the body of this middle-aged Negro man:

Bite marks on his neck.

Whoever he was, there was nothing she could do for him now—drained, partially eaten, it was obvious he'd gone through several sunsets, so he was victim only, not fated to walk this world as a vampire. It saddened her that she had no idea who he was, what his name had been, or if he had a family who now wondered where he'd gone. In Martin County, Florida, 1956 was a hard time—work was hard to find, money was scarce. Perhaps there was a wife and children somewhere who thought, unfairly, that this poor man had run off to seek his fortune in richer climes.

A soft splash off to her right made Asha tense and back away from the body. It could be an alligator that had caught the smell of free food, but it could be something else entirely. This was Cajun country, and those hard, heavily accented men and women weren't known for their friendliness to outsiders, especially Negro folk. Asha slipped away rather than risk a nasty confrontation, letting her shadow blend with the deep greenness of the vegetation. But she'd be back.

Because that wasn't the only vampirized body she'd found in the swamp this week.

Laurent was waiting for her when Asha got back to their small shack. Settled comfortably on the weather-cracked rocking chair on the front porch, the middle-aged Cajun woman sucked on her old hardwood pipe and regarded her for a few moments without speaking. Smoke from the cheap tobacco swirled above her head, and while Asha didn't like it, she had to admit that the tobacco smoke helped to keep the biting insects away.

"Find 'nother one?" Laurent asked around the pipe jammed between her lips. At Asha's expression, the woman nodded. "Uh-huh. Evil's afoot, all right." She raised an eyebrow. "Gonna have to hunt it down."

"I know." Asha sighed and forced her fingers through the tight curls on her head, wishing for the tenth time that week that she could just cut it all off like a boy's. Laurent wouldn't allow it though, said that while it would be easier to care for, it'd be like a big sign pointing to her, marking her as being different from the rest of the colored girls in their small town. And she *was* different, but she didn't need everyone else in Port Buck to know that; enough bad stuff happened there already, and she was supposed to help *stop* it, not become a target.

"Where're you gonna start?"

"I'm . . . not sure. I guess I could go into the swamp tonight."
A risky business, doing that—her eyesight was keen but not like
the animals, which had the advantage of a better sense of smell
to boot. If there was no moon she'd have to carry a lantern. A
light might lead her along the right path and keep her from stepping on an alligator, but it could also draw a few creatures her
way that were far worse than the reptiles.

Laurent said nothing, as usual. Asha had been with her for
nearly twelve years, but the sturdy woman was still a mystery in
many ways. Beneath gray-flecked black hair, Laurent's skin was
leathery from a lifetime in the Florida sun, and her eyes were as
black as Asha's own. She didn't talk much, but she said volumes
in looks and gestures—like the one she was leveling at Asha right
now, a gaze filled with unvoiced disapproval.

"Or I could go to town instead," Asha ventured, trying to read
Laurent's eyes. "See what's going on there."

Still silent, Laurent rocked a few times, and Asha knew from
the last decade of seeing this move that Laurent thought this was
the better choice. Sometimes she wished the woman would talk
more, but all things considered, maybe Laurent had seen so much
that she'd just run out of words. Perhaps she'd used them all up in
explaining the way of the world to Asha as she'd grown from the
orphaned five-year-old whom the eccentric Cajun woman had
taken in, to the Vampire Slayer she now supervised as a Watcher.

"You just listen. And watch your back," was all Laurent said as
she pushed herself up from the rocker and then went inside the
shack. Asha followed, grateful to get out of the humid heat of
midday. There were black beans in a pot on the unlit woodstove,
and the two women ate them cold with a chunk of homemade
sourdough bread. Afterward, Asha crawled onto her small bed in
the corner and tried to sleep for a bit, knowing that tonight

might be long and, if she found a vampire or two, physically demanding.

Were there vampires in the other parts of the country? The world? It was hard to imagine any place but this one, their small town with the one side where the white folks lived behind their painted picket fences and houses with flowerpots on the windowsills, the other side where the poor Negroes and Cajuns—the ones like Laurent who weren't reclusive—stayed in shacks and houses that were one step above collapsing at any moment. This was the life Asha had been born into, it was the only life she knew.

But even that life had changed drastically a couple of times, once when she was five and her father had been found hanging dead from a black tupelo tree in the swamp, again two years ago when Laurent had sat her down and explained about the vampires and the Slayers and the Watchers, and told her that the last Slayer had been killed and so now it was Asha's turn to take over. Sometimes Asha thought that was the day that Laurent had used up whatever quota of words had been given to her by God, because the woman had rarely said more than a sentence at a time since. At least Asha had finally understood why Laurent had insisted that as early as age nine, she start learning to fight. At the time, her guardian had told her it was so she could defend herself against the neighborhood bullies. She must have known the day was coming when Asha would be called.

There must be vampires elsewhere, Asha realized. She had never heard of something called a "Slayer" before Laurent had told her she was one. One thing that happened regularly in a small, mostly poor town was gossip. With little else to occupy their time, the residents talked—about anything, everything, and everyone. Stories were brought in from as near as down the road to as far away as Palm Beach and Saint Lucie counties, probably farther, although such news was reserved for the more affluent. Asha didn't know how Laurent had found out the other Slayer had been killed, and the woman had never said. Had someone told her? Or sent her a rare piece of mail?

In any case, the previous Slayer certainly hadn't been from around here or Asha and the rest of the people in Port Buck would have known something about it. Asha couldn't help wonder what the nameless, faceless Slayer had been like. Had she been colored, like Asha? Or a half-breed Cajun like Laurent? Certainly not white—all the white girls Asha had seen were soft and pampered princesses who did nothing but giggle and talk about boys—Asha couldn't imagine one of them not fainting if they'd had to face one of the twisted-looking monstrosities she'd fought, and the thought of one of them driving a stake through such a beast's heart was laughable. *Shoot, most of them don't seem strong enough to pick up a sack of potatoes.*

At least she had a purpose now, something to look forward to in her life besides the complacency of day-to-day existence in the swamp or even marriage and a handful of screaming babies hanging off her skirt. She hadn't met any boys who interested her like that, but had she not been called as a Slayer . . . who knew what might have happened? Life around Port Buck was pretty languid, and someday Laurent would be gone; there'd always been someone else in her life—first her father, then Laurent—and the odds were probably pretty good that she would want company other than her own lonely self in the years to come. At least she'd always thought so, until her calling.

Now things were different, she *felt* different. If not more at peace with herself and the world, then more accepting of the way things were in it and her place in that plan, her destiny. Asha didn't know where that destiny would take her, but that was all right, too. There wasn't much else around here to do, so she might as well follow the path and do some good along the way.

Asha rolled over and faced the wall, feeling herself start to drift toward sleep. Her eyelids fluttered closed, then opened again, not really focusing on the cracked plaster of the wall a few inches from her face. Down at the other end of Port Buck, on the white side of town, there was a drive-in movie show, and she'd heard tales about it, how images of real people and things moved across the screen while their voices came from speakers folks hung on their car doors. The wall in front of her was kind of like that, showing semi-coherent pictures from her subconscious and her half-closed eyes as Asha hung on the very edge of sleep . . . and finally slipped over.

The swamp is as green as ever, but night-dark now and filled with the hoots of owls and dark-time insects. Everything seems so much bigger because she is so small—in the eyes of a child a kitchen table can look huge—and she is only five years old. Even back then she knows the swamp and the creatures that live in it, because her daddy has taught her; what he hasn't shared with her is how cruel a group of men can be to another, based on superficial things like skin color and religion.

Her Daddy has left her alone in their little house while he's gone out to visit a neighbor down the road a piece. He's done this before, and Asha knows she is supposed to stay in bed and sleep, and when she wakes up in the morning he'll be home. Tonight, for some reason she cannot say, she disobeys and follows him instead, scampering behind him in the nighttime shadows as though they are playing hide-and-seek.

She thinks Daddy is on his way to visit the Greens, or maybe the Ropers, but he never gets there. He is walking on the side of the road, alone on the long, empty stretch between the two houses, and she is maybe a hundred yards behind when a car speeds up beside him, a black one, huge and smelly. It careens to a stop just in front and all the doors open at once, then figures garbed in white robes roll out of the automobile like bright ghosts with flapping wings.

Asha sees her daddy start to run, but they are on him too quickly, as many of them as she is years old; her daddy goes down amid a hail of punches and kicks, but he is still fighting as they drag him into the underbrush and disappear. The whole thing has happened so quickly that she didn't even have time to scream.

She is too afraid to follow, so she hides in the bushes next to the road and she waits. It isn't very long before the white-costumed figures return, and they are laughing and joking among themselves, their eyes glittering behind the holes cut in the strange, pointed hoods on their heads. Still, her daddy isn't with them. Finally they all climb back into the big car and drive away, and Asha doesn't know what to do—should she look for her daddy? Or should she go home?

Asha woke with a start, drenched in sweat and slapping away a mosquito—she calls them insect-shaped vampires—that was sucking greedily at a spot on her forearm. The dream memory replayed clearly in her head instead of fading as dreams normally did. She hadn't thought of that night in years, nor of the white-robbed figures—members of the Ku Klux Klan—and her father's abduction. The Klan was a part of life in Florida, and she knew it was called the Invisible Empire in the rest of the country, but it was a quiet chapter here in tiny Port Buck, not usually much in the public eye. Now and then there were rumblings about the organization regaining its strength and returning to its glory days, but nothing had happened yet—why was she suddenly remembering the night her father had been killed?

Asha sat up and swung her legs over the side of the bed. The rough, clean-swept floor felt good beneath her feet, solid footing in a life that had turned upside down more than a time or two.

"Sun'll be setting soon."

The sound of Laurent's scratchy voice made her blink away the last of her sleepiness. She primed the pump at the kitchen sink and rinsed her face and hands, enjoying the chilliness of the well water.

Then she changed her clothes, trading the boy's T-shirt and denim jeans for something more girlish that wouldn't stand out. They didn't have money for fancy here, so she'd leave the petticoated skirts and the ribbon-trimmed blouses to the town's white girls; a simple cotton dress and comfortable shoes over hidden cut-off denim jeans would do just fine.

She brushed her teeth and fought with her hair for a bit, then gave up on the unruly curls as she stared into their only mirror. *Do I look like my mother?* Her mother had died giving birth to her, so she had no idea. Although some people had told Asha she was beautiful, Asha didn't see that beauty in her own reflection. A white girl could hide in plain sight, blend in with the towns-folk, but even dressed like this, like "normal" people, Asha's dark skin would make her stand out if she went where she shouldn't. She would have to be very, very careful to stay unassuming.

"Here."

Laurent pressed two quarters into her palm, and Asha frowned down at the money. "What's this for?"

"You don't need to be wandering the streets like a penniless waif," the older woman said. "You're in town, you get yourself some supper like the other teenagers."

"No, we don't have money to throw away on that." Asha tried to give the coins back, but Laurent only folded her arms and looked at her sternly.

"You want to hear what people are saying, then you got to be where they're saying it. There's still a chance that a colored girl will just get tossed out the door, but depending on how greedy the owner is and if no one notices, your money might spend like anyone else's."

Asha pressed her lips together but finally nodded. Her Watcher was right—she stood a better chance visiting the local hangout if she had money than if she didn't. "All right." She glanced in the mirror a final time as she tucked the coins into the deep pocket on the left side of her skirt, then went back to her bed and withdrew the sharp-tipped stake from beneath her pillow. That went into the right pocket, where she'd reinforced the bottom of the fabric with a strip of heavy leather. "I'll be back later."

As always, Laurent didn't say good-bye, just mumbled a few words to herself as Asha left. The Slayer wondered if the other woman realized that Asha knew what they were, had figured them out the third time she'd gone out to face the vampires—

"God willing."

As much as Laurent could do such a thing, Asha supposed it was her way of sending her off with a blessing.

She didn't know why, but Asha found herself following that same dark stretch of road from twelve years previous.

It had to be the dream, of course, bringing back to the surface memories that she'd thought were long held at bay by the protective shell of time. Between the dream and that same old swamp, that barrier was disintegrating rapidly—tonight might as well have been a decade ago. Déjà vu swirled through her mind, and Asha could swear the same owls hooted overhead, the same insects buzzed in the undergrowth, the same sweet smells of butterwort, orchids, and lizard's tail hung on the night air, the same cricket frogs croaked somewhere out of sight.

Twelve years ago she had been too frightened to do anything as her father had been dragged away. She had passed this same spot hundreds of times since then, but it hadn't been until this afternoon's nap that she had finally made the connection between the white-costumed figures and the Ku Klux Klan. Now she would not be so timid.

Asha stepped off the road and pushed through the bushes, not making much of an effort to move quietly, almost *daring* someone or something to challenge her. The vegetation was dense, but there was an area where it thinned out, an old path not much used anymore; she followed it, forcing her way where necessary. Night things made sounds all around her, but they were natural, nothing to set off the alarms in her head. She could hear the bellow of a 'gator somewhere in the distant swamp as it warned away another reptile, the splashing of water flowing over rocks in a tiny creek close by. She felt strangely excited but at peace, one with the night and about to discover some great secret.

The lush greenery abruptly ended and Asha stopped. The starry night sky was cloudless and lit by a three-quarters moon that sent a cool, butter-colored glow over the clearing she now faced. Here the ground had been trampled flat a long time ago, but sparse tufts of grass had found life again and were spreading. The undergrowth was trying to reassert itself where it had been hacked away, sending forward tentative branches of growth that would eventually tangle together and eliminate this irregular spot in nature's plan. In the center of the clearing were two mature black tupelo trees, and Asha stared up at them, frowning. The lowermost branches of the biggest one had been sawed off to a height of eight feet; she could see the bottommost one and the lighter scar that ran around it, two feet away from the trunk where something had rubbed away the bark—

The men drive off in their big, smelly car, and five-year-old Asha crawls out of her hiding place in the bushes, moving like a skittish salamander. Her dress is torn, and she knows her face is streaked with dirt and tears, and for a little while she stands in the middle of the muddy road and wonders what to do. Where is her daddy?

She waits, but he does not come out of the trees. The night is dark and cool around her, but not as scary as those bad men in the car.

She decides she would rather face a snake or an alligator than them, so she finds the space where the men and her daddy went into the woods and decides to follow it. It's a path, easy to walk by the moonlight. She's never done this sort of thing at night, and it's almost fun, an adventure—

—until she reaches the clearing.

Her daddy hangs from one of the trees, swinging by a rope looped around his neck and pulled tight below his chin by the weight of his body. He is not so far up that Asha can't see his face. It is utterly devoid of expression—his eyes are open and sightless, his mouth, lips swollen from punches, is slack and soundless. The breeze makes him swing slightly from side to side.

"Daddy?" Asha whispers, but even at her tender age she knows it is useless. She puts her small hands around his ankles and tries to pull him down, but that, too, is futile. After a while she gives up, sits on the ground below him, and cries.

Time passes, but she does not know how much. She hears movement, someone coming, and she knows she should run, but she is too tired from weeping to be scared or to care. The lone figure that steps into the clearing is small and sturdy, features shadowed by the brim of an old hat. When it steps up to Daddy's body and looks upward, the moonlight shows Asha that it is a woman, a Cajun, and her tanned face is as lined from the Florida sun as the leather of her hat is cracked. She turns the body gently until she can see the other side, and Asha also sees what the woman is looking for—two bloody punctures on her daddy's neck, a couple of inches below the rope.

The woman shakes her head and releases Daddy's legs. Then she lifts Asha into her arms and carries her off into the swampy night.

All these years, Asha realized as she stared at the trees, and she had blocked that memory, hadn't wanted to remember the way her father had looked. He hadn't been the victim of a hanging at all—that was just an easy way to camouflage the vampire attack in this heavily Ku Klux Klan–infested town. And of course they wouldn't have made her father drink and rise again—the last thing they'd want was a Negro vampire among their ranks.

The pointed white hoods where only the eyes were revealed, the near immunity the Klan enjoyed in Port Buck . . . they could feed on the coloreds, the Jews, the Catholics, and any other race or religion they decided to target. What more perfect way for a vampire community to feed and grow undisturbed than from beneath the costumes of an organization that *expected* its members to hide their identities behind masks? And for how long had the bloodsuckers been living behind the protection of the KKK? Ten years? Twenty? Or longer? Hangings might not be so easily brushed off anymore, but as the corpse she'd found this morning testified, there was always the swamps and the 'gators to help get rid of the leftovers. A poor and backwoods Florida town had given them the perfect method, and the perfect setting.

But not anymore.

The town of Port Buck was just as the tourists described it when they passed through—a ragged hole in the swamp with no more than fifteen hundred people stuffed into it. Most of the locals choked out a living over in Indiantown at the milling plant, the Tampa Farm Service, or the big citrus groves. There wasn't much to bring or keep visitors, who had better things to look for in Florida than a half dozen churches and a VFW hall, a Dairy Queen, and Main Street with its standard shopping fare—grocery store, hardware store, Laundromat, a couple of struggling antique and crafts places. Visitors found that in particular they could live without the unfriendly stares of the Port Buck locals, the surly responses to requests for directions, and the repeated attempts of local merchants to price gouge on things like cigarettes and eight-ounce bottles of Coca-Cola.

In all honesty, the atmosphere wasn't much better for the considerable number of Negro people who called Port Buck home.

A few tried to get out, but if cash for day-to-day food and clothing was hard to come by, finding money to go gallivanting elsewhere to hunt up your fortune was like stumbling over that rainbow's end pot of gold. As a result, the colored folk generally kept to themselves and stayed out of trouble, watching the noises about equality made by people in the rest of the country with a keen and hopeful eye. The white people tolerated them as long as they kept to their place—back of the line and the town's only bus, mind you—provided cheap labor, and stayed on their own side of Port Buck.

Which is why Asha knew it would be an unexpected sight for people to see her, a young Negro woman, walking right down Main Street like she had the God-given right.

In her mind and her heart, Asha felt she *did* have that right, but she wasn't out to debate equality here, or start a conspicuous battle over it. She did, however, want to draw some—just a bit—of attention to herself. If she was lucky, the unseen ears of certain KKK vampire powers would hear about her; from there she'd be marked as a target. Not a threat—she would do nothing to let them know that she knew their true nature, nor that she could actually do something about it. Tonight she just wanted to be noticed.

And, oh, was she ever.

Humidity notwithstanding, it was a rare and lovely Florida night, not too hot, not too cool. Most of the smelly automobiles had been left at home, and there were a fair number of people out and about, taking their evening strolls or going home from church socials and Bake-Offs—God was a big-ticket item here in eastern Florida. A few teenagers, those who didn't have Dad's rusting old Ford or Plymouth to go off and make out in, loitered around the Dairy Queen parking lot and lounged at the picnic tables set along the front sidewalk.

As Asha passed from her own side of town to the other, she felt the gazes of them all, most surreptitious, a few bolder and openly hostile. She was less concerned with that than with the occasional snippets of conversation she heard, thanks to a Slayer's intensified senses. It seemed everyone had something interesting to pass along, no matter their race or point of view:

"Pastor Johnson says eight folks from his parish have gone missing since February."

"Annabelle Thomas's husband didn't come home last Saturday."

"I heard that a couple from the Catholic church on Maple Street rang the priest in the middle of the night asking for help, but when he got there the house was abandoned. No one's seen those folks since."

"Elijah Peterson sent his son James to the store for a sack of flour and he never came back. Boy's only ten years old, but the sheriff won't bother looking for him."

"You hear about that Jew family, the Steins? Deputy Pique says they moved out of town, but George Sanders says he went over and found the house open, and all their furniture and whatnot still inside."

"Better be sure to keep your mouth shut and don't get noticed around here, that's for sure!"

Negro men and women, Jews, Catholics, even children and entire families seemed to be falling victim to the unseen evil here, and as she moved from one part of town to the other, the comments changed. After hearing what she had, Asha wouldn't have thought it possible, yet the words took on an even darker connotation, more fragmented and secretive. But the message, at least to her, was frighteningly easy to comprehend.

"—meal's a meal. Don't make no difference. Maybe that's what they were made for to begin with."

"—*easy to catch 'em coming out of those evening Masses they have all the time.*"

"—*pick off one of their kids and you stop a whole line of breeding. Just like killing a mosquito.*"

"—*non-Christian heathens, they ain't no better than the darkies.*"

As a rule, Asha didn't come into town very much, and certainly not onto the white side of Port Buck—since her calling, most of her vampire battling had been done in the swamps and on the edge of Port Buck. Now she realized her mistake. She'd always believed the evil was outside, trying to get in. It really had never occurred to her that it might be inside trying to expand *out,* and the concept was an ugly and eye-opening revelation.

At the Dairy Queen she stood off to the side and changed her tactic a bit, worked at not being noticed until there was no one else in line. Then she stepped to the walk-up window and placed a twenty-five-cent piece on the ledge. "I'd like a malt, please." She kept her voice carefully even, but she didn't lower her gaze.

There were two people in there, one back by the sink working on the dishes and one guy at the window to take orders. The dishwasher never glanced up from his chore, but the order taker looked like a typical Florida teenager—tall with blond hair, blue eyes, and well-tanned muscular arms poking out of a uniformed shirt with the name *Joey* stenciled above the left pocket. If it hadn't been for the *smell* of him, she'd have probably mistaken him for a normal all-American boy, doubtlessly a member of the Port Buck high school football team. But Asha knew the scent of death all too well, and this kid *reeked* of it.

Joey looked at her, then at her money, then back at her. Had there been other people in line, Asha was sure he would have refused to serve her, but her strategy of waiting until no one else was around had worked. After a final glance out the window to make sure no other white folk were around, his hand snaked out and snatched away the quarter, came back a moment later with five cents change. A ten-cent overcharge, but now was not the time to count her change.

"One malt, coming up." Asha had heard tales of people doing stuff to the food they served Negroes—spitting in it wasn't uncommon—so she watched him while he scooped out the ice cream and added the milk and malt. He must have had other things to think about than adding something nasty to her drink, because he never so much as tried to turn his back to her. He even smiled when he poured it into a big paper cup and set it on the serving counter.

"Don't see many of your kind over here," he said conversationally. "You lost or something?"

Asha had been trying to figure out a way to get the boy talking, and he'd opened up the door on his own, even given her an idea. "Yes, I am," she told him as she took a sip. The malt was a rare treat, and she let herself enjoy the rich taste for just a second before getting back down to the dirty business at hand. "Kind of new to the area, you know. I heard about this meeting place, and I was trying to find it. . . ." She let her voice trail off, knowing he would assume she had no clue about who, what, or where in the town. He'd think she was dumb as a rock; after all, she was colored *and* a girl.

Joey put his elbows on the counter and leaned toward her, and Asha had to force herself not to wrinkle her nose and pull away—did vampires have no idea that they smelled so bad? Perhaps it was only to her heightened senses. "If prayer's your kind of thing, I hear they hold big prayer meetings every other night at that bingo hall over on Hickory and Thirteenth Streets," he said.

"Really?" She gave him a bright, vacant smile, although she wanted more than anything in the world to ask why a white boy would know about Negro prayer meetings and bingo halls.

"Sure." Joey smiled back, and she could almost *feel* his hunger, the way his fangs wanted to slide forward. That he held back gave her hopes a little lift—at least vampires weren't so common in Port Buck that he could just change right there in the DQ window and attack. Now he looked her up and down, then licked his lips, probably didn't even realize that she noticed. "Anyway, pretty colored girl like you . . ." He paused dramatically, trying to play up his concern. "Well, let's just say you might not want to be walking around the white part of town at night, you know?"

Asha looked at him with wide eyes, hoping she could act the innocent. "Oh, my—I never even thought of that. I guess I'd best be heading home straightaway." It pained her to act so submissive, but there was a greater good to be served here—far better that she keep her identity and abilities a secret than pound this ugly-hearted weasel into road kill—or better yet, vampire dust—in the middle of the white half of town. She gave him a final smile and picked up her cup, felt the gaze of his hot, hidden vampire side as he watched her walk away.

Would he follow her? Probably. Asha could well imagine Joey getting the other kid to cover for him for a few minutes. Not wanting to get too far ahead, she kept her walk steady but not overly rapid, and three blocks out of the main shopping strip where the DQ was centered, she set her paper cup against the wall of a building, then slipped into the doorway of a darkened store a couple of yards away. If her counter boy decided to hunt, her malt cup would draw him like a bread ball would draw a catfish.

She smelled him before she heard his stealthy footsteps, the scant breeze easily carrying the scent of his rot to her hiding place. He was reaching for her malt cup when she stepped from the doorway.

"Looking for me?"

Joey jumped back, then grinned. "Well, yeah. I wanted to make sure you got through the neighborhood okay, and I thought we could, you know, talk." He shoved his hands in his pocket, going for the shy teenager act.

Asha wasn't fooled, but she let him think she was as she stepped closer. "About what?"

"Well . . ." For a second it seemed like he might try to continue the charade, but his impatience won out. "How about something to *eat?*" His face twisted suddenly, the features running together like hot wax and instantly reforming into a beast of the night.

But Asha only grimaced at him. "You looked a lot better when you were human."

Joey jerked and blinked at her. "Say what?"

"Is there something wrong with your hearing?"

Rather than argue, he growled and grabbed for her. Asha leaned out of his reach and swatted him aside, her blow hard enough to make him bring a hand up to his mouth in surprise.

"What the heck—who *are* you?" he demanded.

She stepped toward him, and he stepped back. What a coward—for crying out loud, she'd only smacked him once, not even hard. "I'm the Slayer," she said calmly.

"The what?"

Golly, Port Buck was so far out of the loop on the rest of the world that they didn't even know. "The Vampire Slayer," she told him. "It's what I do—slay vampires."

Joey gawked at her. "You mean it's like your *job* or something?"

"Exactly." Asha gave him a condescending smile. "So that's what I'm going to do—slay you."

For a second, the boy just gaped at her. Then it sank in—the way she'd tracked him when he'd thought he'd been hunting her, her rapid-fire reflexes, the easy-looking blow that had rattled his brain but good. He looked around wildly, searching for a way to escape. Then he realized Asha had angled him into the corner where another building stuck out farther from the rest; he was trapped. Whatever thoughts he had of fighting her fell apart when he saw her pull the stake from her pocket and realized she wasn't fooling around.

"Listen, I can help you, I can tell you stuff, lots of stuff, or at least about something that's going to happen—" He was practically babbling in his fear. "About that bingo hall I mentioned? You know, that one? Except if I do you have to let me go, okay? Because I wasn't going to hurt you, I would never do something like that, I was just clowning around—"

"Of course you were," Asha said amiably. Her left hand shot out and she wrapped viselike fingers around his throat, then slammed him against the brick wall. "Now what's this about the bingo hall—no no, you just keep your hands right down there where I can see them. That's right."

"Y-Yeah, the bingo hall." The cold flesh of Joey's throat worked against her hand as he tried to talk, and he shuddered. Asha thought she ought to be the one doing that. *God, I hate touching these creatures.* "See, the Klansmen in town, they got this idea—"

Asha's long fingers tightened momentarily and his words gurgled off. "By 'Klansmen' I'm guessing you mean vampires?"

Joey tried to nod, then found his voice again when her grip relaxed enough to let him speak. "Y-Yeah, and so they found out about the Negroes' eight o'clock prayer meeting at the bingo place, the one I told you about, and so they're going there tomorrow night and. . . ."

He didn't finish, and Asha grimaced. To give Joey a little encouragement, she brought up the stake and dug the sharp end into the center of his chest; he started to struggle, but that went south in a cry of pain when his own movement made the point sink in about a half an inch. "Hey, that hurts!"

"It's not supposed to tickle, you fool." She let her fingers crawl upward a bit, going for the nerves just under each side of the back of the jaw. The boy hissed in pain and frustration. "You're saying they're going to have a little feast? But what are they planning to do with all the bodies? I don't suppose they want a bunch of colored vampires running around Port Buck, do they?"

"Gonna bomb the building afterward—get rid of the bodies plus show all the Negroes who's boss."

For a second, Asha was stunned. "*What?*"

Joey tried to bolt.

He went sideways and the end of the stake scraped across his chest but didn't do any real damage. He darned near got away, but Asha lunged after him and grabbed his collar—better that than the blond crew cut that wouldn't have given her anything to hang on to. She jerked him off his feet and heard his shirt rip, knew that if the fabric went, her hold on him was also gone. He aimed a haymaker at her head, but she ducked it with barely a thought, then turned the hand holding the stake inward and drove a hard uppercut into his jaw. He went all the way down and she leapt on him and positioned the piece of wood for the final kill.

"Wait!" Joey cried. "I thought we had a bargain!"

Asha only looked at him coldly. "Your mistake," she said. "I don't bargain with vampires."

And hammered the beast into oblivion.

Beneath her bed, Asha kept a battered, musty-smelling crate full of weapons, and in the morning she dragged it out and checked the contents. There was nothing fancy about the box or what was inside—a dozen extra stakes, several wickedly sharp hunting knives, one equally sharp but smaller blade that could be hidden in the palm of her hand. She set out several of the stakes, then inspected each of the knives for a good edge and chose the best one.

"You'll need some help this time, uh-huh."

When Asha glanced up, the calm-faced Cajun woman was awake and sitting on the side of her own bed against the far wall, watching her. Laurent had been sleeping when Asha had come in last night, and the Slayer had risen earlier than normal, her dreams and rest troubled by what she might face this evening.

"Help?" Having someone else battle these creatures with her was something she'd never considered, but Laurent was right—she'd fought a bunch of the creatures since her calling, but never more than two or three at a time. Her toughest battle had been early on, when first two, then another had risen from the murky green waters of a swamp bog like sea monsters, surrounding her. She had been prepared for the first two but the last one had surprised her, ripping a chunk from her shoulder as it tried to chew its way up her neck before she'd battered it away and finally killed it. How would she face a whole crowd of these savage things by herself?

They were smart and would not go down easily—no doubt the white boy she'd killed last night had already been missed and questions were being asked. Had anyone noticed him talking to a pretty colored girl at the Dairy Queen? Had he told anyone he was going to follow her? Possibilities for doom spread through her mind like a spider with long, sticky legs.

"Yes," she finally said. "I do." She studied her fingers. "I was thinking to get there early, stop the meeting before it starts, and send everyone home. There's been so much talk about coloreds disappearing in Port Buck, I don't think it'll take much to get them out of there. Then when the vampires show up . . ." She didn't have to finish.

"There'll be more of 'em than you've ever seen in one place, uh-huh." Laurent nodded matter-of-factly. "I've trained you as best I can," she said. "If we have to, we keep our backs together and don't let them separate us, and we'll do all right."

"Yes," Asha said again, wishing she felt as confident as she was trying to sound. She checked another of the hunting knives one more time, then put it aside—later she would change to denim jeans and a shirt, and tie the knife in a sheath on her belt.

Her Watcher got up and began to make a plain but filling morning meal—drop biscuits and smoky pieces of thick-cut bacon, a couple of eggs for each. Knowing she would need strength tonight, Asha ate well even though she was too nervous to be hungry. To Asha, this was a huge thing they were about to do, her biggest battle yet; her insides churned with excitement and more than a little fear, but as always, Laurent was silent during the meal, giving no insight about her emotions. Afterward the older woman took her pipe and went out to sit in the rocker on the front porch; Asha could hear the chair going back and forth, back and forth. Laurent was such a strange, closed-up person. *Does she have any fear? Any love?* After all these years, Asha had no idea.

Asha spent the day training lightly in the front yard, focusing more on skill and speed than a hard workout that would overtire her muscles. Laurent watched from the porch, occasionally coming over to offer a comment or two, or to correct something in the way Asha kicked or blocked an imaginary punch. Somewhere in between they ate a midday meal, beans and bacon, biscuits left over from breakfast and lightly warmed in a pan on the stove. The hours passed swiftly, too much so—it seemed as though the sun was high in the sky one minute, then only a few inches above the tree line the next. The daytime chatter of the birds quieted, surrendering to the hum of evening insects; soon the frogs and owls would join in the swamp's nightly song.

It was time.

The preparations were done, and they were as ready as they could be. Both were dressed like men, in denim painter's pants—lots of pockets—and cotton shirts, leather boots. The eight-inch hunting knives hung from their belts because while a stake was the weapon of choice for the killing—they each had several stashed in deep pockets—there was nothing like a trusty blade to sever the hand that might be around your throat. Asha had slipped the smaller knife into the ruler pocket down the right side of her leg just in case, and if she didn't exactly feel self-assured, she did feel strong and ready.

The swamp, the Slayer decided, had never seemed so beautiful and serene to her as it did on the walk to Port Buck. It might be because the worst of its hidden creatures had all gathered somewhere else in preparation for their grand attack on the bingo hall tonight, but Asha intended to enjoy the feeling nonetheless. The lushness of the alder, elm, red bay, and ash trees was nearly surreal, and damselflies flitted from the arrowhead flowers to the wild pine to the swamp and spider lilies. It looked and felt like some strange tropical paradise instead of the swamp that Asha had grown up in, filled with tiny, harmless things like vinegar flies and leaf beetles rather than the deadly cottonmouths and 'gators she knew hid in the wet undergrowth.

That magical feeling disintegrated as soon as they crossed the line into Port Buck and houses quickly cropped up along the hard-packed road. They kept to the dirt-packed side streets to avoid being seen, using the darker doorways of closed businesses when they could, simply forging ahead when they couldn't. Like most towns, the numbered streets in Port Buck counted down the closer a person got to the center of things; at Thirteenth and Hickory, the bingo hall where the Negro folk met for prayer and games was well away from the town's main shopping area.

While it was a pretty good size, like most of the structures on the poorer side of town the building wasn't fancy. But it was clean, with whitewashed clapboard siding and shining windows below a tin roof that was, like most things metal in this climate, losing a battle with rust. Cheerful light spilled from windows over which were fitted iron security bars, and Asha and Laurent could see the shadows of people already moving around inside. It was only seven-thirty—no doubt the vampires would wait until the meeting started to make sure they had as many victims inside as they could. They walked around to the back and found only one other door at the rear, propped open with a flowerpot so that air could flow from front to back through the building.

"Guess we'll go on in," Laurent said when they'd gone back to the front door. The Watcher stroked her pipe for a few seconds, but the tobacco inside had long burned away. She tapped it against the heel of her boot, then slipped it into her shirt pocket.

Asha didn't bother to say anything, just led the way through the door. She wished she felt more confident and in control, but the truth was she felt more afraid tonight than she had ever before. She should have spent more of her time over the last two years in town, getting to know the people and learning, *realizing,* its dark undercurrent. How many vampires *were* there in this town, how many of the creatures had multiplied while she'd ignorantly fiddled around out in the swamp and staked the stragglers?

Still, she couldn't dwell on the past or her fear, couldn't let it cloud her judgment and senses. Inside there wasn't much to speak of but people—at least forty or fifty—and a bunch of folding metal chairs. The walls were unadorned, and because tonight was a prayer meeting, the long tables, also folding, had been pushed up against the walls where they would be out of the way. A plain wooden podium stood at the back of the room, its sole decoration a good-size basket of lovely great laurel flowers. Against the wall behind it were a couple of tall stands holding lit, pine-scented candles.

Asha eyed the room and chewed her lip, trying to decide what to do. This wasn't right at *all*—Joey had said eight o'clock. She and Laurent had planned on arriving and stopping the prayer meeting before it began, finding the bomb, then dealing with the vamps when they arrived and found an empty building—in the best of all possible words, Asha and her Watcher might be able to trap the creatures inside the very building they planned to destroy. But the boy had obviously lied to her about the time of the attack—this meeting was already in full swing, the seating almost full. Laurent had said they shouldn't split up, and she was right, but there were two entrances. Would the vampires come through the front or the back? Or both? Finally she motioned to a couple of chairs in the middle of the rows. "Let's sit there," she suggested.

Laurent followed her without comment, ignoring the stares of the other people. She and Laurent had never been churchgoers to begin with, so their faces were unfamiliar in the God-fearing circles of the town. Where Asha might have normally blended in, her men's clothes made her stand out and brought giggles from the children and teens, disapproving frowns from the men and women. Laurent was an outsider, plain and simple—Cajun she might be, but she was still white, and this was a Negro gathering. No one told her to leave, but the expressions on the dark faces around them were without a doubt completely bewildered and more than a bit suspicious.

Still, the people here were gathered for a prayer meeting and pray they would continue to do. At the podium an older man with close-cut salt-and-pepper hair clapped his hands to get everyone's attention. When he had it, he gave the crowd a warm smile. "Welcome," he said and cast a gaze toward Asha and her Watcher. His voice was deep and melodious, the kind of calm tone that folks would like listening to. "Would the rest of you all quiet down a bit so we can continue, please?"

His words made it clear the meeting had started some time

ago. The last of the people who'd been murmuring did as he asked, and when everything was still, he held up a Bible where everyone could see it. "For those who just joined us"—he looked again toward Asha and Laurent—"my name is Wilson Ray, and I'm the deacon of the Hickory Street Baptist Church. We've come here this evening to pray together and ask for God's guidance and support in the troubled town of Port Buck." His expression was solemn. "We all know about the recent happenings, people of color disappearing from their homes or the streets, people of other faiths—the Jewish, the Catholics—doing the same. The truth is these things have been going on for a long time . . . just not to this extent. For as long as I can remember, the Negro people in this town, in this *county,* have been prey for an unseen darkness, an evil that has just recently begun to run rampant in this community."

Asha's eyes widened as she listened. Did Deacon Ray, and perhaps other people, know about the vampires? And if so, what were they planning on doing about it?

"Tonight," the deacon told them, "we will bow our heads and pray that the Lord in his Glory brings us salvation from the scourge that has been set upon us, from those who hide their hatred beneath robes of white and bring misery to others who have different skin or beliefs."

"Amen!" called someone in the crowd, and it was echoed around the room at least a half dozen times.

Asha barely hid her disappointed frown. Prayer wasn't going to help these people, only standing up and fighting for themselves, for their *lives,* would. To sit around like this and basically do *nothing*—they were like bait in a box, just waiting to be snapped up by the hungry.

"Guess you never thought of yourself as the answer to anyone's prayers," Laurent murmured from her side.

Asha turned and stared at her Watcher. "Me?"

"Uh-huh."

She opened her mouth to reply, then closed it as she realized Laurent was right. These people—they were innocents and had no true idea what manner of beast stalked them. They were praying for salvation, for something, or some*one*, to save them. And here she was, Chosen a long time ago by some power greater than all of them combined. As Laurent had said: *the answer to their prayers.* Now, Asha realized, was not the time to hesitate—they would have to clear this building the hard way, with an old-fashioned "run for your lives" kind of announcement.

"In the course of the great darkness that has overtaken us," Deacon Ray continued as Asha was about to get to her feet, "we need to hold tight to one another and. . . ." Without warning his words faltered and stopped, and he gazed over the crowd toward the main entrance.

Trusting Laurent to keep her eye on the other exit, Asha turned to look and was surprised to see the longtime Port Buck sheriff, Gabe Jenner, amble through the door and into the bingo hall, with one of his deputies not far behind. Sheriff Jenner wasn't a large man, but he was sturdily built and muscular, with dark hair and hazel eyes that Asha had always thought held a hint of down-home meanness; it wasn't hard to imagine them peering out from the circular eyeholes of a tall, Ku Klux Klan hood.

"How're y'all doing tonight?" His voice boomed over the group, falsely cheerful. When no one answered, he grinned and rested one hand on the butt of the revolver holstered at his side, then scratched at his ear with the other. She'd risen an inch or two off her chair, but the gun was something Asha hadn't considered, a weapon for which she had no match, and she had to sink back onto her seat. She wouldn't do anyone any good if she was arrested and taken away, or worse, left with her lifeblood leaking onto the dusty floor.

Standing there and smiling, Asha thought Jenner looked anything but friendly, more like something stupid but . . . *predatory.* She didn't like the way his gaze scanned the crowd, but he was too far away, and there were too many people here for her instinct and sense of smell to kick in and help out, too many overwarm bodies mixing it up with the sweet, heavy aroma from the basket of flowers; instead she tried to think if she'd seen Jenner out and about Port Buck during the daytime recently. No, she was sure she hadn't. "I thought this was supposed to be a prayer meeting, but it don't seem to me like y'all are in a talkative mood at all."

Asha sensed Laurent stiffen beside her, and when the Slayer glanced back toward Deacon Ray, she saw that another uniformed deputy had appeared at the back door. Just visible in the outside darkness, he was standing there and smoking a cigarette, trying to look nonchalant. "I guess we'll just have to change our plan," Laurent said beneath her breath.

"Tell you what," the sheriff said loudly. He spoke like he and everyone in the room were old friends and it was the most natural thing in the world for a white lawman to walk into a Negro bingo hall. "Me and my friends, we'd like to join you. Maybe that'll bring a little excitement to whatever it is you're asking God for tonight."

Uh-oh, Asha thought.

And vampires poured through the two entrances.

Sheriff Jenner's face changed at the same time his deputies' did, the eyes and brows pulling back into the familiar, sharply angular expression, teeth elongating and turning dirty yellow. Asha lost count of how many came through each doorway, thought that all told the number might be as high as twenty. The last one through each slammed the door, then shoved a key into the dead bolt and locked it. The windows were useless, the security bars that had been meant to keep the bad guys at bay now trapping the humans inside the building. These prayerful people would be no match for the stronger vampires.

The creatures waded in, and the screaming started as they bit whomever looked the tastiest and smacked away the troublesome, terrified attempts of some of the men who tried to stop them. Asha saw immediately that she and Laurent would never be able to stay together as they'd hoped—too many people would fall victim to the creatures if they didn't take the initiative. As Laurent headed toward the podium end of the room, the Slayer yanked the hunting knife from its sheath with her left hand and leapt forward with a stake in the other. Unable to escape, people ran in all directions, their faces contorted with terror as they tried to dodge the vampires; a few tried valiantly to pull the beasts off their friends and family.

Asha staked one in the back, then left another writhing on the floor in agony as she buried the knife under his rib cage and pulled it around as she passed. She punched and kicked, her knife hand flashing out again and again, its sharp edge finding purchase far more often than the killing point of her stake in all the uproar. The windows broke as people threw chairs against them, but the security bars did their job all too well—if the vampires had any say in it, no one was getting out of here alive.

One of the vampires gave Asha a punch in the jaw that made her stagger and drop to one knee; she used the metal chair she grabbed for support to brain the creature senseless. Before it could jump on her again, Deacon Ray was there with a well-timed kick to the vampire's head that sent it momentarily into dreamland. Asha didn't miss the chance to make sure it stayed there, and the preacher gaped at the swirl of dust.

The Slayer didn't give him time to think about it. "Here," she said, and shoved her stake into his hands. "Use this, but don't be a hero. It's more important to try and get these people out of here, *now!*"

Wisely, Deacon Ray didn't ask for an explanation. Asha spun and kicked one of the deputies when he tried to grab her from behind, then buried her fingers in his hair and slammed his head against the flat of her other elbow. He howled and tried to jerk away, then looked down in surprise when Asha gutted him like a catfish. He sank to his knees and she kicked him aside and went for a more dangerous target—he might not be dead, but he'd have a hard time fighting with his insides hanging out.

Still, she and Laurent were outnumbered. The Cajun woman was holding her own at the far end, but she was older and not as strong as the Slayer, and at least ten people lay here and there among the chaos of overturned chairs, their bodies drained of lifeblood. She and her Watcher had killed or maimed perhaps a third of the attackers—they had to do better before more innocent people died.

Asha dodged in front of a vampire as he lunged for a screaming woman and buried the point of her hunting knife in his eye. His bellow of fury was cut short as she yanked a spare stake from a pocket in her pants and jammed it into his chest. Rage swept her as she glimpsed the sheriff ten feet away; he grinned evilly and clamped his mouth on the neck of a boy who couldn't be any older than eleven.

She headed in that direction, offhandedly pulling an older man out of the way as a female vampire grabbed for him. Without even thinking about it, she hit the woman-beast across the collarbone with the outside of her arm, leaning into the blow and hearing a satisfying crack as the creature's collarbone shattered. With her arms now hanging uselessly at her sides, the vampire screeched and ran in panicked circles.

Concentrating on his meal, Sheriff Jenner's mouth opened and he bellowed in shock when Asha circled behind him, slipped her left hand over his forehead, and dug her first two fingers into his eyes. His child-victim fell to the floor, but quickly recovered and crawled away. *Thank God for the strength of the young,* Asha thought. She dragged the vampire lawman backward and tight against her, then shoved her other arm under his and to the front of his chest. His fighting ceased abruptly when he felt the deadly end of the stake press against it.

"Call off your dogs or die," she said grimly. "I won't ask a second time."

He wasn't stupid enough to think she was kidding. *"Stop the attack now!"* he roared. *"No more!"*

The remaining vampires froze where they were, their hideous faces confused and incredulous. When they saw their leader taken hostage, they released the men or women in their grasps, sneering at the humans as they stumbled away. As Asha had expected, they began to inch toward her; she, in turn, dragged the sheriff toward the podium end of the room where Laurent waited. The older woman's chest heaved with exertion but she still looked triumphant.

"Unlock the door and let the humans leave," Asha ordered. She kept her fingers hooked into Jenner's eye sockets, working off the man's hiss of pain.

"And then what?" he demanded. "Us against you?"

Then what, indeed? The truth was Asha had no idea how to get out of this situation. She'd never had the lives of so many people dependent on her at any one time, and they were badly outnumbered; if she didn't find a way to keep the upper hand, a whole lot more people would die. She'd never considered having to make a decision like this, and the responsibility was nearly suffocating. "Then we'll talk," Asha managed to reply. Despite her fear, her voice was strong. "Otherwise I'll send you straight to hell right now."

Jenner growled in frustration, but he really had no choice. He couldn't even move in Asha's hold. "Do as she says," he ordered.

Two of the vampires moved forward, one heading toward each door. "Oh, no," Asha said, and stopped the second one with a frigid stare. "You just stay right up front there with your ugly friend. Then"—she jerked her head at Laurent—"pass my friend there both sets of keys. In fact, *all* of you disgusting vampires get over to one side where I can keep an eye on you, *away* from the window. And hurry up—the sheriff here wouldn't want my fingers to get tired."

Laurent moved to the front and yanked the keys from the hands of one of the deputy vampires. In another second she had the front door wide and the fresh, night air was pouring through the opening. Asha hadn't realized how quickly the room had filled with the metallic scent of blood and the heavier smells of death and decay. People were crying and babbling as they rushed for the exit, some crawling, others pulling the injured to freedom. Asha wouldn't let the misery playing out in front of her distract her or loosen her hold on Sheriff Jenner. The last one at the door was Deacon Ray, and he paused and looked to her and Laurent for instructions.

"Close it behind you," Asha ordered. "No, don't argue. Just do it." Her grasp on Jenner tightened and he winced. "I'm going to have a little talk with our town's friendly lawman."

Deacon Ray looked anything but pleased at the notion of leaving her and Laurent in here with perhaps a dozen vampires, but ultimately he did as she commanded. When the door finally closed, Laurent didn't need to be told what to do; she hurried forward and locked it, then stepped to the window and sent both sets of keys sailing into the outside darkness.

For a moment, no one said or did anything, then the expressions on the faces of the vampires went from smugness to fear and dismay.

"You two are already dead," Sheriff Jenner snarled. Spittle ran from his twisted mouth. "You just don't know it. We wired this building last night." He held out his hand, and from her position behind him, Asha could just see it over his shoulder. He was holding something small and boxlike, and as she focused on it, Sheriff Jenner pushed down on it with his thumb. There was a soft, dull click somewhere behind them, and Asha staked him before he could say anything. The world would definitely be a better place for his absence.

With nothing in her grip but vampire dust, Asha realized the room had gone unaccountably silent. That sound of just a moment ago, so small and insignificant . . . what had it been? She looked at the faces of the unmoving creatures in front of them and saw only dull acceptance mirrored in their eyes, like the surrendering of a mouse caught in the talons of the nighthawk. No one tried to run, or even talk.

Disbelieving, Asha turned toward her Watcher and their gazes locked. Laurent gave her a slow, sad smile. "Guess we're going on to Glory together," she said. She reached out a rough hand and touched Asha's cheek, and it was the first sign of affection the Slayer could remember since the night the Cajun woman had plucked her from beneath the hanging body of her dead father. If nothing else, Asha knew she had done a measure of good in her small world, and she had been loved by someone besides.

Then . . .

Detonation.

About the Authors

After obtaining a degree in wildlife illustration and environmental education, **Doranna Durgin** spent a number of years deep in the Appalachian Mountains, where she learned not to get cocky about Things That Go Bump In The Night. When she emerged, it was as a writer who found herself irrevocably tied to the natural world and its creatures (even the ones no one else sees). Doranna hangs around with three Cardigan Welsh Corgis and an amazingly sane Arabian, and drags her saddle wherever she goes. Her online home is at *http://www.doranna.net/*.

Christie Golden is the award-winning author of seventeen novels and fifteen short stories published in the fields of fantasy, science fiction, and horror. Her historical fantasy novel *A.D. 999*, written under the pen name of Jadrien Bell, won the Colorado Author's League Top Hand Award for Best Genre Novel of 1999, competing against novels from every genre including romance, mystery, and western as well as fantasy. A history buff, Golden has always been intrigued by the legend of the white doe of Roanoke Island, which has been around in one form or another for the last few centuries. When primary research sources yielded such choice tidbits as the fact that the Croatoans had tales about the walking dead, she knew she was on target with her idea. Golden lives in Colorado with her artist husband Michael Georges, two cats, and a white German Shepherd. Readers are welcome to visit her website at www.sff.net/people/Christie.Golden. She feels compelled to inform readers that, while she thinks very highly of fellow writer Christopher Golden, no, they are not related.

L.A. Times bestselling author **Nancy Holder** has written over two dozen projects for the *Buffy the Vampire Slayer* and *Angel* series of books. She has worked with a number of *Buffy* and *Angel* authors, including Christopher Golden, Jeff Mariotte, and Maryelizabeth Hart. Her love of France and her passion for history inspired her to set her Slayer's Tale in Revolutionary Paris. She has visited the Palace of Versailles and stood in the Hall of Mirrors . . . where she found, to her dismay, that she cast no reflection. She keeps to the shadows in San Diego with her daughter, Belle, and their all-female cast of supporting characters—Dotdog and the cat sisters, David and Sasha.

Yvonne Navarro is a Chicago area novelist who has written a bunch of stuff, including novels, movie and television novelizations, and short stories. In the Year 2000 she had three novels published, *Buffy the Vampire Slayer: Paleo, DeadTimes,* and *That's Not My Name.* Two of those novels, *Paleo* and *That's Not My Name* (and one of her short stories), took first place in three different categories at the state level in the Mate E. Palmer Communications Contest in early 2001. Yvonne used to draw and publish illustrations, but alas, she hasn't had time to make pictures in years—in the world of fiction publishing, one picture is *not* worth a thousand words!

Some readers might not be surprised to learn that her first published novel, *AfterAge,* was about the end of world as orchestrated by vampires. In her second novel, *deadrush,* she worked on zombies; both *AfterAge* and *deadrush* were nominated for the Bram Stoker Award. *Final Impact* (which won the 1997 CWIP Award for Excellence in Adult Fiction and the *Rocky Mountain News* "Unreal Worlds" Award for Best Horror Paperback of 1997) and its follow-up, *Red Shadows,* tell the story of some really nifty people struggling to survive when the Earth is nearly destroyed by a celestial disaster. Yvonne wrote the novelizations of both *Species* and *Species II,* as well as *Buffy the Vampire Slayer: The Willow Files, Vols. I and II* and *Aliens: Music of the Spears.* She also authored *The First Name Reverse Dictionary,* a reference book for writers.

Currently she's about three-quarters of the way finished writing a supernatural thriller called *Mirror Me* and still plans to someday write sequels to most of her previous solo novels. She also studies martial arts and loves Arizona (she has been scheming to take over the Phoenix area for years), dogs, champagne, and dark chocolate. Visit her site at www.yvonnenavarro.com, where you can read more of her stuff and see funny photos, plus find out how to get books autographed and keep up to date. Come visit!

Mel Odom lives in Moore, Oklahoma, with his wife and five children. In addition to writing novels for *Buffy the Vampire Slayer,* he's also written for *Angel* and *Sabrina the Teenage Witch.* His new fantasy hardcover, *THE ROVER,* has just been published. His e-mail address is mel@melodom.net, and he welcomes comments and questions.

Greg Rucka is the author of seven novels, including five about bodyguard Atticus Kodiak and his companions. He is the author of several short-stories and comic books, and currently writes the adventures of Batman in Detective Comics, and the adventures of Tara Chase in Queen & Country. His favorite slayer is Faith.

the Vampire Slayer™

tales of the slayer

By Joss Whedon, Tim Sale, Gene Colan, P. Craig Russell, and others!

Buffy the Vampire Slayer is the latest in a long tradition of young women who've been trained to give their lives in the war against vampires. We've gotten glimpses of these other women over the years on T.V., in comics, and in books. Now for the first time, the writers from the television series, including the show's creator **Joss Whedon**, and one of its stars, **Amber "Tara" Benson**, present the tales of these girls, with help from comics' greatest artists!

Gene Colan, co-creator of Marvel's *Blade*, returns to Dark Horse for the story of a young girl in 1970s New York battling vampires. Tim Sale, artist of recent epics *Batman: The Long Halloween*, teams with Joss Whedon for a grim tale of a medieval slayer. P. Craig Russell (*Dr. Strange, The Ring of the Nibelung*) and international rising star Mira Friedmann (*Actus Tragicus*) also join the line-up. A must have collection of stellar tales!

On sale November 2001 at your local comics shop or bookstore!
To find a comics shop in your area, call 1-888-266-4226

Check out the Dark Horse Comics website for a complete list of Buffy the Vampire Slayer comics and graphic novels!

For more information or to order direct:
•On the web: www.darkhorse.com
•E-mail: mailorder@darkhorse.com
•Phone: 1-800-862-0052 or (503) 652-9701
www.darkhorse.com   Mon.-Sat. 9 A.M. to 5 P.M. Pacific Time

www.buffy.com